"Ellie." The [barcode] d her.

Elizabeth te [barcode] oo difficult to grasp [barcode] "Will you still be the [barcode] only part of my nig [barcode]

"Open your eyes, *ee kwai wah*."

With eyes still closed, Elizabeth smiled at the Shawnee word sliding smoothly from his lips. "What did you call me?"

How could he explain that the simplest translation of the word was *woman,* but that it meant so much more. It conveyed the essence of woman; gentle and tender to those she loved but tough to anyone who threatened her loved ones, soft but with an inner strength that would rival forged iron, giving, caring, compassionate.

"It means . . . my woman." His booming voice was lowered to a whisper. "Open your eyes, *ee kwai wah*, I'm far too big to disappear like a puff of smoke."

"Daniel . . ." His name was a caress as she stood, stepping forward. He reached out. "Daniel."

She was in his arms as she had longed to be, his body solid against hers, his breath warm against her cheek.

"You're home . . . you're home . . . you're home," she whispered.

"I am now." Daniel buried his face in the soft crease of her neck and breathed deeply. "God, I've missed you."

"Daniel . . ." Effortlessly, he picked her up and carried her away from the cabin. With her head nestled against his shoulder and her fingers buried into his shirt, Elizabeth didn't question his destination. She would be content to stay in his arms until the end of time. . . .

CAPTURE THE GLOW OF
ZEBRA'S *HEARTFIRES!*

PAMELA K. FORREST
RIVER OF DREAMS

ZEBRA BOOKS
KENSINGTON PUBLISHING CORP.

ZEBRA BOOKS are published by

Kensington Publishing Corp.
475 Park Avenue South
New York, NY 10016

First Printing: January, 1994

Printed in the United States of America

for my Ethel Mae, *with love,*
Ethel Tuthill Wade

One

"*Mama?*"

Daniel LeClerc clutched his pounding head between his hands as pain ricocheted gun-fire quick through his skull. His body, exhausted by both the lack of sleep and too little food, slumped in the saddle while his equally fatigued horse plodded on through the darkness.

"*Mama, me be good.*"

The relentless agony that had begun nearly two weeks earlier robbed even his formidable willpower of the strength to continue. From far too many past experiences he realized that the pain was reaching the crescendo he had learned to dread. When it stopped he'd have relief from the tortuous punishment. But the freedom from pain would be bought at far too high of a price.

"*Mama, peeze . . . scared, Mama . . . Mama?*"

"I'm coming, baby, I'm coming," he whispered to the voice as real as his own.

"*Mama? Mama!*"

"Too soon! Give me just a little longer!" he

begged, tears of torment tracing silent paths down his drawn cheeks. "She's only a baby! Not yet, please God . . ."

"Mama?" The pitiful cry thundered through his head.

"I'm almost there. Please, little one, I'm almost there!"

"Mama!"

Daniel's scream shattered the silence, bouncing off the surrounding trees, vibrating through the night as his head fragmented into countless pieces of a rainbow. The pain, a dull blade, became shards of red and blue, yellow and green, as he lost his tenuous hold on consciousness.

The horse, no longer guided by the man on his back, slowed to a stop. In spite of the weight of his rider, the animal rested on three legs, his head lowered, too tired to nibble at the tender spring grass peeking from the dirt.

Night drifted past with the whisper of the wind and the stirring of nocturnal creatures newly wakened from their winter sleep. Daniel hung from the horse, his evenly distributed weight and the stillness of the animal keeping him in the saddle.

The voice in his mind whispered again, too softly to disturb him, to reassure him. Soon, it, too was quiet.

Daniel woke as he felt himself slipping off the horse. He grabbed a handful of black mane but was only able to slow his descent. His shoulder

8

hit the hard ground with a jarring impact and he rolled onto his back. Looking up at the morning sky through the still bare trees, he realized that his headache was gone, leaving behind it a heartbreak that threatened his sanity.

He listened to the sweet song of the birds and the gentle whisper of the breeze. The sky was too blue, the sun too bright, the day too perfect for the knowledge that murmured through him.

If he could hide, he'd gladly run to the very end of the earth. But he knew that for him there was no escape except, perhaps, death. He had no choice but to go on, find what he was destined to find, then return home to search for a solace that would be denied him.

His family would ask no questions or intrude on his privacy. They would wait patiently until he had come to accept what he could not change. Their love would surround him in warmth, a fragile wall of security.

Until the next headache began and once more he was forced to follow where it led—to heartbreak and one step closer to the promise of madness.

Climbing unsteadily to his feet, Daniel ran his hands through his vibrant red hair. Deep shadows beneath his black eyes gave testimony to his exhaustion, as did the slump to his usually square shoulders and the sallowness of skin surprisingly dark for a redhead.

Moving like a man ten times his age of twenty-six, he gathered enough wood for a fire and prepared a small pot of water for coffee. While he waited for it to heat he pulled the saddle and blanket off his horse and carefully rubbed its matted coat.

"We've been through hell, haven't we, boy?" He talked quietly to the horse as he inspected its hooves for stones and fed it some grain. "It's almost over now. We'll find her later this morning and then we'll go home."

Patting the animal on his rump, Daniel knelt down beside the fire and dug some food out of his sack. He halfheartedly ate the dried meat and drank the bitter coffee. His stomach rebelled at the food, the first he'd had in nearly a week, and he fought to keep it down.

Because of neglect and the all-consuming demand of the headache, his massive body had been forced to consume its own resources, leaving him weak with hunger but nearly unable to accept the nourishment he so badly needed.

Daniel ate slowly until he knew the food would remain in his stomach, but stopped when eating began to require too much effort. The hot coffee coursed through his system but brought no warmth to his chilled blood. Nothing would warm him until he returned to the security of his home and the family who loved him and accepted him as he was.

"Mama?"

Shock vibrated through him, making him spill the hot coffee down his chest but he was immune to the scalding pain. As the voice whispered through his mind, Daniel concentrated on the sound only he could hear.

This had never happened before. Previously, when the headache ceased so did the voice, never had it continued after the pain was gone. He tried to ignore the unwanted thought that his mind had finally been shattered by one nightmare too many.

"Mama? Me 'ungry! Let me out!"

"Oh, God, you're alive . . . thank God, you're alive!"

Not trusting the voice, afraid that it was desperation speaking to a mind that had finally slipped over the edge into insanity, Daniel waited to hear her again.

"Mama, peeze? Where you at, Mama?"

"I'm coming, baby, I promise. Just a little longer."

"Mama?"

His hands shaking with renewed urgency, Daniel put out the fire and saddled his horse. He had to force himself to slow down when excitement made him clumsy, causing him to waste precious minutes. Following an instinct that had never failed him, he headed toward the silent sound.

He heard the reassuring whisper of the little girl several times during the morning. He knew that she was safe, frightened and hungry. Her nearly constant demand for food had actually brought a smile to his face.

As he approached the scene of total destruction, all humor fled. Impatient to arrive at his destination, sure that this time he'd wouldn't be too late, he was unprepared for the sight that confronted him. Two wagons, gutted by fire, still smoldered. Clothing, broken crockery and prized personal possessions were scattered all around the campsite.

The Shawnee training of his youth was not necessary to read the signs of ambush and devastation. Two couples, younger than himself, had traveled into the wilderness. While they slept, they had been attacked, possibly by the Iroquois that frequented the area, but just as likely by some of the river rats who ambushed inexperienced travelers.

He found the two men with their throats slit, their bodies still sprawled in their respective beds, obviously murdered in their sleep. The women hadn't been so lucky.

Daniel closed his eyes at the vision of the young, lovely women, tortured beyond belief, twin expressions of horror frozen on their faces. Death had come slowly for them, but it had brought their only means of escape from a terror beyond their control.

Turning away from the sight, he searched the area for the barrel. It lay on its side, the lid hammered tightly into place. His hands drew into fists and a snarl of rage contorted his mouth as he wished for the opportunity to inflict some of his own justice on the men who would deliberately torture a small child.

She had been put in the barrel and the lid closed too tightly for her to open, promising a slow, lingering death by starvation and dehydration.

Daniel curbed his natural impatience to go to the child and free her from her prison. He knew she wouldn't understand the death and destruction that surrounded them. He didn't want the last memory of her parents to be of them covered in their own blood.

He found a shovel with a broken handle among the wreckage and began to dig. Once or twice he heard the child call, but it was no longer in his mind. Her voice was reassuringly real, drifting to him from the wooden barrel as he finished the chore. Using whatever was at hand, he carefully covered the newly turned dirt so that scavengers, human or animal, wouldn't easily find the lonely graves.

There was nothing that he could do about the burned-out wagons but he managed to gather up some of the possessions and stack them in a pile. He found several articles of clothing for the little girl and bundled them together in a colorful patchwork quilt. When the site was as respectable as he could manage, Daniel walked over to the barrel and prepared to meet the child who had forced him to this place of sorrow.

Setting the barrel upright, he slowly pried the lid off, careful to hold it so that it wouldn't fall back onto her. When it was free, Daniel threw it to the side and looked down at the child.

He was greeted by scraggly, carrot red hair that would defy taming, a nose full of freckles and bright blue eyes. A cat, skin covering bones, was clutched in her arms. It hung lifelessly and if it hadn't blinked Daniel would have thought it was dead.

"Hello, baby," he said softly, trying to moderate his naturally thunderous voice.

"Me no baby! Me Jenny Sue!" A pouty lower lip wobbled threateningly. "Mama?"

Daniel stared at the child and wondered how he could explain death to someone too little to understand.

"Your mama isn't here, baby. Would you like to come home with me?"

"No!" She squeezed the cat to her until Daniel was concerned that she'd inadvertently kill it, but it made no protest at her rough handling. "Me want Mama!"

"I know you do, little one." Daniel reached into the barrel, attempting to pull her free.

In the limited confines of the barrel Jenny Sue dodged his hands, throwing the cat at him. Daniel grabbed it, gathering it against him. Green eyes stared unblinkingly into his. The animal's claws stretched out threateningly, then as if sensing there was no danger, they rested against his arm before it began to purr so loudly he wondered if it would shake itself out of his arms.

"Hello, kitty," he said quietly, softly stroking the tiger-striped golden fur. "Bet you're hungry."

"Me 'ungry," Jenny Sue said plaintively from the barrel.

"Come with me, kitty, and I'll find you something to eat." Daniel stood and started to walk away. "I don't have any milk but I think I can fix you up with something."

"Me 'ungry!" Jenny Sue repeated, standing up in the barrel that came to just beneath her eyes.

"It's a shame Jenny Sue doesn't want to go with us," Daniel continued as he slowly moved away from the barrel. "We might be able to find her something to eat, too."

"Me 'ungry!"

Daniel turned, swallowing back his smile as her blue eyes peeked at him from the rim of the barrel. "Did you say something?"

"Me 'ungry!" she bellowed.

"Would you like to go with us?"

She nodded and held her arms up to him, firmly wedging her way into his heart. Images of his little sister, Dara, drifted through his thoughts as he approached the child. Raised with six older brothers, Dara knew no fear of men—even men the size of Daniel. In fact, theirs was a special relationship, the oldest child and the youngest, both red-haired, and Daniel feared, both sharing the same curse that had haunted his life.

"What do you think, kitty?" Daniel stroked the animal whose contented purr vibrated through him. "Can you wait a little longer to be fed?"

"Peeze?" Jenny Sue asked and Daniel saw the charmer behind the disheveled red hair and bright blue eyes. "Me really, really 'ungry!"

Knowing that his size combined with his naturally booming voice were intimidating to strangers and possibly terrifying to this tiny child, Daniel moved slowly. He shifted the cat to one arm and reached in for Jenny Sue with the other. A lump clogged his throat when her small arms wrapped confidently around his neck as he pulled her free. Easily balancing her on one arm, he willingly let her take the cat from him.

"Hello, angel," he said softly.

"Me no angel!"

He smiled, having little doubt that truer words had never been spoken. She had the appearance of finding or causing more trouble than any three kids, but, in spite of her plain appearance, he knew he'd never seen anyone more beautiful.

"You're an angel to me," he told her quietly, reveling in her slight weight in his arms.

"Me 'ungry!"

"A hungry angel, then." With a smile and a lightness of heart that had been denied him for far too long, he turned and headed toward his horse. He grabbed the bundle of clothes as he passed and after putting Jenny Sue onto the animal's back, he tied them to the saddle. Swinging up onto the horse, he shifted her until she sat across his legs.

"Let's go find us something to eat. Suddenly I'm as hungry as a bear."

Jenny Sue's troubled gaze lingered on the wagons, the tragic evidence of the end of the only life she had ever known.

"Mama . . ."

Two

Elizabeth Spurlin looked at the tiny, ramshackle cabin and felt her determination dip to a new all-time low. A bitterly cold wind tugged relentlessly at the pins holding her hair in a semblance of an accepted style beneath a ridiculously frivolous hat and viciously sought to discover each inch of bare flesh beneath her skirt. She wondered if the chill dancing across her skin was from the wind or from the desperation that sought a firmer hold on her.

The children behind her, two elegantly dressed little girls and three bedraggled boys, shifted restlessly. She knew that they were as tired as she and longed for the home she had recklessly promised was waiting for them at the end of this journey.

She didn't dare turn her gaze to the boys, whom she suspected were familiar with less than this cabin or to the girls, whom she knew were accustomed to much more. It would break her heart to see the acceptance and unconditional love shining from their faces. They expected so little and she couldn't even provide them with that.

She stared despondently at the miserable structure that made a mockery of her promises. Hardly large enough for one person, she couldn't imagine living in it day after day with five children. There was chinking missing from between the logs of the windowless cabin, and even from the ground she could see holes in the roof and a bird's nest sticking out of the top of the chimney.

"It's a mite small," Elder Jacobs said, his thumbs hooked through the suspenders over his shoulders. "But it'll be a roof over your head, Mistress Spurlin, and with you bein' a widow and all, I figure you'll be grateful to have someplace to be keeping your youngens. We didn't plan on hiring a teacher with youngens. In fact, we've been looking for a man. But the Lord sent you to us, so we'll manage."

"Thank you, Elder Jacobs." Elizabeth forced the words from her tight throat.

This pious, obnoxious man had preached and lectured to her since their first meeting in town two hours earlier. It would feel good to tell him exactly what she thought about both him and this poor excuse for a cabin, but she knew it would be the end of her teaching job, a job she desperately needed, in the small Indiana settlement of Richmond. She had already lost one position, she couldn't chance losing this one, too.

She had been promised a teaching post in Cincinnati. After making the long, arduous journey from Virginia to the growing Ohio settlement, she had discovered that it had been filled by a man, one possessing less credentials than she, if his limited vocabulary was an indication of his education. There had been no apology for the inconvenience or reimbursement for the expense of traveling to the town.

"You understand that we don't have no money to pay you," Elder Jacobs continued.

"I understand."

"We'll be bringing out a sack of flour and coffee and some other victuals. Time to time somebody'll give you a bolt of cloth or maybe a side of beef."

"That will be fine, Elder Jacobs." Elizabeth had already been informed that the method of payment for teaching the settlement children would be in food and goods rather than cash. She longed for the man to get on his way so that she could begin the mammoth job of making the cabin livable.

"School will begin every day at eight and let out at noon, 'cepting when harvesting time comes. Crops are more important than schooling."

From the corner of her eye Elizabeth saw eleven-year-old Belinda poke eleven-year-old John in the ribs. She knew that it was in retaliation for something John had done first—John always struck first!

"Children." The single word, spoken in a

softly accented voice, held a wealth of meaning for the youngsters.

"Well, guess you'll be wanting to get settled. I'll be bringing you a load of wood out in the next day or so. Mind that you're at the church building before eight tomorrow. We won't tolerance our teacher being late."

"I would appreciate it if we could postpone classes for a couple of days so that the children and I can get settled in," Elizabeth stated quietly.

"Ain't much settling to do." He looked at the cabin, either ignoring or not seeing the obvious faults in the structure. "Ain't no reason school can't be started tomorrow."

"I'll be there, Elder Jacobs. So will my children." She forced a pleasant expression to her face, hoping that he would leave before it slipped.

"If you don't live a moral, proper life here with your youngens we'll be asking you to leave," he warned. "We don't hold with no whoring ways."

Elizabeth had enough of his thinly veiled threats. Miss Edna Smothers of the Tidewater School for Young Ladies Who Wished to Make Their Way in the World, would have been proud of her former student as Elizabeth applied every lesson in etiquette and decorum she had ever sat through. Hands folded primly at her waist, head up, shoulders squared, she looked at the man.

"I can assure you," she enunciated precisely,

"that my morals will never be in question. I intend to live here with my family and to teach your children as much as they'll learn about reading, writing and history."

"See that you do!" He climbed back into his wagon and set off down the road.

"Old windbag!" nine-year-old Wilson stated.

"Ya, old windbag," his seven-year-old brother Benjamin parroted.

"That's enough, boys." Elizabeth sighed with fatigue as she bent to pick up her cases. "Let's go see if the inside is better than the outside."

The children grabbed their own miserably small bundles of possessions and followed her into the cabin.

If the outside had been deplorable, the inside was wretched. The door refused to budge until the two older boys, John and Wilson, with considerable help from Elizabeth, forced it open. The smell that assaulted their noses made them regret their efforts as they coughed and gagged.

"Somethin' done gone and died in here!" John said in disgust.

From the safety of the doorway, the children looked around in fascinated revulsion. Elizabeth put her hand over her nose and entered the cabin—walking straight into a huge spider web that stretched from one end of the room to the other. She batted it away from her face, keeping a careful eye out for the creature that had spun it.

The dead thing was easy to spot in the corner of the nearly empty cabin. It no longer resembled whatever it had been and Elizabeth didn't take the time to try to figure out what it was. The room was dark, dank and smelly. The only light entered from the doorway, the hole in the roof and from the holes between the logs.

It was going to take a lot of work and effort on everyone's part to make it a home. And there was no doubt that the first chore had to be removing the remains!

Elizabeth rushed back to the open door. The children parted to allow her to leave the cabin and she breathed deeply of the fresh air.

"What was it?"

"Ya gonna bury it?"

"Can I go see?"

"I'm not gonna live in there!"

"It stinks!"

She smiled at the comments of the children. "Yes, Elaine," she replied to the youngest child. "I agree with you, it does have a distinctive odor."

"Ya, like shi—"

"John, that will be enough," she cautioned quietly.

"I ain't gonna bury it!" he replied, crossing his arms over his thin chest.

"Me neither!" the other children chimed in together.

"Well, thanks, I guess you expect me to do the nasty deed?"

Five pairs of eyes, two pairs of blue, two brown and one pair of green, stared determinedly at her.

"Draw straws?" she asked hopefully. It had become their way of deciding who should do a particularly loathsome task. The negative shakes of their heads were her answers.

"Extra piece of pie at dinner?"

"We ain't got no pie and it don't look like we'll have us no dinner, either," John answered wisely.

It had to be done and Elizabeth silently cursed the man who had dumped them here like unwanted baggage. They were unwanted, she reminded herself, she and the children. But together they would be a family. And she'd fight anyone who tried to take the children from her.

"Benjamin and Wilson gather firewood, John build a fire." She looked around the area and found a clearing not too far from the cabin. "Over there should be good. We'll have to clean the chimney before we can light one inside. But we need someplace we can get warm."

Folding the edges of her cape back over her shoulders and unbuttoning her sleeves and pushing them up her arms, Elizabeth tried to prepare herself for the task at hand. "Girls, there has to be water around here somewhere. Take the bucket and go see if you can find it. Don't get lost!" she cautioned as all of the children started on their assigned task.

When they were all gone but for John, he scrapped the toe of his tattered shoe in the dirt, his hands buried deeply in the pockets of his equally ragged trousers.

"I'll help you bury it, Miss Elizabeth," he said

quietly. "But don't you go telling the other kids that I did."

"Thank you, John," she replied softly.

"Want me to look in the shed out yonder and see if there's a shovel?"

"Please do, and bring back anything else that might be of help."

She watched as the boy ran off. He had only been with her family for two weeks and he still tried to maintain his aura of indifference with the other children. But Elizabeth understood his fear of rejection and saw through his guise to the child who longed to love and be loved in return.

In time he would learn that there was a place for him in the family and that he was very much wanted by her. She hoped he would come to think of himself as the oldest brother and that nothing would separate them.

If security was an unknown in his young life, hardship was not. She had nearly bitten through her lower lip the first time she'd seen the criss-crossed scars on his thin back. He had glared at her defiantly, his blue eyes daring her to comment, brashly provoking her to abandon him as his own father had done, the father who had sold him to her for the price of a bottle of whiskey. Fighting to keep the pity out of her gaze, she had pointed to the bucket of water and the sliver of soap and told him to wash if he intended to eat.

He had washed and eaten. When darkness came he slept away from the rest of them, wrapped snugly against the cold in the blanket she had provided. To her surprise he had still been there in the morning. To her delight, he had decided to travel with them.

He worked hard at any task she assigned him and fought harder, seeming to be ready to start swinging at the slightest provocation. At the tender age of eleven he had appointed himself her protector but refused the simplest sign of affection. He had volunteered little information about himself and she had respected his wishes. Maybe she would never know about his past, but she promised him and herself that his future would be better.

"That shed's in better shape than the cabin." John's voice interrupted her reverie.

She turned to find him carrying a shovel and a hoe in one hand and dragging a slab of board in the other.

"Figure how we can scrape it up on this here board and carry it out back somewheres. Could bury it iffen the ground's not too froze up."

Reluctantly turning to enter the cabin, Elizabeth wrinkled her nose at the waiting chore. Taking a deep breath, she headed straight for the corner praying that she didn't spend the next few minutes gagging up her last meal.

By the time the other boys returned with armloads of firewood, Elizabeth, with a lot of help from John, had removed the carcass from the cabin and carried it deep into the woods.

John carefully removed leaves and debris from the ground and built a small fire. Belinda and four-year-old Elaine returned with a bucket of water, wet shoes and the first flowers of spring.

"How pretty," Elizabeth said as she accepted the flowers from Elaine's grubby hand. "Thank you for thinking of me, sweetie." She hugged the little girl to her. "Why don't you look through the box of cooking utensils Elder Jacobs provided and see if there is something you can put them in."

She turned her gaze back toward the cabin. "Who wants to climb up on the roof and clean out the bird's nest?"

The children, being children, began to argue over who got to do the job. For a change, they all wanted to do it. John took matters into his own hands by agilely climbing the logs and reaching the roof while the others were still arguing.

"Be careful!" Elizabeth called, fear for his safety evident in her voice.

A strange sensation of warmth drifted from the top of his head to the tips of his toes as he looked down at her worried face. He couldn't remember anyone ever worrying about him. It still surprised him that this lady, as beautiful as the angel he'd once seen in a picture book, really cared. Tears clouded his eyes, making his young voice gruff.

"Ain't nothin' gonna happen to me!"

"You just make sure of that, young man!" Elizabeth called back.

"Women!" he muttered just loud enough for

her to hear. The warmth stayed with him as he pulled the bird's nest free. It was there as he inspected the chimney for further trash and examined the hole in the roof.

As he nimbly descended back to the ground and saw the look of relief that crossed her face, John decided that he could easily learn to like the feeling, too easily. It wouldn't do to become dependent on her, she might use it against him if she knew. He couldn't afford the possibility of her abandoning him as everyone else in his life had done.

"The water's boiling," Belinda called.

With John safely on the ground, Elizabeth turned her attention to other matters. The noon meal consisted of the last of their food. She ate the small amount she allowed herself, watching as the children eagerly disposed of their portions.

"I'll be goin' huntin' this afternoon," John said quietly as he wiped his plate clean.

"Oh, John, I'm sorry," Elizabeth muttered, feeling the weight of her responsibility rest more heavily than usual on her shoulders.

"Ain't no problem, Miss Elizabeth."

"Promise me that you'll at least try to find *wild* game."

In the short time that he had been with them, John had shown that he was very adept at finding food. But he had little concern if dinner was a wild rabbit or a chicken from someone's coop.

A rare smile lighted his features, showing the

promise of arresting masculine beauty and an unusual hint of mischief.

"John, I will be forced to use discipline," she warned sternly.

"You ain't gonna beat me!"

Elizabeth was shocked at the suggestion. "I would never beat you or any of my children!"

"What you gonna do, send me to bed without supper? It ain't the first time I'd try to sleep with my belly growling."

John's stance, head raised determinedly, hands knotted in fists and legs spread, showed that he wouldn't be intimidated. Elizabeth placed her plate on the ground and rose. She took several steps toward the child, watching as a cornered look entered his face. If he had been one of the other children, she would have taken him into her arms, reassuring him with her touch. But John wouldn't allow her to touch him.

The top of his head came to just beneath her chin and his clean sandy brown hair, now free of lice and other crawling things, lay in gentle waves. So old, she thought, for one so young. She mourned the loss of innocence he would never know.

"John, I promise you that you will never be beaten or sent to bed hungry," she said softly, aware that the other children were avidly listening. "But stealing is wrong."

"So is going hungry!"

There was no way she could fight his childish

logic, no way she could battle his longstanding sense of injustice.

"You're right, going hungry is wrong, but we need to find a way to provide for ourselves that doesn't involve taking something that belongs to someone else."

"You figure it out, Miss Elizabeth, while I go huntin'." Reaching to his back pocket to reassure himself that his slingshot was within easy grasp, John turned and walked away. He had become fairly proficient with the weapon, but it would only bring down birds or squirrels, rarely anything as large as a rabbit

From experience, he knew it took a lot of birds or squirrels to feed a family of six. Far more than he was usually successful in finding.

Elizabeth watched until he was out of sight. It shouldn't be his responsibility to find food for the family and yet, he was usually the one to do so. Wilson was taking lessons from the older boy but she wasn't happy that those lessons meant stealing from someone.

She looked at the other children and knew her work was cut out for her if she was to raise them all with a sense of right and wrong. And stealing, for any reason, was wrong.

But so was starving.

"All right, we have a lot to do before dark." She clapped her hands to get everyone's attention. "Let's get busy.

While Belinda and Elaine cleaned up the dishes, Elizabeth assigned Benjamin the task of gathering more wood. With a rag securely tied to the end of a long stick, Wilson pulled down the cobwebs. Elizabeth began the formidable task of clearing years of ashes from the fireplace.

The children worked hard all afternoon without bickering or grumbling. John returned with a dead chicken clutched in each hand. Elizabeth tried to think of the many reasons that stealing was wrong but gave up by the time the air was filled with the delicious aroma of stewing chicken.

Before darkness arrived the cabin was habitable—barely. Beds were made on the dirt floor. As usual, Belinda and Elaine shared blankets for extra warmth, as did Wilson and Benjamin. John chose a spot across the room, directly beneath the large hole in the roof where he could look out at the stars.

There was little space left on the floor of the tiny cabin when Elizabeth spread out her bedding, but there was a roof over their heads and a door to close against unwanted visitors, providing a welcomed illusion of security.

The small fire in the fireplace did little to warm them as the bitterly cold night wind whistled through the open spaces between the logs. The days showed the promise of spring warmth but winter returned each night with the reminder that it still dominated.

Elizabeth listened to the familiar sounds of the sleeping children. A sense of accomplishment filled her with a previously unknown satisfaction. Obstacles could be overcome, challenges met with determination.

Tomorrow would be the beginning of their future. Somehow, with love and tolerance, she would turn these bedraggled children into a family.

With a contented sigh, Elizabeth closed her eyes. For the first time in her life she would have the thing she most wanted—someone who needed her, someone to love.

Three

"I guess this is it, angel," Daniel whispered to the child sleeping confidently in his arms. He looked at the well-cared-for house with trepidation. It sat just outside of the small Indiana town of Richmond, a growing settlement of several hundred people.

The three-story structure boasted a new coat of whitewash with dark green shutters framing the windows. A white picket fence circled the small front yard and he had seen several outbuildings in the back.

He had spent two days searching without success for any of Jenny Sue's relatives. It had been simple to backtrack the wagons for several miles but then other tracks soon wiped out the trail. It had not been an easy decision, but Daniel knew he could travel faster and further without having to care for his precious burden. His chances of finding her family would vastly improve if he didn't have to be concerned for her.

After making several inquiries, Daniel had

been sent to this house. The mostly Quaker populace of Richmond had established this home for children, practicing their principle of feeding the hungry and providing for the needy. They promised Daniel that they would continue his search for her relatives and reassured him that if none were found she would still be well provided for.

The sign on the front gate read RICHMOND'S SOCIETY OF FRIENDS' HOME FOR UNWANTED AND ORPHANED CHILDREN and a shiver of dread ran up his spine as he opened the gate, carrying his trusting treasure up to the door. His knock was answered by a woman in a plain black dress with a white scarf over her head. She didn't smile in greeting, but her eyes were gentle when they rested on the child sleeping in his arms.

"Her name is Jenny Sue," Daniel said quietly. "Her parents were killed on the trail and I can't find any relatives. They told me in town that she could stay here."

"She will be well taken care of," the woman said quietly. "Her tender years will be a time for her to begin learning about death, eternity and life. We will teach her to overcome the frivolity of youth and prevent her from joining unsuitable company. When she is older she will be apprenticed to learn a way to provide for herself."

Several young children gathered behind the woman but there were no greetings or laughter, no teasing or shows of childish curiosity.

"We will tend her body and soul so that she

may enter the light when her day of judgment comes," the woman continued.

But will she learn to laugh and play? Daniel thought, gazing at the solemn faces of the other children. *Will she pick flowers in the spring and run in the tall grass of summer?*

He rested his cheek against her red hair and tried to convince himself that this was the right thing for her. There was a possibility that she had family in the area, grandparents, aunts and uncles, someone who would want to raise her. Maybe he would find them and her time here would be short.

"Her cat?"

"The animal can stay in the barn out back. We have several others that keep it free of rodents."

"She won't be happy without the animal near her." Daniel had discovered that Jenny Sue clung to the cat with jealous ferocity. Holding it while she ate and slept, carrying it constantly on their journey.

"She will adjust," the woman replied calmly.

He didn't want her to adjust! He wanted her to be happy and content. Daniel sighed as he handed Jenny Sue's bundle of clothing to the woman.

"Wake up, Jenny Sue." Daniel rubbed his beard-roughened cheek against the top of her head. He watched as sky blue eyes opened and then looked guardedly around.

"You're going to stay here for a while, sweetheart," he said quietly. "These people will keep you safe while I search for your family."

"No! Me stay with you!" She clung tightly to his fringed coat, her tiny fingers wrapped around the buckskin.

Daniel carefully pried her fingers loose and handed her, cat and all, to the woman. Afraid to linger, he turned and headed down the walk.

"'Peeze? Me be good. . . ."

He had heard those same words for nearly two weeks before he had found her, only then she had been pleading to be freed from the barrel. Those simple words in her childish voice had forced him to keep moving long after exhaustion should have claimed its toll.

Now she was begging him for help and he was walking away. He nearly stopped. His steps slowed and he nearly turned around. The quiet closing of the door helped him to take the necessary steps back to the horse.

Untying the reins, Daniel turned and stared for long minutes at the dark green door. Children should laugh and play and get into trouble, not be examples of adults in miniature. Knowing that it harbored the tiny child who had stolen his heart, he fought a nearly overwhelming urge to go back, knock on that door and tell the woman that he had changed his mind.

Daniel mounted the horse, trying to convince himself that this was for the best. If he couldn't come back she would be safe here, given both physical and spiritual guidance. And there was a chance her family would be found.

Somehow, all the reasons why he should leave her here did nothing to release him from an overwhelming sense of guilt. He was deserting her.

It was so final. . . . She was gone.

Remembering a tavern a few miles back down the trail, he turned his horse in that direction. He rarely drank, but now he welcomed the promised oblivion.

Several hours later, Daniel stumbled out of the tavern. It took an excessive amount of concentration for him to put his foot in the stirrup and an even greater effort to pull his body up into the saddle. The horse stood patiently as he fumbled with the reins and searched with his right foot for an elusive stirrup.

By accident of a drunken mind or intentionally by one still sobered at the memory of a tiny voice begging him not to leave her, Daniel rode back toward the orphanage. Somewhere in the back of his mind he was aware of the low hanging clouds and the occasional snowflake that drifted past his face, but his concerns weren't about the weather.

He had known she'd be there. Standing at the fence, the cat pressed between her and the wood. Her fingers were wrapped around the pickets, her eyes peeking between the slats.

Pain ripped away the haze of liquor as if it had never been. Daniel stopped the horse at the gate and stared down at the fuzzy red hair and the tiny button nose. Her joyless blue eyes spoke with an eloquence far greater than words.

Tears traced silent silvered paths down her freckled cheeks.

"Me be good . . ."

Lacy, delicate snowflakes swirled and twirled in an unleashed dance of lunacy. Nearly weightless flakes piled one upon another until branches of mighty trees bowed in defeat of a more powerful force. Gently bubbling streams became dangerous rivers of ice, trapping the unwary, destroying the unheeding. Distraction was disastrous, carelessness was fatal.

Daniel raised his head and sniffed at the air. The faint smell of smoke drifted to him, but from where? It teased with savage cruelty, promising warmth and safety. But the wind buffeted it around his head making it impossible for him to detect its direction.

He let the horse travel as it would, hoping that the animal would instinctively find its way to shelter. He cursed his own stupidity for not staying in town but he had wanted to get away from the place where he had nearly deserted Jenny Sue. Now he could only hope to find a cabin that would provide refuge until the storm abated.

Jenny Sue and her cat were beneath his coat and two blankets covered his head and shoulders, keeping the upper part of his body fairly warm. But his feet and legs felt frozen and he frequently wiggled his toes, worrying about the very real possibility of frostbite.

Blizzards this late in the winter were rare, but not unknown. Weeks of nearly balmy weather made this storm seem even worse. Daniel knew he had no choice but to try to find someplace for them to wait out the storm. Had it only been himself to consider, he would have stopped and tried to build a lean-to, but he feared for Jenny Sue if she had to stay uncovered for the length of time it would take to construct. He knew that his own body heat was keeping the child safe for now but her tiny body had no reserves to draw on for her own warmth.

As long as the horse could walk, they'd stay on his back. But if he should falter, Daniel would have no choice but to struggle on without him, carrying the child in his arms.

Since this was unfamiliar territory, he didn't bother to look for landmarks but he did raise his head periodically to smell for woodsmoke.

Jenny Sue complained frequently, and loudly, about hunger, but he didn't dare stop. If he didn't soon find a shelter hunger would no longer be a problem.

The children sat closely together on the wobbly benches at the equally rocky table. The bitterly cold wind howled mournfully, making even the dubious protection of the cabin a welcomed sanctuary.

The girls, with their expensive coats and heavy wool dresses, fared better than the boys, who wore whatever extra clothes they possessed.

They all had blankets wrapped around their shoulders and over their heads. With fingers too cold to hold a spoon, they tried to eat their rapidly cooling soup.

The fire burned feebly, the wet wood pouring smoke into the room only to be swept away by the wind blowing through the cracks between the logs, but not before it caused eyes to water and noses to drip.

The first day of school had been less than successful, with only three children from the settlement in attendance. Word had not yet spread that the teacher had arrived and with the threat of a winter storm even the children who had come to school had left early.

Elder Jacobs had not delivered the promised load of wood and the amount the children had gathered was pitifully small. Everyone had worked hard all afternoon preparing for the storm but Elizabeth kept to herself the very real fear that the storm could outlive their meager supplies.

Knowing that a storm was imminent, Elizabeth and John had tried to patch the roof. Having no nails, they had placed a slab of wood over the hole and used several large rocks to hold it in place. The patch had proved successful until the first strong gust of wind had viciously blown it free, allowing snow to drift to the floor where it melted and turned the hard-packed dirt to mud. The temperature dropped steadily once the sun had gone down and now the mud was turning to ice and the snow beginning to pile up.

Elizabeth used her spare clothes as rags to stuff between the logs, but there were more holes than she had gowns. The late winter storm that had started as a few gently falling flakes earlier in the afternoon had become a full-blown blizzard as night progressed.

She doubted that they had enough wood to keep the fire burning all night and worried that without its frail heat they would freeze to death. She had never been so cold in her life, even the cup of hot broth she held between her hands failed to help warm her numb fingers.

"This snow sure would feel good in the middle of summer," Belinda murmured.

"If we live that long!" John replied, the usual harshness gone from his voice.

"I'm cold!" Elaine whined, rubbing at her dripping nose.

Before Elizabeth could respond, John unwrapped his blanket, pulled the little girl onto his lap and rewrapped them both. "Now we'll both be warmer."

It was such an unusual move for the boy, that Elizabeth stared with amazed surprise. The sudden, unexpected pounding on the door made them all jump.

"What on earth?" she asked as all eyes turned toward the door. Before anyone could move the thundering bang was repeated.

"What'll we do?" Belinda asked, fear suddenly crossing her features. Strangers at any time

40

caused suspicion but banging on the door during the middle of a blizzard created fear.

"We can't let them freeze to death," Elizabeth replied, aware of the very real danger they faced.

"Ain't gonna be no warmer in here than out there," John stated. He pushed Elaine off his lap, wrapping her in his blanket. Straightening his narrow shoulders, he walked over to Elizabeth. "Let them stay outside."

"We can't do that, John." She turned her gaze to the door when it seemed that their uninvited visitor intended to break it down with his knocking.

"Open the door, Belinda," Elizabeth instructed as she grabbed a piece of wood to use as a club. She was aware of John taking up a defensive stance across the room from her and prayed it wouldn't be necessary for the child to try to defend them.

Belinda approached the door and lifted the bar that kept it closed. They all gasped when it opened, revealing a man—at least they thought it was a man.

"Gor, it's a real snowman!" Benjamin whispered in awe.

The man was huge, filling the doorway. Snow covered him from head to foot, icicles weighing down the fringe on his coat and hanging from the edges of the blanket thrown over his head. Without a word, he entered the cabin, slamming the door closed behind him.

Daniel looked at the bewildered, childish

faces staring so intently at him and knew that he was more frightening than usual. His gaze wandered to the woman wrapped in a cape, a piece of wood held in her hands, and he wondered if she really thought that tiny piece of kindling would protect her. He could snap it in two without the slightest effort.

He wanted to take the time to offer reassurance, but his greatest concern at the moment was Jenny Sue. It had been a couple of hours since he'd felt her move and he prayed that she had simply fallen asleep.

He let the ice-covered blankets slip from his shoulders but his frozen fingers had trouble working the buttons of his coat. Finally, he managed to get it open and heard their startled gasps when it revealed the sleeping child and mangy cat.

"Jenny Sue." His deep voice rumbled through the silence. "Wake up, little one."

Obediently, Jenny Sue opened her eyes. When she saw the strange faces staring intently at her, she clutched tightly to Daniel's shirt.

Painfully aware that the wood was no means of defense against so large a man, Elizabeth's fear evaporated when she saw the child wrapped against his massive body. No man that protective of his own child would bring harm to her children. She dropped the piece of wood and approached them, her smile a gentle greeting.

"It's not much warmer in here than outside, but you're welcome to stay until the storm clears." She reached out to stroke the cat's furry body, amazed by its warmth, until she realized that snuggling against this man would be like snuggling against a burning fire.

"I'm Daniel LeClerc," he introduced himself, his voice vibrating through her in the strangest way. "And this is Jenny Sue. We appreciate your offer."

"Come sit by the fire, feeble as it is, and try to thaw out a little." Elizabeth stepped back to allow him entrance into the room, which seemed even smaller with his large presence. "If nothing else, it should warm your fingers and toes."

Four pairs of eyes peeked curiously from behind blankets as Daniel knelt by the fire, Jenny Sue carefully balanced on his knee. He had seen a boy, obviously the oldest child, across the room, his hands knotted in fists and a look of fierce determination on his thin face. He recognized and respected the boy's grit but hoped the child would realize that he presented no danger.

Daniel stifled a moan as the heat warmed his fingers, bringing life back to the nearly frozen flesh with a painful vengeance.

"Let me take your daughter while you warm up," Elizabeth offered, her arms outstretched to take the child.

Jenny Sue's eyes widened, panic clearly evident, and she buried her face in Daniel's shirt, her fingers clinging frantically to the cloth.

"It's all right, *m'eudail*." The Gaelic endearment rolled softly from his tongue as he gently rubbed her tiny back. "You can stay right where you are." Her fingers did not loosen their grasp nor did she lift her head, but he felt the relaxing of her body.

Daniel raised his head and stared at the woman, disappointed that he could see so little of her. The hooded cloak covered her from head to toe, hiding even her hair and the color of her eyes. But her husky voice teased every nerve ending in his body.

"Your name, mistress?"

"Elizabeth," she replied, mesmerized by something in his voice and a burning deep in his black eyes.

"Elizabeth." Her name was a caress, rippling down her back with a shiver of awareness that he was a man and she was a woman.

"Eliz . . . Elizabeth Spurlin," she stumbled, trying to shake off the strangeness that filled her. She turned slightly, her hand waving toward the inquisitive faces behind them. "And these are my children: John, Belinda, Benjamin, Wilson and Elaine."

All of the children, except for John, nodded politely. Daniel's gaze lingered on the boy, seeing the hostility and dislike on the young face.

"I apologize for barging in, but we appreciate the invitation to stay until the weather clears." He scanned the sparse cabin, noticing the clothing stuffed between the logs and the hole in the roof. The pot of soup hanging on the hook over the fire seemed to be more broth than meat and the smoky fire made his eyes water but provided very little heat.

Elizabeth stepped back when he stood, cradling Jenny Sue, his head nearly touching the rafters of the roof. She wondered if his fiery red hair was warmer than their fire and was startled to realize that she wanted to touch it to find out.

"I need to take care of my horse," he stated.

"There's a shed to the side of the cabin, but I'm not sure you can see it through the snow."

"I'll find it." He softly caressed Jenny Sue's hair. "I'll leave her in here with you, but I don't think she's going to be happy about it."

Elizabeth smiled. "I think we can manage. Surely between the children and myself we can watch one little girl for a few minutes."

"She can be a handful," Daniel warned.

Elizabeth watched as he whispered to the child and saw her hand tighten on his shirt. He carefully pried her fingers free and handed her to Elizabeth. Jenny Sue didn't scream or cry when Elizabeth's arms folded around her but her body stiffened, making it difficult for Elizabeth to hold her.

"Point me in the direction of the woodpile and I'll bring some wood in when I come back."

"We don't have a woodpile," Elizabeth mumbled as she tried to get a firmer hold on the child.

"What? Everybody has a woodpile." He shook his head in disbelief.

"Everybody with an ax or a hatchet, maybe, but we don't have those either." Feeling Jenny Sue's stiff body slowly sliding out of her grasp, she fought to get a firmer hold on the child. "The only wood we've had are pieces the boys have found that are small enough to fit into the fireplace."

Belinda walked up to Elizabeth and pulled the cat from Jenny Sue's grasp. She carried it back to the table and the other children gathered around, eager to have a chance to pet the animal.

"Kitty!" Jenny Sue bellowed, fighting free from Elizabeth.

Seeing his chance to escape while Jenny Sue was otherwise occupied, Daniel opened the door and stepped outside, wrapping his coat tightly around him.

"My kitty!" Jenny Sue bellowed again, but hesitated approaching the children. Her lower lip quivered but her blue eyes showed no sign of tears. "My kitty," she stated again.

"May we hold your kitty?" Elizabeth knelt beside the child, softly pushing her tangled red hair from her face. "My children don't have a pet of their own to play with."

"My kitty!"

"I'll bet kitty would like something to eat." Elizabeth took a chipped bowl from the only shelf in the cabin and filled it with milk one of the settlement children had brought to school that morning. She crumbled up some bread and set the concoction on the floor. Picking up the purring cat from Belinda's lap, she set it in front of the bowl and the children watched with fascination as the cat fastidiously sniffed the food

46

before sitting down and delicately licking at the milk.

"Are you hungry, too?" She poured a cup of milk and ladled some soup into another bowl.

Never one to miss a meal, Jenny Sue looked at the other children. "My kitty!"

Hiding a smile, Elizabeth nodded. "Your kitty," she agreed, helping the child to climb up on a bench. Clear blue eyes watched that no one touched the cat as she ate her food.

Daniel entered without knocking, snow covering his heavy coat. He shook the snow free but didn't bother removing his coat. He carried a few pieces of wood in his arms which he slowly added to the fire, being careful not to smother the flame.

Dropping Jenny Sue's bundle of clothing on the floor, he began to unwrap another package. Everyone's eyes widened when they saw the haunch of meat he exposed.

"Killed this deer yesterday," he explained. "Hate to waste good meat and would have packed it all if I'd known we'd be stopping here, but I cooked what I could last night and only packed this piece for today."

Elizabeth's mouth began to water at the thought of the meat. It had been a long time since there had been enough food to go around and she had been aware of her gowns hanging loosely on her body rather than hugging curves.

Daniel had seen that all of the children except one, the boy she introduced as John, had bowls of steaming soup in front of them. John had only a piece of bread, and though it dripped with honey, it still wasn't as filling or as warming as the hot soup. He didn't normally interfere when something wasn't any of his business but he couldn't stand back and watch as a child was denied something as simple as a decent meal.

"It'll take a while for the meat to cook, but there'll be plenty for everyone." Daniel turned his gaze from John's dinner, making it clear that he didn't approve of her partiality to the other children over this one boy.

His black eyes burning into hers, Elizabeth understood his unspoken criticism and wondered if he'd believe that John had chosen his own meal, claiming it was his punishment for the chicken he'd provided for their supper. The honey had been at her insistence and had been applied generously.

"Leave her alone!" John came around the table, his hands clenched into fists. He stood in front of Elizabeth, ready to provide whatever protection he could.

"What I eat is my business! Ain't nobody gonna say that Miss Elizabeth ain't being fair."

"Thank you, John," Elizabeth said quietly, placing a gentle hand on his shoulder. She felt him stiffen at her touch but he didn't pull away. "Mr. LeClerc is naturally curious as to why you have only bread for your supper."

"It ain't none of his business." Her hand felt good on his shoulder, sort of warm and comforting. She was so sweet and nice and didn't know how cruel life really was. Why, look what she'd done for him, paid good, hard money to his drunken father for him when she already had four other kids to provide for. She'd even had trouble starting a fire before he'd come along. And according to the other kids, there had never been enough to eat.

But her voice was always soft and her words kind. She smiled at a flower and laughed for nearly any reason. And the others weren't at all afraid to ask for a hug or a kiss; she was always willing to give the smallest sign of affection to them. He knew that the offer was open to him, too, but it was hard to accept something he'd never had before.

He blinked back tears of frustration at his knowledge that he couldn't protect her from this giant. He was little, still had a long way to go before he was grown, but he swore to himself that this man would only get to Elizabeth by killing him first.

Hoping to offer silent reassurance, Daniel carefully maintained a relaxed stance, his admiration for the boy going up several notches when the child had shown that he would try to protect the lady. He still had not seen beyond the hooded cape but he had thought that she was the mother of this brood. By John's own choice of titles, Daniel now knew that he, at least, wasn't her son.

"John decided on his own supper," Elizabeth offered. "He feels that punishment is necessary but knows that I disagree with him."

"Punishment?"

"I got the chicken," John hissed, hating to explain anything to this stranger.

"Why should you be punished for that?" Daniel asked.

"'Cause I raided a neighbor's coop."

Daniel shook his head with confusion. There was more here than the surface appearance. No woodpile, ax or hatchet; a dilapidated cabin not fit to house a family of skunks. Five kids, one he knew wasn't hers and four others he was beginning to wonder about.

The little girls were dressed in the latest fashion, their cloaks made of fine wool. But the boys wore ragged clothing either too small or several sizes too large.

A kid far too tough for his age, admitted to stealing so that the others wouldn't go hungry but accepted only bread as his own meal because he knew stealing was wrong.

And hidden in the concealing depths of a dark cape, was a lady with a soft, well-educated voice whose gentle southern accent skimmed across his skin with the supple sensuality of mink.

Four

"Kitty!"

Jenny Sue's bellow of rage successfully broke the deadlock between the man and the boy without either one being forced to back down.

"My kitty!" Tiny hands were doubled into fists and her face glowed an angry red as she tried to grab the animal away from one of the boys.

"Wilson, please give the cat back to Jenny Sue," Elizabeth said quietly.

"You said we had to share our things," Wilson stated firmly, holding the docile animal above the little girl's reach. "I just wanted to hold it. I won't hurt it."

"I know that, Wilson, but Jenny Sue doesn't. Maybe tomorrow when she knows us better she'll allow us to hold her pet." A cloud of snow burst from the hole in the roof and settled on Elizabeth. She shivered, shook the covering of white from her shoulders and pulled the cape tighter around her neck.

"Dumb ole cat," Wilson muttered as he carefully handed it back to Jenny Sue.

"My kitty," Jenny Sue stated needlessly as she clutched the animal to her. "Burr, kitty . . . burr . . ." Having accomplished the rescue of her pet, she turned melting blue eyes toward Daniel.

"Ma'am, if we don't do something about getting some heat in here none of us may be around tomorrow." Daniel wrapped one of his blankets around the little girl, adjusting it so that only her eyes were visible.

"I realize that, Mr. LeClerc, but we are nearly out of wood. I was hoping that we'd have enough to last through the night." She looked at the miserably small stack of broken branches and large twigs.

Daniel said nothing, his eloquent expression implying that only a fool would have come to that conclusion. Elizabeth squirmed, grateful for the cape, as his black eyes tried to penetrate its concealing folds. She wanted to deny to herself that she was grateful for this Scottish giant's presence but the security she felt just knowing he was in the room was unquestionable. She tried to blame the shiver that ran up her spine on the storm, but that didn't explain the sudden light-headed breathlessness that made her reach out for the support of the table. A gust of wind blew through the logs, releasing her from his gaze and unnecessarily reminding them that freezing to death was a very real possibility.

Darkness combined with the blowing strength

of the storm made it impossible for Daniel to venture out in search of wood. More than likely he'd just get lost and freeze to death. A quick scan of the room showed him that it held only the personal items of the family . . . and the table and rickety benches.

Kneeling down on one knee, Daniel grasped one of the empty benches and applied a light pressure. The creaking sounds proved his suspicions, the wood was old and dry. If he could splinter enough of it, it would burn hot, providing them with much-needed heat.

Elizabeth's eyes widened with amazement as she watched him break the bench apart using nothing but his bare hands. It brought back to her with painful clarity that her plan to defend them with what amounted to nothing more than a twig was ludicrous. Nothing short of a cannon would stop this man if he was determined to accomplish something.

Placing several pieces of the bench into the fireplace, Daniel watched with satisfaction as it caught fire and burned with a blue flame. He swung the hook with the pot attached over the heat so that the watery broth could come to a boil.

"I'll cut up some of the meat and add it to the pot." Elizabeth approached him cautiously, his size and strength once again intimidating her.

"Add most of the meat that I cooked last night, " Daniel instructed as he reached for the rest of the demolished bench. "It'll be ready sooner than the raw meat and the kids can have a decent meal before they go to bed. We'll cook the rest of it later."

Knowing his show of strength had caused her sudden apprehension, he felt an overwhelming desire to reassure her but words from a stranger were useless. Perhaps, if the storm eased up, he and Jenny Sue could leave in the morning.

As if laughing at his thoughts a strong wind blew another storm of white into the room. Daniel again looked around the dilapidated room. He knew he couldn't leave the woman and her children until he had helped make some much-needed repairs.

"Sometimes it's safer to trust what your instincts are telling you than what your eyes are seeing." Kneeling on the floor, his eyes on level with her chin, his normally booming voice was lowered so that it traveled only to her.

She wasn't surprised that he had accurately interpreted her anxiety, he seemed to be aware of things that most people ignored. "I have five children to protect," she stated firmly.

"And I can destroy a wooden bench using nothing but my hands." He looked down at his hands then up at her. His massive shoulders shrugged, his black eyes burning into hers with something more than reassurance.

"Don't fear my strength, appreciate it. You have to take my word for it when I tell you that I'd never use it against you or the children." He wrapped his hands around the bench and proceeded to demolish more of it. "Without an ax

54

or a hatchet this is the only thing between warmth and freezing to death. It may be our only hope of surviving the night."

Knowing she had no choice but to trust him, Elizabeth took a deep breath, picked up the knife and began to hack on the frozen meat. "Watch out for splinters."

A sheepish grin crossed his face, reminiscent of a little boy who'd been caught with a fistful of cookies. He rose to his feet and approached her, holding out his left hand. Standing so close to him, she was again overwhelmed by his size. She briefly debated asking him to take off his coat since the heavy fur only added to the impression. Deciding it would be cruel and foolish to ask him to freeze so that she wouldn't be intimidated she cupped his hand in both of hers and looked at the splinter of wood imbedded into his flesh.

"I think I can pull it free, but it might hurt." She unconsciously stroked his calloused palm with her thumbs.

"I think I'll survive." Daniel smiled at the thought of something as minor as a splinter causing him pain. He had felt the wood enter his skin but hadn't given it much thought until she'd spoken.

"I'll try to be quick." She lightly rubbed the angry flesh, strangely unsettled at the thought of causing him pain.

The gentle strokes of her fingers were far from soothing and he briefly closed his eyes to regain control of his wayward thoughts. He opened his eyes and stared into the black void beneath her hood.

"I think I should see the person who's going to cause me undue agony." His voice wasn't as teasing as he'd have liked as he reached up with his free hand. The material fell back from her face and Daniel stared at the vision of femininity it had hidden.

Elizabeth had long been accustomed to the admiring stares caused by her beauty but remained mystified by them. When she looked into a mirror she saw a face: eyes, nose, lips, forehead, chin. She often felt that she was cursed by her face; her life would have been easier had her looks been plainer. Many of the offers she had received were made by men who were enthralled by her loveliness and wanted her as a prized possession to parade upon their arms. None offered more than a house, clothing, money; things granted to a mistress for the use of her body. Marriage was never offered to the beautiful bastard daughter who could bring only herself to the union.

As the hood slid free from her head, Daniel's muffled gasp of surprise startled only him. Eyes the color of a stormy winter sky calmly met his. Golden blond hair, glossy red in the flickering fire, was pulled severely back from a face sculptured by a loving hand.

Daniel's perusal was interrupted by the intensity of an angry stare directed toward him. He turned his gaze from hers and collided with angry blue eyes. Old beyond his years, John's face

56

was filled with the knowledge that he understood and resented Daniel's thoughts. Hands clenched in fists, his intentions to protect Elizabeth spoke clearly in his stance.

"Mistress, perhaps it would be better if you quickly remove the splinter and free my hand from your grasp. Your young champion is not happy with our present circumstance." Daniel directed her gaze toward the child.

"Thank you for your concern, John," she said softly, smiling at the boy. "Mr. LeClerc has need of my assistance."

"That ain't all he be awantin'," the child said wisely.

"Maturity allows you to want but willingly accept only what is given." Elizabeth spoke to John but looked at Daniel. "Mr. LeClerc is going to get my help in removing the splinter," she continued. "Should he want anything else he'll just have to be satisfied with what is freely given."

"Would more be freely given?" he couldn't resist asking.

"Only the removal of the splinter, Mr. LeClerc." Elizabeth forced her hands to hold steady. The thought of offering him more caused a curious weakness. At a tender age she had learned that men such as this one would eagerly satisfy their needs on her body but offer no hope of achieving her own desires.

His gaze studied her intensely as she pulled the splinter from his hand. His dark eyes seemed to try to read her thoughts, to find the answers to questions he wouldn't, or couldn't, answer without her help.

"All done." Elizabeth bit back a sigh of relief as she released his hand. She didn't want that knowing stare to penetrate too deeply, to hunt for answers to questions that shouldn't be asked. Picking up the knife, she again hacked at the meat.

"Just be sure that one of your fingers doesn't suffer the same fate as that meat you're hacking up. I'd hate to bite down on a fingernail!"

"Thanks to your generosity we're no longer in so dire need of meat that I'd willingly give a finger to fill the pot."

Her teasing reply brought his head up with a snap. "You had considered such a thing?"

Elizabeth looked at her long slender fingers, the nails broken and torn to the quick, callouses forming where none had been before. "Our situation was desperate, but I hadn't quite reached the point that I was willing to sacrifice parts of my body, Mr. LeClerc."

"Would you have done so?"

"Whatever is necessary," she answered without hesitation. "These children will not suffer if it is within my power to prevent it."

Daniel was speechless. It was her acknowledgment that she would do anything to provide for the children, even if it was something so repugnant it would affect the rest of her life.

He knelt in front of the fragments of the bench and pushing with one hand while pulling with the other, easily snapped it into manageable size. With the splintering of each new piece, his anger grew at the unfairness of life. He, who because of his size and his sex had never been at the mercy of another, wanted to demolish the person responsible for forcing her to even consider selling herself to save the children.

Who had left her alone to protect and provide for five children? What man had turned his back and walked away? Why was she in the middle of nowhere living in a structure not fit for animals? Well educated, dressed in expensive clothing in the latest styles, it was glaringly obvious that she was accustomed to more in life than this hovel.

The mystery of this woman grew with each passing hour. He knew she appreciated his help and yet he felt that she would have managed, somehow, if he hadn't come along. That the children loved her was obvious, but he began to wonder about their parentage.

Daniel knew that John was not her child, yet the boy was extremely protective of her. From the corner of his eye he watched as she spoke softly to the boy, her hand reaching out to him. The child stepped back, away from her touch, but still within the space he had deemed necessary to provide protection.

So many questions, so few answers.

Little was said as Elizabeth continued cutting the meat and adding it to the pot while Daniel further increased the growing stack of firewood. Snuggled beneath blankets, the children sat quietly watching the adults work, except for John, who stood protectively close to Elizabeth, a blanket thrown around his thin shoulders at her insistence.

With each new piece of wood added to the fire, the heat grew. A bone-chilling cold breeze still wove its way insidiously through any available crack but the children crowded up close to the fire, tiny hands held out in supplication to the heat.

The pot soon began to bubble and delicious smells vied with the warmth for attention. As Daniel began breaking apart another bench, Elizabeth filled bowls with the meat-rich broth. Little fingers, warmed by the flame, held spoonfuls of broth to appreciative noses and breathed deeply of the mouth-watering aroma. Childish voices were stilled in favor of slurping, which was ignored by the adults who shared in the warmth and the food.

Outside, the wind howled, the ferocity of nature undeniable. Snow blew through the hole in the roof, piling onto the floor where it began to melt in the heat from the fire. Daniel dug a trench toward the door, allowing the water to run away from them. The hole in the roof was the first thing that needed his attention. Tomorrow, snow or not, he intended to patch it.

He removed the clothing Elizabeth had crammed into the cracks between the logs. The gowns, of silk and lace, polished cotton and velvet, were extremely expensive rags.

Turning them inside out to protect the delicate fabric and dainty lacy, he twisted them into neat rolls then filled in the worst of the cracks at the lower level of the cabin. It would help stop the wind from blowing over them once everyone lay down for the night.

Warm at last, tummies pleasantly full, little eyes began to droop and yawns filled the air.

"Bedtime," Elizabeth stated firmly.

No voices were raised in protest, no complaints to stay up for a while longer or requests for bedtime stories. The children wandered to their chosen places on the floor and lay down. The two girls, Belinda and Elaine, shared their blankets while Benjamin and Wilson did the same. Only John lay by himself, his face turned so that he could watch Daniel.

"Where me sleep?" Jenny Sue asked, the cat clutched in her arms.

"Up! Everybody up!" Daniel's voice boomed through the room.

"What on earth . . ." Elizabeth exclaimed as the children jumped up and huddled together, bewildered by the unexpected command.

"Tonight we sleep together! Girls on one side, boys on the other, adults on each end, everybody's feet pointed toward the fire.

"How many blankets, capes and coats do we have?" Daniel asked as he began to organize the children. He instructed everyone to remove their coats, knowing they would be warmer snuggled together without them. He watched with natural curiosity as Elizabeth untied her cape and pulled it from her shoulders. Her printed cotton dress was slimly cut so that it hinted at her curves, the high-waisted, low square-cut neckline emphasized her cleavage, allowing his imagination to run rampant.

Elizabeth watched as he slowly unbuttoned his coat. Her eyes were drawn downward as his fingers worked the bone buttons free. It slid from his shoulders leaving him in a linen shirt that accentuated the width of his shoulders and the narrowness of his hips. She was startled to discover that the coat had not added to his size, but rather hid the fact that he was truly a giant.

In front of the fire, Daniel spread his coat open, making a warm, soft bed for the three little girls. He rolled their coats into pillows and topped them with two of the blankets. More blankets were placed on the floor and coats rolled into pillows. Benjamin and Wilson snuggled together while John made it clear that he would not join the group.

"You next, mistress." Daniel spread a blanket on the floor and waited for Elizabeth to comply.

Feeling silly, Elizabeth smiled at the children as she sat down on the blanket. "There are only three blankets left. I can cover up with my cape.

"No need." Daniel looked at the remaining child. "John, snuggle up on that side of her. It'll help keep her warm and you two can share blankets."

Elizabeth smiled at the child and softly patted the blanket beside her. "Come on, John, you can be my bed warmer for tonight."

Daniel turned away to add more wood to the

fire, alert to the sounds as the boy settled in beside her. When everyone was situated to his satisfaction he found another shirt in his pack and pulled it on over his head. Taking the remaining blanket, he wrapped it around his shoulders and sat down beside Jenny Sue.

"You'll be cold with only one blanket," Elizabeth said quietly from the far side of the group.

"I'll be fine."

"But you can—"

"I'll be fine!"

The popping and crackling of the fire gave its own form of comfort as the wind whistled through the rafters. Elizabeth said a silent prayer of gratitude for the unexpected arrival of Daniel LeClerc. With him she was no longer afraid, no longer concerned that they would make it through the long, cold night. He would guard over their sleep and nothing, not even the temperature, would win against him.

"Quit wiggling, Elaine," Belinda said softly.

"There's a lump!"

"Benjamin's kickin' me!"

"Am not!"

"Are too—"

"Settle down children."

It was still bitterly cold, but with feet toward the fire and blankets to snuggle beneath, the children soon forgot the terror of the storm. Daniel leaned against the wall, the blanket thrown around his shoulders and over his head. He intended to feed the fire carefully, hoping to make the wood last through the night. If he was very careful they had a chance of surviving the night. He prayed that the sun would shine tomorrow, bringing the temperature to above freezing.

"He hit me!"

"Did not!"

"Did too!"

"Elaine, stop wiggling."

"The lump—"

"Ouch, that hurt . . ."

"That's my pillow . . ."

"You're taking my part of the blanket . . ."

"Children," Elizabeth interrupted the arguments before they could get out of hand. "It's been a long day for all of us. It's time to settle down and go to sleep."

"But he hit me . . ."

"Did not . . ."

"My bed's lumpy . . ."

"That's my blanket . . ."

". . . my pillow . . ."

"Where's my . . ."

"Enough!"

Daniel's roar brought a sudden, complete silence to the complaints. The whisper of the wind and the crackle of the fire filled the void.

"He scared me," a little voice said in the dark.

"Boy can he yell!"

"Wish I could yell like that!"

"Children, that is more that enough," Elizabeth stated firmly. "Mr. LeClerc is tired and you know how grumpy we get when we're tired."

"My name is Daniel!" he stated through clenched teeth.

"Oh, excuse me," she said quietly. "Daniel is tired and you know how grumpy we get when we're tired."

"I'm not tired."

"Sounds tired to me," Wilson mumbled.

"Sounds grumpy, too," Benjamin agreed.

"ENOUGH!"

In the silence that ensued not a whisper was heard, or complaint or even deep breathing. Suddenly, Jenny Sue threw back her blankets and climbed to her feet.

"Where do you think you're going, little one?" Daniel asked gently, fearing that he had frightened her.

"Gotta wee."

Laughter filled the room at the tiny girl's statement and Daniel had a hard time hiding his own smile. "Of course, I should have known."

Smothering a chuckle, Elizabeth climbed to her feet. "I'll handle this." She took the child by the hand and led her to a far corner and a pot she had placed there just for that purpose.

Everyone else seemed to need something, too, and it was some time before they were again settled into place. Daniel added more wood to the fire and checked to make sure that blankets covered small bodies.

Elizabeth was amazed at his gentleness as he tucked the blankets around the children. Giving each child a few moments of individual attention, he caressed the girls cheeks with gentle fingers and lightly tussled the boys hair. His deep voice was the rumble of quiet thunder through the cabin as he instructed them to stay beneath the blankets.

Elizabeth had not perceived how frightened they had been until she listened to him reassure them that he would keep the fire burning through the night while they slept and that if anything got into the cabin it would have to go through him before it could reach them. They had never given her any indication of the extent of their fear. A deep sadness filled her as she realized that, in their own way, each child had tried to protect her by hiding his apprehension.

She had promised them that they would be safe but it was agonizingly clear to her that she was failing them. How could they feel safe in a flimsy cabin that couldn't even keep out the elements? What security was there for them wondering what, or even if, they would have food to eat when they were hungry?

Knowing that her exhaustion and her own fear was adding to her feelings of incompetence, Elizabeth closed her eyes and sought sleep. She listened as Daniel spoke quietly to John, treating the boy in a more mature manner than he had the others.

Her eyes flew open when she felt him carefully tucking the blanket around her, too. It had been a long time, a lifetime ago, since someone cared enough to tuck her into bed. Elizabeth knew he wasn't giving her special attention, he was treating her exactly as he had the children, but the unexpected sweetness of the gesture left her craving more.

The remembered pain of a little girl being deserted in a strange place by the father she had adored threatened to fill her eyes with tears. She mentally shook her head in disgust. Twenty-two years old and still hurting by abandonment fifteen years earlier. Would she always feel the pain? Would the hurt never go away? She was an adult now, with an adult's understanding that a bastard daughter wouldn't be wanted by the new wife, couldn't be placed above the legitimate children that would be born. She didn't even hate her father or his wife any longer. So why did the pain still prick her heart?

"Good night, Elizabeth," Daniel whispered, his fingers softly caressing her cheek.

" 'Night, Daniel," she replied, her voice fighting to break through the paralysis his touch was causing.

Security such as she had never felt before filled her with wonder. She watched him walk to the far side of the room and sit down, his back against the wall. As she forced her eyes to close and waited for sleep Elizabeth allowed herself to dream of someone like Daniel LeClerc truly caring. What measure of security and safety could she find in such capable hands? And if he loved, ah . . . if he loved. . . .

Five

Through the haze of sleep Elizabeth became aware of whispering voices and childish giggles. She snuggled deeper into the cocoon of blankets, reluctant to face the cold air nipping at her nose. Even the hard, lumpy floor was tolerable when compared to the temperature of the room.

She fought the urge to stretch luxuriously and give away the fact that she was awake. Guilt that someone else was taking the responsibility for the children wove its way insidiously through her, but she forced her eyes to stay closed. Surely, just this once, it was all right to be a little bit lazy.

After a few short minutes Elizabeth discovered that pretending to be asleep had its own drawbacks. She was forced to use senses other than vision to comprehend what was happening. And so much seemed to be happening.

Why were the children giggling? Her dawning smile receded when she realized that she couldn't remember hearing such a happy sound from them.

Something sizzled over the fire. What was cooking? And that delicious smell wafting its way beneath her blankets, could it be coffee? Surely not, she decided with a silent sigh. She hadn't had coffee in months and tea was an expensive treat she doubted she'd taste for a long time to come.

Her thoughts were interrupted when an owl hooted softly, its age-old question drifting through the room. An owl? In the middle of morning? In the cabin? A few seconds later when a turkey gobbled she nearly opened her eyes. Delighted giggles and pleas for more were met by the song of birds, the grunt of a pig and the extremely realistic cry of a wolf that sent a shiver of fear up her spine.

Quiet cries of amazement filled the room and suddenly Elizabeth knew she wanted to be a part of the happy group. Again, she nearly opened her eyes when a voice stopped her.

"How'd you do that?" John asked in an awed, respectful tone she'd never before heard from him. "You sounded just like all those animals."

"I was raised with a Shawnee brother." Daniel added some wood to the fire, his eyes turned toward the lump under the blankets. He knew that Elizabeth was awake by the stiffening of her body when he'd howled but he decided to let her stay abed a bit longer. She had slept so deeply through the night that he wondered how long it had been since she had felt secure enough to close her eyes and let oblivion claim her.

"A real Injun?" Wilson's voice reflected both fascination and horror.

"Nathan Morning Hawk is full-blood Shawnee," Daniel replied. "He's also my brother and my best friend. When his mother died in a measles epidemic that killed most of the tribe, Hawk was only a newborn baby. His father, Limping Wolf, left him with my mother and father when the tribe moved west."

"Gor! You know a bunch of Injuns?"

Daniel hid a smile at the amazed looks on the childish faces. "Hawk and I were raised by my parents and his. Limping Wolf would come and get us and we'd spend months with his people. After a while my mother would want us home and my father would come and take us back. We both learned the best of each other's heritage."

"And you learned to make the animal noises from the Indians?" John was filled with fascination as he listened to the story.

"Among other things," Daniel confirmed.

"Like what?"

"Well, like how to track and hunt." Daniel moved the pot of gently boiling coffee away from the fire. "We learned to respect animals and kill only what we needed to survive. We were taught how to live in the wilderness with little more than a knife in our possession."

Elizabeth listened to Daniel's deep, soothing voice with the same attention as the children. As they asked question after question she realized that Daniel was an experience none of them had ever had . . . the undivided attention of a man who didn't abuse them, neglect them or demand untold things from them.

None of the children had ever had gentle concern or attention from a father. Elaine and Belinda had been in her care for over four years and not once in that time had their father been to see them. He had provided everything they needed: a lovely home, nice clothes, the care of an educated governess, everything but the attention all children need from a loving father.

She had found Wilson and Benjamin living under the boardwalk of a town, stealing to survive in an existence little better than wild animals. They had been raised by a grandmother who had died, leaving the boys alone with no one to care if they lived or died.

And John . . . She shivered at the memory of the drunken man who had sold the boy to her for the price of a bottle of whiskey. From the little she had learned of the child she knew it hadn't been the first time. In fact, John had been sold and resold numerous times. It was up to him to escape after a day or two and return to the abusive man who soon sold the child again.

She listened as Daniel patiently answered each question as he continued to prepare breakfast.

"You speak Injun?" Benjamin asked.

"I speak Shawnee," Daniel replied. "As well as French and Gaelic."

"What's Gaelic?" Belinda questioned.

"It is the language of the people who live in Scotland and French is the language of the people of France."

"Say something!" they begged.

Daniel easily completed a sentence that sounded to Elizabeth as though it had combined all of the languages into one.

"What'd you say?"

"I said that it's time for opossums to wake up or breakfast will be burned."

Knowing she had been found out, Elizabeth smiled and rolled to her stomach, propping her head up on her folded hands. "Can't I have breakfast in bed?"

She looked as innocent as the children who gathered around the table watching Daniel remove the food from the fire. Her smoky gray eyes, still warm with sleep, unknowingly enticed him to join her.

"You may not have breakfast in bed, *meanbha aon*. You may, however, have the use of the only remaining bench, which might well be the last time it is used as such since we are nearly out of firewood."

"*Meanbha* what?"

"Gaelic—means little one," Daniel informed her.

"Easy for you to say. Everyone is smaller than you," Elizabeth mumbled as she climbed from her warm cocoon.

"I have four brothers who are equal to me and we all follow our father in size."

"Good heavens, a family of giants! Is everyone a redhead, too?"

"Only me and my little sister, Dara. We get it from our mother."

Daniel watched appreciatively as she stood. Her dress had managed to work its way up her thighs and he had a satisfying view of nicely shaped legs and slender ankles. Her golden hair was in total disarray, tangling enticingly over the cleavage that hung threateningly—promisingly—from the square neckline of her dress. The creamy, silken flesh beckoned, inviting him to caress with his hands, to taste with his lips.

Clearing his throat of its sudden tightness, Daniel forced his gaze away from her. Too much imagination was a bad thing for a man, he decided. It made him forget that five pairs of innocent eyes watched every move he made. And one pair of far-too-young-to-be-so-knowledgeable eyes, seemed to understand every lustful thought that went through Daniel's mind.

Elizabeth straightened her dress and pushed her hair back from her face as she joined everyone at the table. She sat regally on the bench and wrapped her hands around the tin cup Daniel placed in front of her.

"Coffee . . . real coffee . . ." Inhaling its fragrance, Elizabeth carefully sipped from the steaming brew.

The children stood beside the table, eagerly consuming the food Daniel placed before them.

"Do you have an Indian name?" Elaine asked.

Daniel rested a lean hip against the table

73

edge. "My Shawnee friends call me Mountain with Voice of Thunder." He thoughtfully rubbed his chin with long, strong fingers. "I never have been able to figure out why."

"Ain't you got no ears?" Wilson's voice was filled with amazement. "You'd make the windows rattle, ifen we had windows!"

"Are you saying I'm loud, boy?" Daniel looked down at the youngster, a smile playing at the corners of his mouth.

"Ah, well, umm . . ." Wilson found that being the center of attention was a scary thing.

"My maman used to say she could hear me whispering a mile away from the house."

"A mile's awful far away," Wilson replied, trying to find a way out of his dilemma. "Mayhaps she just had real good ears."

Daniel threw back his head with a roaring laugh. His eyes twinkled merrily when he looked down at the child but his voice grew serious.

"When you make a statement that's right, and you know it's right, stand your ground, boy. It makes no difference who challenges you, if you're right then nothing else matters." He reached over and gently ruffled the down-turned head.

"The Indians named me Mountain with Voice of Thunder because they say I'm loud and there's no one who can deny that I'm big."

"Must be nice to be big," Wilson mumbled. "Then nobody can push you around."

Daniel's heart went out to the child. "You'll

grow soon enough, son. Being a man is a life-time thing, but you can only be a child for a short while. Enjoy what's left of being a child. No one's going to pick on you while I'm here."

"You mean it?" his voice wobbled as he fought back tears. "You won't let anyone pick on me?"

"I promise that no one will mistreat you while I'm here to prevent it." Daniel's gaze lifted from the boy and connected with Elizabeth's. Her eyes were so filled with sorrow that he watched her bite her lower lip to prevent the tears from flowing.

"No one will mistreat any of you." Daniel looked around the table, his eyes resting briefly on each child. "That's a promise."

"But you ain't gonna be here long," John stated.

"I'll be here for a while longer."

Elizabeth's head snapped in his direction. "I thought you'd be leaving this morning."

"It's still snowing." As if that statement explained everything, Daniel lifted the coffee cup to his lips.

"You ain't gonna stay," John repeated.

Daniel sighed. "My home is far from here, but for a while I'll stay."

Elizabeth watched as the light faded from the children's eyes with acknowledgement that Daniel's stay was only temporary. Far from the noisy beginnings of the day, breakfast became a quiet meal, each person lost in his own thoughts.

When she was finished, Elizabeth carried her

cup of coffee over to the door and pulled it open. Snow was continuing to fall lightly, but the sky showed patches of blue, promise of clearing later in the day.

Evidence of the blowing wind could be seen in the piles of snow. In some places it was pushed into drifts at least three feet deep while in many spots the ground was bare, showing blades of spring green grass. The bitingly cold air quickly drifted beneath her dress, threatening to freeze her bare toes. She soon closed the door to preserve the little heat that remained in the room.

Placing her empty cup on the table, Elizabeth began to fold the blankets that had served as bedding. Finding her shoes hidden beneath the pile, she looked for the bench to sit on so that she could put them on and realized that Daniel was feeding it into the hungry fire.

"No school for you today," she told the children, leaning against the table for balance as she pulled on her stockings and then stepped into the leather shoes, struggling to tie them and maintain her balance at the same time.

She reached to the shelf for her brush and comb, grimacing as she attempted to free the snarls from her hair. Silently ridiculing herself for not putting her unmanageable hair in its usual nightly braid, Elizabeth was unaware of her appreciative male audience.

Daniel watched with pleasure as the long strands floated away from her brush, seemingly with a life of their own. He felt a growing urge to bury his hands in the golden mass and discover if it was half as soft as it looked.

Memories from childhood were stirred from a forgotten corner of his mind. He thought of the many times he had watched his father brush his mother's long fiery red hair until it lay smooth and glossy down her back, then burying his face in its warmth. His parents were always touching each other in some loving way and as a child he had accepted it as natural, not understanding the sensuality of the simplest caress.

As a man, Daniel knew. Good Lord above, how he knew!

Watching the innocent feminine routine of brushing the snarls from her hair became a torture so refined in its exquisite agony that he had to force himself to turn his back on the scene or face the very real possibility that he would do something to embarrass himself. How could something so guileless become so erotic?

Shrugging into his coat, Daniel walked across the room and opened the door. The wind had died sometime during the night and the temperature was slowly rising though he instinctively knew it was still below freezing.

The two older boys, John and Benjamin, joined him at the doorway, their worn coats little protection against the cold.

"We've got enough food for a day or two but firewood is a serious problem. If we don't get some gathered today we'll freeze again tonight."

He talked to the boys as if they were adults rather than children.

"There's an old ax in the shed but it's so rusted you couldn't cut a piece of bread with it," Benjamin volunteered.

"We gotta fix the roof," John stated. "Ain't never gonna stay warm with that hole letting all the heat out."

"I can do somethin'!" Wilson stated, not wanting to be left out.

"Sure can, boy. Everybody'll have something to do before the day's over." Daniel smiled at the small child.

"Not the girls," Wilson explained solemnly. "Girls ain't good for nothing but cookin' and washin' clothes."

"Everybody will help out, including the girls. Let's go see what other surprises are stored in the shed." Daniel led the way outside, the boys following eagerly at his heels.

Elizabeth watched them leave as she finished rolling her hair into a knot low on her neck. She draped her cape around her shoulders, pulled the hood over her head and securely tied the ribbon beneath her chin.

"Belinda, I want you to watch the younger children. I have to go to the school in case any of the village children arrive. I don't know what the other parents will do on a day like this but I have to be there just in case. We don't want Elder Jacobs to think that I'm neglecting my duties."

She smiled warmly at the children as she

headed for the door. Giving them several chores to do, she instructed them to seek out Daniel if there was a problem, then headed out into the cold.

The school building was less than two miles from the cabin and on a warm day it would be a pleasant walk. Today, with snow knee deep on some parts of the trail it was far from agreeable.

Snow lay in the branches of the trees and decorated the new spring leaves. Tiny flowers wore a crown of white, a delicately beautiful composite of spring and winter. Appreciative of the unusual merging of seasons she wished she could linger to enjoy it, but the cold soon penetrated her clothing.

Elizabeth pulled her cape more tightly around her, trying to prevent the frigid air from finding a way inside to add to her discomfort. Burying her fingers into the layers of the fabric she turned her thoughts to Daniel.

His arrival had been so unexpected, so startling. His size had intimidated her. No, she corrected herself, his size had plain scared her to death! But he had shown how gentle he was beneath his large exterior. She'd had no second thoughts about leaving the children in his care, in fact, she hadn't even considered whether or not it was a wise thing to do. Elizabeth was startled to realize that she'd simply put on her cape and headed out the door, leaving the children with a virtual stranger.

Praying that she had not made an error in judgment, Elizabeth walked faster. The sooner she arrived at the school the sooner she could go home. In the open, the path had been free of snow, but it now headed into the woods. In some places it was piled knee high and soon Elizabeth's shoes were cold and wet.

Had she been foolish to venture out into the snow, leaving her children unprotected. What did she really know about Daniel LeClerc? He was an incredibly strong giant of a man who could maim or destroy tiny bodies with his brute strength. He had entertained the children during breakfast with stories of his past, but was that simply to lull her into accepting him and not questioning his true motives?

None of the children, including John, would stand a chance of defending themselves against a man his size. They expected her to protect them. She had promised them that they would be safe in her care and she had failed their trust by leaving them defenseless.

By the time Elizabeth reached the school-house she was shaking with cold and fear, no longer certain that Daniel was a good person to leave her precious children with. Fear for their safety grew as she entered the empty structure.

The room was bone-chilling cold and the empty woodbox held no promise of warmth. Encased in frozen leather, her feet felt numb and her fingers were clumsy as she tried to work the stiff laces free. Several long minutes later, huffing and puffing with the effort, she pulled her feet free. The sodden stockings thumped to the floor beside the shoes as she sat down on one of the wooden pews that served as desks during school days. Elizabeth bent her knees, folding her cold feet beneath her legs. Chills raced up her spine as her nearly frozen flesh made contact with the warm skin beneath her skirts.

Wrapping her cape around herself, Elizabeth sought every bit of warmth from her own body. It became vital that she warm her feet as quickly as possible so that she could return to the cabin. Why had she ever thought of leaving the children alone? She remembered Daniel's size, the booming volume of his voice seemed to echo in her thoughts. He was so dangerous, a stranger, and she had deserted her children to him.

Again his voice bounced through her mind, but when it happened for a third time she realized that it wasn't her imagination. The door opened, bringing the man of her fears closer with each step.

"What do you think you're doing, woman? It's colder in here that it is outside. Do you really think any of the parents are uncaring enough to send their children out today for something as ridiculous as school?"

"School isn't ridiculous," she mumbled inanely. Elizabeth sat with her feet folded beneath her skirt and watched as he approached. Her memory hadn't been wrong about his size, he was the largest man she'd ever seen.

But she had forgotten his eyes. One look at his warm, black eyes and Elizabeth knew she'd allowed her imagination to invent things that would never be.

"I agree, school is vitally important, but so is staying healthy. And taking a two-mile walk with the promise of another blizzard doesn't seem too smart to me."

"I . . . I couldn't take the chance that some of the children would show up and I wouldn't be here," she explained. "I need this job too desperately to chance angering Elder Jacobs."

"Why didn't you come to me?" Daniel saw her wet shoes and the pinched look of her face. "You knew I had a horse. I could have brought you to the school."

"I didn't think . . ."

Kneeling in front of her, Daniel raised her skirt enough to find her legs. He forced her to unbend her knee and took her cold foot in his hand.

"What do you think you're doing?" She tried to pull her foot away from him but had trouble maintaining an indignant voice as the heat from his large hands penetrated the cold.

"Excuse me if this seems insulting, it is my intention only to warm your feet so that we can go back to the cabin. I left John and Belinda in charge of the children." His eyes twinkled merrily. "Unfortunately, there was no one to leave in charge of them. They were already giving each other dirty looks when I rode out. If we delay our return too long we may not like what we find."

"Oh . . ."

Daniel reached for her other foot. Nestling her right foot in the warmth between his massive thighs he rubbed her left foot briskly between his hands. She squirmed away, giggling involuntarily.

"Ah, ticklish?" Wicked delight entered his warm gaze as he lightly rubbed the bottom of her foot.

"Oh, please . . . no more!"

She wasn't sure it was better when he stopped. He deftly maneuvered her free foot beside the other one between his thighs. Her cheeks blossomed with color as he began to rub her calves, his hands reaching as high as her knees.

"And I distinctly heard Jenny Sue yelling for her cat as I rode out of the yard," he continued as if their conversation had never been interrupted.

"She's . . . she's nearly as loud as her daddy." It was hard for her to form a coherent thought with her flesh pressed so intimately to his and his hands rubbing up and down her legs. What if someone came in and saw them? She'd never be able to explain the situation.

It was scandalous!

Daniel wanted to let his fingers linger, to test the strength of her muscles, to caress the softness of her thighs. It was delightful!

"She isn't my daughter." Daniel reluctantly moved his hands away when he felt his own flesh heat with the innocent touch.

"Not yours?"

Carefully leaving out the events leading to the discovery, he implied that finding Jenny Sue had been pure luck. Told in a straightforward, matter-of-fact way, he left little room for her to find questions to ask. He wasn't ready to explain to a stranger about the visions that had led him to the little girl.

Daniel grabbed her shoes and realized that she couldn't put the frozen leather back onto her feet without chancing frostbite. Without warning he stood, dropped the shoes into her lap, then bent and picked her up.

"What are you doing?" Elizabeth frantically grabbed for her shoes with one hand while wrapping her other arm securely around his neck. She couldn't remember ever being carried. It was thrilling. It was scary.

It was a long way down!

"Put me down! I'm far too heavy for you to carry. You'll hurt your back."

Daniel smiled at her slight weight in his arms. "I'd say you weigh a might bit more than Jenny Sue but a whole lot less than my horse."

"Your horse—!"

" 'Course, I've never tried to pick him up. He's a very cooperative animal but I don't think he'd take too well to that." Daniel closed the schoolhouse door with his foot and carried her to the animal, where he settled her onto the saddle.

Concern about riding the horse vied with trying to protect her modesty, Elizabeth attempted to gather her skirt around her while holding on to the animal's mane. Distressed about her exposed legs and bare feet, she was startled when Daniel stepped into the stirrup and swung up onto the saddle behind her.

The horse stood docilely as Daniel shifted his weight until Elizabeth was sitting across his thighs. He looked down at her bare feet hanging in the cold air.

"Can you fold your feet up under your skirt?"

Elizabeth looked skeptically at the limited space, already cramped by his size. "We'll be home soon, I can warm them then."

Daniel grabbed her legs, capturing her feet between his leg and the horse's side. It was an uncomfortable position, to say the least, but incredibly warm. When Daniel flicked the reins, the horse turned his head to look back at his riders. With an almost human expression of disbelief, the animal shook his head then started to walk.

Elizabeth tried to sit away from Daniel, but each time she bounced up she'd come back down on his lap. Finally, out of desperate concern that the wrong bounce would put her into painful contact with a delicate portion of his anatomy, Daniel wrapped his arms around her, pulling her against his chest.

She didn't fight it, she couldn't fight it. Elizabeth rested her head beneath his chin and prayed that no one would see them.

Warm and safe, protected as never before. The thick fur of his coat tickled her nose and gave her a soft pillow for her head. His arms kept her in the saddle, while his leg provided warmth for her bare feet. She decided it would be nice if the horse walked real slow . . .

Six

"Mistress Spurlin! I trust that you have an explanation for this indecent display!"

At the sound of the harsh, nasal voice, Elizabeth's eyes snapped open and her head popped up from Daniel's chest.

"Eh . . . Elder Jacobs . . . good morning." She tried to put a respectable distance between herself and Daniel but found that extra room in the saddle was extremely limited.

"I'm waiting Mistress Spurlin!"

Daniel looked at the smaller man, his eyes narrowed dangerously. "Are you the man responsible for leaving Miss Spurlin and her children in that dilapidated cabin?"

"Who are you, sir, and what business is it of yours?" Elder Jacobs was accustomed to respect in the small frontier community. He held a position of some authority, plus being the major landowner in the town. Few questioned his actions, and those who did soon found reason to regret their behavior.

"Was it you who left them without firewood for heat or even the means for them to cut their own?"

Elder Jacobs bristled under the younger man's stare. "That is none of your affair, sir!"

Daniel walked his horse closer to the man. "Did you leave them there with virtually no food?"

"I repeat, it is none of your affair, and I resent your questions!"

"And what did you do during the blizzard?" Daniel asked, the very soft rumble of his voice a warning that his anger was rising. "Did you stay snuggled up in front of your own fire, a warm cup of mead at hand? An abundant stockpile of wood waiting to be burned? A hearty stew cooking over the fire?

"Did you, for even a passing moment, give thought to this women and five young children who were in every danger of freezing to death? Or were you too concerned for your own selfish comforts to worry about them?"

"Mistress Spurlin, I will not be spoken to in this manner!" Elder Jacobs bristled as Daniel hit too close to the truth. "I do not know who this man is or why you are so wantonly spread across his horse, but I warn you, if you don't have an adequate explanation I will be forced to rescind our offer to you to teach our children!"

With her arm wrapped around Daniel's neck for support, Elizabeth felt him stiffen with each word from the odious man. She unconsciously stroked the long hair that hung below his collar, her fingers lightly rubbing his warm flesh.

"Daniel, please, let me handle this," she murmured softly before he could respond. Glittering black eyes met hers and she knew he was fighting for control.

"Mr. LeClerc and his daughter arrived at the cabin last evening just after dark," she began to explain, only to be interrupted.

"I am also the man who found wood to burn so that they stayed warm and food to eat so that they didn't have to go to bed *hungry* and cold!"

"Daniel . . ."

"And, I venture to add," he continued, ignoring her plea, "if I had been a few hours later I would have found six frozen bodies, covered in snow blown in through the hole in the roof!"

"Are you implying that I would have left Mistress Spurlin and her children to freeze to death?" Elder Jacobs asked, his voice maintaining the correct amount of disbelief that anyone could possibly think such a thing of him.

"I don't imply." Daniel's voice rose slightly in volume, but was still far softer than his normal level. "I am stating it as a fact! You were too concerned with your own creature comforts to be worried about anyone else, even a lone woman and five children!"

Elder Jacobs turned his gaze from this too-confident adversary and struck out at a weaker opponent. "Mistress Spurlin, I am growing tired of waiting for your explanation as to your present circumstance!"

"Mistress Spurlin walked to the school this morning, through the snow and freezing temperatures, because she was concerned that a child might show up and she wouldn't be here," Daniel stated before Elizabeth could open her mouth to speak. "She is such a conscientious person that *she* didn't consider the danger to herself. Her only concern was for *someone else!*"

"Daniel, please, I can speak for myself." She smiled gently at him and lightly stroked the warm flesh of his neck, unaware that while her innocent touch was soothing one type of tension it was creating an entirely different kind.

"Elder Jacobs, the children and I owe Mr. Le-Clerc a considerable debt of gratitude. If he hadn't arrived last night and provided for us I'm not sure what would have happened." She thought of the happy faces of the children this morning as Daniel prepared breakfast and realized that he seemed a natural and fitting part of her ragtag family.

"When Mr. LeClerc realized that I had left the cabin on foot this morning he came after me. He was concerned for my welfare. We were on our way back to the cabin when you arrived."

"I would be interested in learning what manner of repayment you intend for this implied debt," Elder Jacobs sneered.

Elizabeth heard the breath hiss through Daniel's clenched teeth and felt the tightening of his body. His hand, resting on her hip, curled painfully into the tender flesh. Because of her innocence, Elder Jacobs's implication was lost on her, but not on Daniel.

"You're overstepping your bounds," Daniel snarled. "You owe the lady an apology."

"Apology? I'm to apologize for stating the facts as I see them?"

"Your kind sees evil in the simplest common courtesy. We were caught in the blizzard and Mistress Spurlin invited us to share her quarters, as mean as they are, rather than letting us freeze to death. In repayment for that I found a source of firewood to keep us all warm!"

Daniel's dark eyes blazed with an anger that would have frightened most reasonable men and warned even those beyond reason. Elder Jacobs cautiously backed his horse away from the larger man, while Elizabeth continued to caress the tender skin on his neck. His rage was stunning and she knew he had no idea that she would bear bruises on her hip for several days from the punishing grasp of his fingers.

Not wanting to let go of the subject, Elder Jacobs ventured to ask another question. "How is it you found wood for the fire when she didn't?"

"I burned the furniture!" Daniel enunciated carefully.

"That was my property! How dare you burn my property!" the older man stuttered in rage.

In a lithe motion, amazing for his size, Daniel slid Elizabeth up on the saddle and swung down to the ground. He grabbed the reins of the horse before Elder Jacobs could move the animal away. Wrapping his hand in the neck of the other man's coat, Daniel pulled him to the ground, shaking him until Elizabeth feared his neck would snap.

"Daniel, don't," Elizabeth said quietly. "He isn't worth a noose around your neck."

Her gentle voice reaching him through his red haze, Daniel threw the smaller man away from him. He turned to her, his gaze resting on her bare feet hanging beneath her dress. Anger brimming just beneath the surface began to swell again, until his gaze met hers.

Soft, warm gray eyes sparkled into his. "Thank you, Mr. LeClerc. Never before has anyone defended me for any slight. Your manner may be rather . . . uh, physical, but it is appreciated."

She looked at Elder Jacobs, still sitting where he landed. "Perhaps you should help the poor man to his feet and then we can be on our way."

Daniel snarled something beneath his breath, grabbed the man's arm and pulled him abruptly up. Elder Jacobs hastily removed himself from Daniel's grasp.

"Be out of the cabin by nightfall," he sneered as he mounted his horse, keeping a wary eye on Daniel. "Your services are no longer needed!"

"Daniel, don't." Elizabeth admonished when Daniel's hands tightened into fists and he made a move toward the man.

They watched Elder Jacobs's rapid retreat.

"I should have put my fist through his face," Daniel muttered.

"Are you usually so violent?"

Daniel looked down at his hands still clenched into fists. He stretched his fingers out then dug them through his fiery hair.

"I've spent a lifetime fighting my own temper. When you're my size you can't let your anger rule you." He looked up sheepishly. "I've never struck out at someone smaller before, unless they were holding a gun on me. The gun always seemed to make up the difference in size."

"Yes, I can understand that," she agreed solemnly, her eyes twinkling merrily. "I'm sure Elder Jacobs would have given anything—even his priceless cabin—for a gun a short while ago!"

"When I think of that wormy little slime—" Agitation showed in his stance and the snarl curling his lip.

"There's a rather large tree just behind you, Daniel, if you'd like to pit your strength against it."

He turned to look at the huge elm tree towering far into the sky, with branches spreading a hundred feet or more and snow decorating its new leaves. He had the good grace to look sheepishly back at her.

"If you'd rather not, do you think we could go home?" She wiggled her bare toes. "My feet are cold."

Daniel swung into the saddle, settled her back into place and took the reins from her hands.

Elizabeth placed a gentle hand against his cheek. "Thank you, Daniel."

"For what? Making you lose your home and your job?"

"Well, there is that, but it's not the first time it's happened." She smiled softly. "Thank you for being my knight. I've never had one before and it's rather a heady feeling to be so protected."

Guilt weighed heavily on his massive shoulders. Because of him she had no job or place to live and here she was thanking him! Her gray eyes were warm, a dark cloud inviting him to drift into their softness. She rested confidently against him and he remembered that she had shown no fear at his rage . . . and that her voice had called him back to sanity.

Sanity.

The word fragmented in his mind. He knew he walked ever closer to the edge of reality with each nightmarish dream and wondered if, perhaps, she could save him from madness. The gentle touch of her hand on his neck had held back a rage that could have turned into violence. With his name on her lips she had stopped him from hurting the smaller man.

Could her gentle voice and tender touch call him back before it was too late and he slipped into the lunacy that was a constant promise?

Had the gods of the Shawnee sent this woman to him as a last chance of hope? Did he dare trust that she would be his salvation? Would she understand if he explained the dreams that sent him in search too late to prevent a disaster or would she turn from him in terror?

He had told his dreams to few people. Their

reactions had varied, but none had doubted him. Even though they couldn't really understand, they believed and tried to help, but they loved him. What would this woman, a stranger, think?

Could he trust her?

"Daniel? Hello, Daniel?"

Daniel blinked and lightly shook his head.

"Welcome back," she greeted with a smile. "Where did you go?"

"Faraway, little one." His voice was husky with the desire to tell her the truth, to find the answers to his questions.

"My feet," she reminded him. "Can we go home?"

He stroked her cheek with a calloused finger. "We'll go home, sweet."

Elizabeth tucked her feet behind his leg and leaned back against him. He was security and gentle comfort. Once again she was homeless, without a job. She had five hungry children to feed and keep warm.

But for now, for the few short minutes it would take for them to reach the cabin, she would close her eyes and pretend. Surely, even she, was allowed to pretend once in a while.

The headache began in the late afternoon. More of a nuisance than the agony that would follow, nonetheless, it promised another tormenting glimpse at madness.

* * *

The snow began again before dark. Gentle flakes, fat with moisture, drifted lazily to the ground. Before long the wind began to blow and the snow became a threat to anyone caught in the open.

Everyone worked steadily throughout the day, hurrying to beat the storm, but taking the time to share a smile or a chuckle. The children never complained about an assigned task; even the two little girls did as much as possible.

By the time darkness hid the storm from view a fire blazed brightly, sending welcoming heat into the cabin. The makeshift patch on the roof kept the howling wind from sending snow onto those below. A majority of the cracks between the logs had been chinked with whatever was available and with blankets and coats on the room was almost comfortable. Fingers no longer numb with cold held spoonfuls of soup to lips rosy with warmth.

Sitting on the floor with his back against the wall, Daniel watched the children eat. He was amazed at their calm acceptance when Elizabeth had explained that they would again be moving on.

"Old patoot!" Wilson grumbled between bites of soup.

"Wilson, it's not polite to speak of your elders in such a manner," Elizabeth corrected in her quiet manner.

"Even if he is an old patoot?" the child asked.

"Even if he is an old patoot," she replied, a smile lurking in her gray eyes.

Jenny Sue sat on Daniel's crossed legs, her soup bowl on the floor was shared with the cat whenever she thought no one was watching. He had finished his dinner with quick dispatch. Experience had taught him that once the headache and dreams were in full force he would be incapable of eating. He knew that he would need the nourishment for whatever lay waiting to entangle him in its snare.

Daniel tried to prepare himself for the night ahead. He knew that as soon as he slept the dreams would come. He would fight sleep with a willpower as strong as life itself. But eventually he would have no choice, his body would take control. He would sleep.

And dream.

The first few nights they would be short bits and pieces: faces, houses, animals, trees. Nothing would match up with anything else in the macabre scenes that would haunt his sleep. Eventually the events would connect into a ghastly event that he would be too late to prevent.

"Where will we go?" Elaine asked.

Elizabeth had waited with dread for that question. Where could she take her family? Where would they be welcomed and accepted?

"We'll go to my home," Daniel answered. He knew his time was limited before the pain drove every other thought from his mind, but maybe, if he was lucky and they hurried, maybe he could get them to the settlement he called home.

"It's a long trip and we'll have to leave tomorrow even if the snow hasn't cleared, but you'll like it once we get there."

"Daniel, we can't impose on you like that." Hope flared in her heart but a lifetime of manners forced her to protest . . . but not too much.

"We leave tomorrow."

Seven

The sun was barely lighting the sky when Daniel left the cabin and the sleeping children and woman. Carrying the ax, he walked a short way into the woods, searching out two saplings of similar size. The quiet morning air soon rang with the sounds of steel hitting wood. With a minimum of effort the two young trees lay on the snowy ground, stripped of branches. Grabbing one in each massive hand, he dragged them back toward the cabin.

Fashioning a halter for the horse out of rawhide strips, Daniel wrapped heavy canvas around the poles to form a travois. It would serve to carry their possessions and the two little girls. The trip was going to be slowed by the children but two-year-old Jenny Sue and four-year-old Elaine would have to either be carried or ride. There was no way they could walk the many miles to Kentucky. The horse stood patiently, occasionally looking back over his shoulder, as Daniel attached the travois to the halter.

"It's going to be a hard trip," Daniel said quietly to the animal. "Six kids, a woman and the dreams coming on, but there's no other way."

Unconsciously rubbing his aching head, Daniel inspected everything a final time to assure himself that it was ready, then he returned to the cabin to waken his charges and hurry them on their way. At the door he glanced back over his shoulder. The rising sun momentarily broke through the low-hanging clouds, sending a bright shard of light toward him. Daniel said a silent prayer to his God and the gods of the Shawnee to allow him enough time to see to their safety before the agony of the dreams consumed him.

To his surprise, Elizabeth and the children were already awake. While they ate their breakfast she carefully packed their belongings, making the packs at light as possible for slender shoulders. Unaware of Daniel's preparations she tried to estimate how much she could carry, what was necessary and what could be left behind.

Daniel watched as she laid several of her dresses aside, carefully folding the children's clothing and adding them to the pack.

"Take it all," Daniel said from the doorway.

"I thought we could put Jenny Sue and Elaine on your horse while the rest of us walk." She looked up at him with an embarrassed smile. "That is if you don't mind, after all, it is your horse.

"You can take it all." At her puzzled expression a smile crossed his rugged features. "Come here."

Daniel opened the door as everyone crowded around him. The horse turned his head at the noise, but continued to rest on three legs.

"We'll load the baggage on this and there will still be room for the little ones" Daniel explained.

He looked at the older children. "I'm sorry, but there isn't room for everyone. You'll have to walk."

"Wouldn't ride on that thing iff'en you wanted me to," John stated bluntly. "Don't look all that safe."

"Is it safe?" Elizabeth asked, concern for the children crowding other thoughts from her mind.

"It's safe. It'll be a bumpy ride but the girls will enjoy it." He put his hand on John's shoulder, lightly pushing the boy out the door in front of him. "Get everything packed. I want to leave before it gets much later."

Daniel pulled the door closed behind him and walked away from the cabin, his hand still resting lightly on John's slender shoulder.

"I'm going to need your help, boy. It's a long trip and we'll be going into some bad territory."

John pulled away from Daniel and looked up at the man he still wasn't sure he trusted. "What do you want me to do?" he asked warily.

Daniel wasn't disturbed by the child's suspicion. John had never been given reason to trust an adult and it would take him time to learn that everyone wasn't like his father.

"I'll be in the front, Benjamin and Wilson can lead the horse while Elizabeth and the girls follow behind it. I need you to take up the rear, to keep your eyes and ears open for anything that doesn't sound natural to the woods. I expect you to yell if you have the slightest doubt."

Daniel's gaze moved in the direction they would soon be traveling. "We're going to be meeting up with men, rough mountain men, savage Indians and even white men who call themselves civilized. They'll take one look at our women and decide they want them for their own. They'd trade everything in their packs for a woman like Elizabeth or a young girl like Belinda. They'll try to take anything they can't trade for. It'll be up to us to make sure that doesn't happen."

"How do I know you ain't just gonna lead us to the middle of nowhere and leave us to fend for ourselves?" The child, so nearly a man, voiced his doubts.

"Instincts, John, learn to follow your instincts." Daniel looked again at the boy. "You can tell a lot about a man by watching his eyes. His mouth may be saying one thing but his eyes will always reveal what's in his heart."

John looked into Daniel's black eyes, trying to read the truth in the dark gaze. "If you do anything to hurt her I'll kill you," he promised quietly.

"Fair enough," Daniel agreed. He would take

the threat from the boy when he would have driven his fist into a man making the same bald statement.

"There's not enough time to teach you how to use my gun, so keep your slingshot and a ready supply of rocks handy. If there's a threat yell your head off and aim for their eyes. You can't kill a man with that slingshot but you can blind him and give me time to get to you."

Daniel held his hand out to the child and John's heart swelled with pride as his reached out to grasp it. Elizabeth and the others needed him and this man was asking for help. For one of the few times in his short life, John felt the satisfaction of being needed. It was a heady feeling.

The children tumbled out of the cabin, each clutching his own bundle of possessions. Daniel carefully packed the travois so that the load wouldn't shift over the rough trail and hurt the little girls.

In spite of its extra weight, he added a supply of kindling and dry firewood. The snow had stopped before daybreak and already the temperatures were climbing above freezing, but the clouds were heavy with promise beneath a watery sun. He suspected that they would be walking in rain before the day was over. It would be a long, miserable day and the children would need the heat of a fire when darkness descended.

At the door of the cabin, Elizabeth stopped and looked around the room that had been their home for such a short time. Empty except for the rickety table and a shelf near the smoldering fireplace, it looked forlorn and dismal.

It was forlorn and dismal, she thought, but for a few hours it had been rich with the happy laughter of children not accustomed to laughing.

Overlooking the patched hole in the roof and the gaps in the chinking, she thought of how it had helped to keep them warm and dry. It had provided a sense of security, flimsy at best, after weeks on the road.

Poor as it was, the cabin had become their home for a few brief days. Given time, Elizabeth knew they would have transformed the structure into a place they all could have been proud of.

"Ready to leave?" Daniel had silently walked up behind her.

"Am I doing the right thing?" she asked quietly. "I've already asked so much of them, should I expect them to just pack up and move again because I say so?"

"Do you have a choice?"

Elizabeth turned her eyes from the cabin to the man standing behind her. "I could stay. The settlement has had such a difficult time finding a teacher I believe they'd return the position to me if I asked."

"But would that make you happy? Could you live with people who suspected that every act of kindness had an ulterior motive?"

"The only person I've had time to meet here

is Elder Jacobs. Surely the others aren't as narrow minded as he."

"Probably not," Daniel agreed.

"They could be much more accepting."

"Could be."

"Not everyone is outrageously suspicious."

"That's true," he agreed noncommittally.

"You're not going to help me make this decision, are you?" she asked with a smile.

"Elizabeth, the decision must be yours, but if you want to go with me we have to leave now." The slight throb in his head needlessly reminded Daniel that his time was limited. "I have to leave today. I have no choice."

She turned and looked at the children waiting patiently beside the horse. The little girls sat quietly on the travois, Jenny Sue's cat regally perched on the neatly stacked baggage. Benjamin and Wilson were throwing stones to pass the time while Belinda talked to the horse. John leaned nonchalantly against a tree, his arms folded across his chest, his eyes glued to the couple in the doorway.

They were prepared to follow her wherever she led, without question or complaint, just as they'd followed her here, her only promise to provide them with a home and a family.

"John needs more than I can give him here," Elizabeth said quietly. "He's really taken to you."

"There are all kinds of people at the settlement who'll help him to become the man he is destined to be."

"If something should happen to me they'd be orphaned again."

A strand of blond hair slipped free from beneath her frivolous bonnet of lace and flowers, the morning breeze fluttering it across her face. Daniel didn't resist the urge to push it from her eyes, his big hand gentle as he anchored it behind her ear.

"You are going to live to a ripe old age, sweetheart." Her concern for the children touched a chord in his heart. "But if you should get run down by a herd of elk, there will always be a home for them."

"Benjamin needs to learn not to steal and Wilson has a real vocation for becoming the world's greatest liar. The girls have never had the chance to know a man, since their father ignored them all of their lives."

"You'll have to tell me how you arrived with this mixed-up family. I just now realized that none of them are yours."

Elizabeth smiled. "They're all mine. I didn't give birth to any of them but I'll fight to keep them."

"I need a decision, lady." Daniel knew he didn't have time to waste while she continued to debate the issue. "Do you go or do I unload the travois?"

Looking first at the children and then back at the dilapidated cabin, Elizabeth stepped back and pulled the door closed. Her wary gray eyes, identical in color to the clouds billowing overhead, met his.

"I hope you won't regret my decision."

"I won't and neither will you."

Daniel put his hand on the small of her back and walked toward the waiting horse and children. It would be a long journey, made longer by the pain hiding behind his eyes.

"You and Belinda walk behind the travois and keep an eye on the little ones. Benjamin and Wilson can take turns leading the horse while John keeps track of things from the rear."

Elizabeth nodded, pulled her cape snugly beneath her chin and waited for Daniel to lead out.

"Just what is the meaning of this, Mistress Spurlin?"

Elizabeth turned, surprise crowding the remaining doubt from her eyes as she stared at the man approaching from the direction of the town. "Elder Jacobs," she greeted him quietly. "I certainly didn't expect to see you here this morning. Did you come to make sure that we were leaving?"

"Leaving? Need I remind you that we have a contract, madam?" he blustered. "I expect you to honor it!"

Elizabeth's mouth fell open in astonishment. She felt Daniel walk up behind her but he remained quiet, letting her make a decision. This was her final opportunity to remain in Indiana.

"Elder Jacobs, when I took this job I was promised a home and I found a structure unfit for bovine. I was promised food, but we would have starved if we had waited for you to provide for us. We nearly froze to death because of the lack of wood, not to mention the holes in the cabin.

"The only person to show any care for us is Mr. LeClerc and he was accused of vile, immoral acts simply because of his concern." Elizabeth felt the heat of righteous anger roll through her as she listed her grievances. "You ordered me and my children off your property. You broke the contract from the very beginning and now you're trying to lay the blame on me."

"The members of the settlement met last night and I persuaded them to give you another chance," he stated, hinting at the generosity of the community in general and himself in particular.

"Did they now? Well, isn't that just wonderful of them and . . . you." Elizabeth smiled, a cold malevolent visage completely at odds with her usual warmhearted expression.

"Of course there will need to be a few changes made. A woman needs a home," Elder Jacobs stated, misinterpreting her smile as one of relief that she didn't have to be dependent on a total stranger to lead her and her family to another place. "And a man to provide for her."

"A man like you, Elder Jacobs?"

"Not just any man is suitable to provide for a widow and her children." The vision of her dainty ankle, glimpsed during the confrontation the day before, had kept him awake most of the night. Sometime before dawn he convinced himself that the woman would be grateful for his generous offer of a home for her children. Perhaps, in time, her gratitude would extend to favors, physical favors, to the man responsible for her blessings.

"Of course not," she agreed.

"It must be a righteous, dependable member of the community."

"Such as yourself?"

"It is completely unsuitable for a young mother to be the lone support of her children when there is an ablebodied man to provide for them."

From his place beside a tree, John snorted then spit at the ground, his actions eloquently, if crudely, expressing his opinion.

"John, I appreciate and concur with your feelings, but that is not reason enough to lower your standards to vulgarity. You must remember to respect your elders, even if they are not deserving of that respect," Elizabeth stated quietly.

"I'll teach that boy some manners." The look Elder Jacobs sent the child was vicious.

"I don't think there is anything you could possibly teach my son." Elizabeth rounded on the man. "There is more honesty in his little finger than in your entire body. You are a narrow-minded hypocrite. Your selfishness knows no bounds and the only emotions you've ever felt have been self-directed."

Elizabeth's voice never rose above her normal, well-modulated pitch as she cut the man off at the knees. Daniel's admiration for her soared at the confident way she handled the man and defended the child.

"I have not had the opportunity to meet the citizens of Richmond, but I will assume they are friendly, likable people. The town is charming and seems to be a good place to raise children, but not if they must prescribe to your oppressive tyranny. I want my children to laugh and play, to run in the sunshine and slosh in the mud, but most of all to remember their childhood as something good. I'd rather that they have no man in their lives than to be forced to suffer your presence."

"You'll regret this, Mistress Spurlin! I'll see to it that you never work in Indiana again!"

"I doubt that your influence is nearly as great as you like to think, but, be that as it may, I will take my chances!"

Turning gracefully, Elizabeth rested her hand on Daniel's arm. "We are ready whenever you are, Mr. LeClerc."

"Remind me to stay on your good side," Daniel said with a grin. "You're vicious when you're angry."

"Mr. LeClerc, I am far from angry. Anger is something that builds quickly and departs just as easily." She smiled sweetly but her eyes spit fire. "I am furious and will probably remain so for the rest of the day. However, I'll do my best to see that you and the children don't unduly suffer."

John moved to her side and put his hand on her arm. "We can stay if you wanna."

Elizabeth looked down at his hand. His touch, so seldom given, was a treasure that wiped away her anger.

"Thank you for that." Her smile was filled with warmth as she looked into his solemn eyes. "Our place is not here, John. But if you and the others can endure another trip, we'll see if Mr. LeClerc's settlement is a happier place for us."

She turned her gaze to the dark eyes watching her. "Mr. LeClerc, you lead, we'll follow!

"Benjamin, hold tight to the reins and mind what you're doing. Belinda, keep an eye on your little sisters. Wilson stay behind Mr. LeClerc."

Elizabeth smiled at Daniel, nodded her head and watched until he reached the front and began to move away. Wilson walked beside the big man, his head hardly reaching Daniel's waist. Benjamin's concentration as he guided the horse was easy to see while Elaine and Jenny Sue giggled as the travois bounced over the rocky trail. Belinda walked just behind them, a smile at their enjoyment lighting her lovely features.

"I realize that you've been given a heavy responsibility, bringing up the rear of our caravan, John. But may I walk with you for a while? I won't distract you with idle chatter, but I would appreciate your company."

"I'd . . . I'd like that . . . Elizabeth," John stammered.

She lifted her head and looked toward the sky. A quick, silent prayer that this was the right decision was her only allowance to the doubt she still felt. The heavy clouds parted briefly, allowing a ray of sunlight to peek through before closing back again.

"It's gonna rain before too much longer."

"Yes, John, I fear that it's going to be a long, wet trip." She looked at the group that had moved a good distance away from them, then down at the child who had become a part of her life, a part of heart.

"Let's go home, John."

Eight

By midmorning Daniel was surprised, pleased and impressed by the children. His admiration for Elizabeth grew tenfold, realizing that it was her loving presence that provided the necessary security that allowed them to display a confidence far beyond their ages.

He was impressed that without instruction from him they were quiet on the trail. There was very little conversation, and that only of necessity. He was surprised that they didn't complain at the pace he set. It was only when he noticed Wilson's face, flushed in spite of the cool morning air, that he realized he was walking at a difficult speed for them and shortened his naturally long steps to account for their shorter ones. He was pleased that they had traveled a greater distance than he had thought possible.

He didn't let himself hope that it would continue, that they'd reach the settlement sooner . . . before the pain that was coming consumed the man that was Daniel.

Stopping on the bank of a gently flowing river, they ate their first meal of the trip beneath a drizzly sky. As the children consumed their food with greedy abandon, Daniel untied the travois from the horse and entered the river. Because of its slowly drifting current he didn't feel that it was very deep, but he wanted to be sure before he brought Elizabeth and the children across. Any unexpected surprises were better handled alone.

He found that the river was scarcely two feet deep at its deepest point, but that was more than enough to drown small children. When he reached the far bank, Daniel dismounted and carefully studied the terrain.

The trail was a well-traveled one and there were several sets of footprints in the muddy ground. With his Indian-trained senses Daniel studied his surroundings. He listened closely but the only sounds were those indigenous to the area. His eyes focused on a distant tree at about chest level for a man. He waited with infinite patience as his peripheral vision observed the movements of plants and animals, finding none out of the ordinary.

With Daniel's movements stilled for such a long length of time the birds resumed their normal songs and tiny ground creatures ventured into the open. When he was satisfied that everything was as it should be, Daniel remounted and made his way slowly back to the other side, where Elizabeth met him with a warm smile and a generous piece of cold meat.

"You need to eat, too."

Rubbing at the slight pain above his brows, Daniel shook his head. "I'll eat later. I want to cross the river before a serious rain starts."

Elizabeth said nothing, but continued to hold the meat out to him. With a sign of recognition that she would prevail and an argument was useless, he took the meat and bit into it. Surprised to discover that he was hungry, Daniel was nearly as greedy as the children had been, quickly finishing the meal.

"Now, how do you suggest we cross the river?" Elizabeth asked once she was satisfied that he'd had nourishment.

A wry smile crossed his features. "I thought maybe you'd have that all figured out by now."

"Would you like to hear my suggestions?" She grinned good-naturedly at his teasing.

"Suggest away, Mistress Spurlin." Daniel crossed his arms over his chest, his sudden seriousness ruined by the twinkling of his black eyes.

"The two older boys first, on the horse with you."

"Why?"

"So that John can be there to alert you to trouble." A dark brow rose slightly as she continued. "The little ones can't stay on the travois. It would be too dangerous if they fell in. Belinda and Wilson can cross next while you pull the travois across. Then the little ones and finally me."

"Have it all organized, don't you?"

"Is there something wrong in my plan?"

"Nope, it's exactly the same as mine except that we're going to have to make one more trip. The travois will have to be unloaded and dismantled. We'll carry the gear across and redo it on the other side."

A frown fluttered over her face. "We're an awful lot of trouble."

"I'm not complaining," Daniel said quietly.

"You'd have been a lot further along the trail by now if you'd been alone."

"Elizabeth, you and the children are not causing trouble." Daniel wanted to reach out and pull her into his arms. He knew that she was so accustomed to having only herself to depend on that it was difficult for her to share the burden with someone else. He read the distress in her face and wanted to reassure her, but their friendship was too new for physical contact.

"You'll tell me if we become a burden?" she asked seriously.

"Of course," he agreed. "And I'll expect you to just fade into the woods and never be seen again."

"Daniel, I'm serious!"

"So am I!"

"You don't sound it."

"Trust me, this is my serious face."

Elizabeth looked at his remarkably handsome countenance; broad forehead, ebony eyes beneath thick eyebrows, well-shaped nose and generous mouth. Vertical slashes beside his mouth deepened as a smile lurked just beneath the surface.

"It's a very handsome face," Elizabeth commented, surprising him with the remark. "However, I have a feeling that your serious face would probably scare away a tribe of Indians bent on mischief."

"Guess I'd better get a looking glass and practice up on serious if you expect me to defend you from marauding Indians with only my face as your protection."

"Oh, you can use your rifle, if your face isn't enough."

"Woman, this conversation has become ridiculous."

"Then why did you start it?" Elizabeth asked, turning to walk away before he could find an answer.

She watched him dismantle the travois, smiling at his willingness to exchange silly chit-chat. She listened as he teased the children, his conversation with them as trivial as it had been with her. When everything was unloaded, Daniel mounted his horse. He pulled Benjamin up in front of him then took several things that John handed up. When the designated bundles were in place, he grabbed John's hand and easily pulled him up behind him.

Elizabeth and the others watched from the bank of the river as they quickly crossed, unloaded both of the boys and the bundles and Daniel started back. The next trip was for the poles, canvas and firewood from the travois.

Two by two the children crossed the river on the horse with Daniel. Belinda and Elaine, then Wilson and Jenny Sue. Soon only Elizabeth remained to make the trip.

"Have I ever told you that I'm not fond of horses?" She looked up—way up—to the man holding his hand out to help her mount.

"There will be plenty of time for you to tell me later."

"He's an unusually large horse," she pointed out needlessly, fidgeting with the edge of her cape.

"I'm an unusually large man," Daniel commented quietly. "Give me your hand."

"The water's not that deep," she hedged, looking at the river. "I'll walk across."

"You'll get wet."

"I'll dry in no time."

"Your hand, Elizabeth."

With great reluctance she started to reach up to him, when the horse moved. "I can swim," she stammered, wrapping her arms around her waist.

"You've been on him before," he reminded her needlessly.

"I didn't have a choice, the children were home alone and needed me."

"The children are across the river alone."

"But I can see them."

He was amazed at her genuine fear of the horse. "I didn't think you were afraid of anything."

"Horses and snakes."

"Why?"

She tried to shrug nonchalantly. "A snake startled my pony when I was little. It threw me and I broke my leg." She turned pleading eyes up to him. "Let me walk, Daniel. I'd rather spend the afternoon in wet clothes."

"I won't let you fall, Lizzie. Give me your hand."

"Lizzie?" She reached up to wipe the hair from her forehead. Her frivolous hat had wilted in the light rain and hung ridiculously just above her ear. "Don't call me Lizzie!"

"Your hand, Lizzie."

"My name is Elizabeth Jane. You may call me Elizabeth, Jane, Beth, or even Janie if you must, or nearly anything else, but don't call me Lizzie!"

"Your hand, Ellie." Irritation began to slip into his voice.

"Ellie's not much better."

"Now!"

She had pushed him as far as he would go and she instinctively reacted to the command in his voice. Elizabeth's hand was swallowed up by his and before she could blink Daniel had pulled her up in front of him on the horse.

"You didn't act this way last time we rode double," Daniel stated as he settled her across his thighs and moved the horse toward the river for the final journey.

"I had other things to worry about." She gasped when she felt the animal move and wrapped her arms around his waist. She was conscious of the rock-hard body beneath her arms but one look down at the swirling water convinced her to close her eyes and think about the impropriety of her position later.

"What other things?" Daniel tightened his hold on her, trying to reassure her that she was in no danger of falling.

"I had just lost my job," she bit back a moan when the horse momentarily lost his footing, sliding on the slippery river bottom. "The children had been left alone and it was starting to snow again . . . and Elder Jacobs was busily ogling my bare limbs."

"I knew I should have given the slimy bastard something else to think about," he snarled between clenched teeth.

Surprised by the anger in his voice, Elizabeth pushed herself away from him so that she could meet his gaze. "Daniel, I'm sure Elder Jacobs wasn't everything he purported himself to be, but I doubt that his parentage was in question."

He smiled at her delicate censure of his language. He watched as her hat slid a little further off center, resting endearingly on her ear. Untying the soggy ribbon beneath her chin, Daniel no longer resisted the urge to pull it from her head. Destroyed beyond hope of repair, he dropped it into the river and they watched as it drifted away.

He pulled the hood of her cape over her head and didn't question why he suddenly wished the trip across the river was longer. He liked the feel of her on his lap, the scent of lily of the valley that drifted from her hair and teased his nostrils, the way her breasts had pressed against his chest.

Elizabeth Jane Spurlin, with her fighting spirit and her undaunted love for five, now six, homeless children, was quickly becoming a danger to him.

"I apologize if my language offended you," he said humbly.

"Your language didn't offend me but dropping my hat in the river is another matter!"

"It was wet." She seemed unaware of the horse leaving the water and coming to a standstill beside the waiting children.

"It would have dried and I could have reworked it," she admonished. "My wardrobe is limited, Mr. LeClerc, and I would appreciate it greatly if you'd refrain from throwing any more of it away!"

"I'll try to remember that, Mistress Spurlin." His dark eyes met hers and suddenly all hint of teasing left them. He felt as if he were sinking into a cauldron of swirling emotions as he watched the smoky light play through her gaze.

Elizabeth was aware only of his burning black gaze. She desperately wanted to know his thoughts but was incapable of forming a coherent question. Her breath felt trapped in her lungs and she tingled where her body touched his.

"Maybe I'm coming down with something," she murmured.

"Then I fear I may be about to suffer the same

ailment," he whispered, making her aware that he'd overheard her.

"What took you so long?" John's harsh voice brought both of them back to the realization of where they were. He'd watched them since before they'd left the other side, and even though they were too far away for him to hear what they were saying, he didn't like the way Daniel was staring at Elizabeth.

"Elizabeth was trying to convince me to let her walk."

"Walk?" The boy looked at her with disbelief and shook his head. "Why walk when you've got a perfectly good horse to ride?"

"My point exactly," Daniel agreed, regretting that the time had come to release his captive.

"That don't make no sense atall," John continued.

"Women are like that sometimes," Daniel said as he climbed from the horse and reached up to lift Elizabeth down. His hands nearly spanned her slender waist as he set her carefully on her feet.

"But why would she want to walk?" John's perplexity showed in the furrowing of his brow.

"Since I'm here, and I rode the animal, I believe that is a question that doesn't need to be answered." Freeing herself from Daniel, she turned and walked toward the others. The memory of his innocent touch, the heat where her hands rested on his forearms, the strength in his grasp, wasn't quite as easily left behind. It haunted her as she watched him reassemble the travois, packing their meager possessions carefully. It teased her when he smiled at something one of the children said or rested his hand on a slender shoulder. She had never been affected like this before . . . and wasn't sure she liked it now.

Daniel glanced repeatedly at the lowering sky and knew it would be only a matter of time before a real rain began. When everything was ready, he loaded the little girls onto the travois and took his place at the lead.

By midafternoon the promised rain began. The trail soon became a morass of mud waiting to catch them unawares. Leather shoes found no purchase on the slippery path and each of them was soon covered by the slime as they fell repeatedly.

Even though no one complained, the rain was cold and the trail was becoming dangerous. Daniel began to look for a place to stop for the night. They weren't too far from the settlement and they still passed an occasional farmhouse. He hoped to find a barn or even an abandoned cabin for the night.

Elizabeth's hood protected her face from the worst of the rain but her nose and cheeks were growing colder as the afternoon progressed. Knowing that the boys' coats weren't as heavy as her cape, she worried that they would get chilled and would become sick long before they reached Daniel's settlement. She didn't know if he would wait for a sick child to recover or if he would insist that they continue on. It was obvious to her that he was in a hurry to reach home and wouldn't tolerate an unexpected delay like illness.

Daniel smelled the smoke long before he saw the homestead. The land around the cabins had been cleared of trees and stumps. It had been tilled and stood ready to be planted. A smaller patch of ground already had inches-high green shoots poking through the dirt. Two cabins, connected by a dog-trot, were surrounded by a split-rail fence. A barn stood to the side and a man walked out of it, closing the doors behind him. As if sensing he was no longer alone, the man looked up, his alert gaze searching.

Daniel stopped and turned. "We're going to see if we can use that barn for the night," he explained. "It might be better if we let them think we are a family."

"You mean lie?" John asked, a smirk on his face.

"I mean avoid telling the truth as much as possible. It would be difficult for even the most understanding people to believe how we've all come together and I can't see confusing them unnecessarily."

Seeing his reasoning, Elizabeth nodded in agreement. "I believe that Daniel is trying to tell you children to keep your mouths shut."

"Exactly," Daniel replied. "Don't volunteer any information. If questions are asked, and they will be, let Elizabeth or me do the answering."

"I'm hungry," Jenny Sue whined from the travois.

"We all are, sweetheart." Elizabeth pulled the damp blanket up higher on her small head. "Pretty soon we'll be warm and dry, and we'll have our supper."

Daniel cradled his rifle openly in his arms and headed for the farmhouse. The farmer spied them as they came out into the open and raised his rifle. It soon became obvious to him that it was a family with several children and he allowed the barrel to point to the ground.

"Evening!" Daniel called as they approached.

"Evening," the man replied. He still maintained his hold on his gun. In this part of the country a man couldn't be too leery of strangers.

"We're looking for a place to shelter for the night and were wondering if you'd let us use your barn. We'll pay for the privilege."

Elizabeth walked up beside Daniel and put her hand on his arm. "I don't have much money," she whispered.

"I do."

"Where you from?" the farmer asked.

"Heading home to Kentucky." Daniel approached the man. "Name's Daniel LeClerc," he nodded behind him. "That's my family. We gave Richmond a try but weren't happy there. The little lady needs to be around her family. You know how women are."

Elizabeth bit her tongue as she watched the man nod. "That's a fact. My wife still ain't happy about leavin' her ma and we've been here almost five years now."

All sign of suspicion left his weathered face. "Come on up, Mr. LeClerc. I'm Harry Wainwright. My wife'll be right glad to have some company overnight. We don't get too many women through here, mostly hunters and mountain men I don't let get a look at her. She'll be pleased as punch to have another woman to gab with."

At a signal from Daniel, Elizabeth and the children approached. A woman came out of one of the cabins, a warm smile of welcome covering her face when she saw Elizabeth and the children.

"This be Minnie, my wife," Harry said. "Minnie, this be Daniel LeClerc and his family. Sorry, ma'am," he nodded toward Elizabeth, "I don't believe I caught your name."

Elizabeth introduced herself and the children. Jenny Sue quickly scrambled from the travois. "I'm hungry!" she bellowed, unconcerned with interrupting the social amenities.

"Well, my goodness," Minnie grinned, "let's get that youngen fed before she starves to death."

"We have food, Mrs. Wainwright," Daniel offered, "if your husband will allow us to use the barn."

"Pssah! Ain't no reason to sleep in that cold, drafty barn when we've got plenty of food in the cabin where it's dry and warm. Come on now, before someone starves to death."

"Remember your manners," Elizabeth cautioned the children as they marched toward the cabin.

"What a wonderful family you've got!" The longing for children was evident in Minnie's voice and in the warmth of her gaze. "Me and Harry ain't never been blessed with none, but I ain't too old yet, so maybe we'll have us a surprise someday."

A fire burned brightly in the one-room cabin and a delicious smell made little stomachs rumble. Damp coats and capes were quickly shed in the warmth of the room. Shoes had been removed at the door and except for Jenny Sue each child cleaned the mud from his own and then carried them to the fire where they would dry overnight. Spotlessly clean, the cabin boasted an oak table and four chairs, a kitchen worktable and a rocking chair placed near the fireplace.

"You have a wonderful home, Mrs. Wainwright," Elizabeth sighed as warmth surrounded her weary body.

"Call me Minnie, dear." She walked to the kitchen area and began gathering bowls and spoons. "Every year my Harry makes something new for me as a birthday surprise." She efficiently set the table, her conversation never ceasing. "He'll work out in the barn every evening for several weeks and I'm never allowed to peek. Then on my birthday he presents me with something he's made. One year it was the table, the next a couple of chairs. He's made the rocking chair, most of the wooden bowls, a chest for my clothes, our bed what's in the other cabin."

Round, childish eyes followed every move the woman made as she placed freshly churned butter and a huge loaf of bread on the table. She spooned out bowls full of soup thick with vegetables and meat.

"Well, come and get it," she invited with a grin when she noticed their hungry eyes. "I ain't never seen anybody wanting something so bad but holding back so polite-like. You sure do have nice children, Mrs. LeClerc."

Elizabeth reddened at the title but didn't correct the woman. "Thank you, but please call me Elizabeth. Children, you may go to the table:"

Daniel and Harry came in from outside, each with an armload of wood. They grinned as they watched the children devour the soup and bread. Jenny Sue sat on her knees on a chair so that she could reach the table, while Belinda, Benjamin and John stood between the chairs.

When they were finished, each child carried his plate to the dry sink then went to sit in front of the fire. Minnie reset the table for the adults and by the time they had finished it was dark outside and the children's heads were nodding.

"Looks like it won't take much for them youngens to bed down. I swear, just give them a blanket and they'd sleep where they are!" Minnie's sweet face beamed as she looked at them.

"We'd better get them out to the barn before I have to carry them," Daniel agreed.

"Ain't no need to go to the barn." Minnie began clearing the table. "We'll fix places for them here on the floor where it's nice and warm. I got plenty of quilts, we'll fix it up real nice."

"Thank you, Minnie," Elizabeth said quietly. "I worried that one of them might get sick out in the cold. It's nice of you to care for them."

"Well, soon as we get them fixed up, you and the mister can go next door and bed down."

"Uh . . . uh . . ." Elizabeth stuttered, "that's not necessary. We can't push you and Mr. Wainwright out of your bed."

"You ain't pushin' us, honey, we're offerin'." She smiled generously. "There's plenty of quilts in that there chest in the corner. I'll clean up these dishes while you get everybody settled."

Elizabeth exchanged looks with Daniel but couldn't read his dark gaze. She didn't want to be alone with him in the other cabin. She still vividly remembered the warmth of his skin, the gentleness of his touch. A night spent cuddled with him in a bed was totally improper . . . but these people thought they were man and wife. There was nothing improper with a man and wife sharing the same bed.

The children were quickly—far too quickly for her peace of mind—settled beneath a mound of quilts. Only John remained awake, as if he waited to find out were Elizabeth was going to sleep.

"Minnie, I think it would be better if Daniel and I slept here for the night. The little ones might waken and need something. That would disturb your sleep."

"Honey, I can't think of nothing more joyful than to get up in the middle of the night because a babe needed me." Her gaze rested on the children by the fire. "Don't deny me that opportunity for one night. You and your mister get a good night's sleep and I'll watch over your children."

"Daniel . . . ?" Elizabeth turned to him for help.

His shrug was almost imperceptible but his gaze traveled to John. "We'll just be next door if they should need us, but I don't expect any trouble out of them." It was a warning to the boy.

Minnie pulled some more quilts out of the chest and laid them on the floor. "You go on now, me and Harry'll be just fine. Take the lantern with you, we've got the fire for light. The bed's made with plenty of coverings so you won't have to worry about the cold."

Reluctantly, Elizabeth followed Daniel out of the room. They walked through the dog-trot porch to the other cabin. It was much smaller than the one designed for living. This one was without a fireplace or furniture, except for a bed—a bed so large it nearly filled the room, leaving no space for Daniel to spread bedding on the floor.

"What are we going to do?" Elizabeth asked, her eyes riveted to the bed.

"Sleep," Daniel replied grimly.

"Together?"

"Together."

Nine

He should have known.

The day had gone so well. The children hadn't complained or squabbled with each other. Once he had shortened his stride they had kept up with no problem, nor had they complained about his pace before then, doing their best to stay with him. Crossing the river had gone smoothly, everyone doing their part to get across safely. Elizabeth had remained cheerful even when the cold rain ruined her hat and dripped into her face. They had found a good place to spend the night, with people who openly welcomed them into their home, sharing their warmth and food as if they were invited guests.

He should have known something would destroy an otherwise good day. But Daniel hadn't planned on this. In fact, he hadn't planned on sleeping at all. He knew that as soon as he climbed into that bed he'd fall asleep and he didn't want that until he had no other choice;

until his body took control and forced him to rest.

It would have been relatively easy to stay awake in the barn. The cold and the hard dirt floor would have made sleeping difficult. And if he had been in danger of falling asleep there would have been plenty of space for him to get up and walk off his drowsiness, even going outside in the cold night air, if necessary.

But a bed . . .

He knew without touching it that a thick feather tick covered the rope bindings. It would invite a body to relax, to sleep. It was a luxury he couldn't afford.

The dreams were waiting. His headache hadn't intensified much during the day but he knew they would come, as surely as he knew the sun would rise in the morning and that he would soon become a man possessed by visions and voices telling of things he didn't want to know. Sleep would give the images an open doorway that he could successfully fight only when he was awake.

Sleep would take him another step closer to insanity.

"Daniel . . . ? Daniel?"

The fear in Elizabeth's voice brought him back from his thoughts. He turned and looked down at the woman by his side.

"What are we going to do?" she asked hesitantly.

Rubbing his hand wearily over his face, he set

the lantern on the floor. "What do you suggest?"

"We could go back in there and tell them the truth."

Daniel shook his head, "They've accepted us as a family, husband, wife and children. Even if we could get them to understand the truth, they'd never believe anything else we told them. And they'd start to wonder, and worry."

"What could they worry about? It's not like we're going to kill them in their sleep and bury them out back so that we can have their cabin."

"But they wouldn't know that. They'd worry that I had kidnapped you or the children, maybe I was forcing you to go along with me. Wainwright might think it's his Christian duty to try to save you. Someone could get hurt if he started shooting."

"But if I told them that you were taking us to Kentucky. . . ."

"Maybe you were saying that because you were afraid of me, afraid I'd hurt one of the children."

"Oh God . . ." Elizabeth sat on the edge of the bed. "What a mess."

Daniel knelt down in front of her and took her cold hands in his. "Elizabeth, I think we should try to get some sleep." He gently pushed the hair from her face. "You're tired, you desperately need to rest. I was so proud of you and those kids today, everybody did what was necessary and no one complained about being tired or cold or hungry.

133

"Tomorrow will be another day just like this one, without the rain, I hope. And we may not find another cabin to sleep in. Tomorrow night you could be sleeping on the hard ground, looking up at the stars."

"But it's wrong . . . us in the same bed." She blushed a rosy red, her eyes turned away from him.

"I won't tell if you don't," he replied soberly.

She looked at him, his dark eyes glistening in the light, his fiery hair turned dark by the night. "I don't even know how to do this."

"Do what?"

"Go to bed."

"Ellie, you've gone to bed every night of your life," he stated.

"Never with a man!"

"Pretend I'm one of the children," he suggested.

Elizabeth looked at him and stifled an hysteric-wrought giggle. "Even I can't pretend that well!"

"Well, then, I guess you'd better just pull back the covers, climb in and close your eyes. Once you're asleep you won't even know I'm here."

"Somehow I doubt that," she mumbled, looking around the tiny room. She rubbed her hands up and down her cold arms trying desperately to find a measure of self-control over the panic that threatened. "I need to change. My dress and . . . uh . . . things are wet. I can't sleep in wet clothes. I need to get my bag."

Daniel tapped the end of her nose then stood.

"I'll go to the barn and get it, then I'll go back and check on the horse while you change. Maybe, if everyone's settled down next door I'll be able to just stay out there."

Elizabeth jumped from the bed. She couldn't sit here by herself and wait for his return, she'd be a babbling idiot by then. "I'll go with you."

At his look, she hastened to defend herself. "I can't just sit here in the dark."

With a nod, Daniel grabbed a quilt and threw it over her shoulders. He picked up the lantern, opened the door and held out his hand. Wrapping the quilt securely around her shoulders, she placed her hand in his. She didn't think how easy it was becoming to touch him. Her hand felt good in his; safe, protected.

The night was still, the moon and an occasional star peeking through the clouds. The yellow glow of the lantern surrounded them in an island of light and the whisper of the breeze provided a soothing night music.

"When I was little I always liked to walk at night," Elizabeth whispered. "I'd sneak out of the school and walk through the woods where I could think wonderful things and have no one to bother me. The darkness seemed to be a friend, a shield protecting me from unseen things."

"You weren't afraid of those things you couldn't see?"

"No, if I couldn't see them then they weren't really there. I was always much more afraid of things I could see!"

135

Daniel's hand tightened protectively. "Little girls shouldn't have to be afraid. That's what daddies are for, to love them and protect them."

"But after I was seven I didn't have a father any longer." He felt and heard pain he knew she wasn't aware of showing. "When something is suddenly taken away from you it takes a while to learn to live without it."

"He died?" Hearing the voice of the little girl who had never really learned to live without her father, Daniel wanted to pull her into his arms and soothe the ache in a broken heart.

"No, as far as I know, he's still alive."

"Then why . . ."

"It's a long story, one I'd rather not discuss." Her tone of voice allowed no argument. "Besides, we're at the barn."

Daniel opened the door and discovered that they were not alone. At the far end of the barn, a light glowed brightly. Harry Wainwright peeked out of a stall, his face breaking into a welcoming grin.

"Just came to settle everything down for the night," he called cheerfully, picking up his lantern and approaching them. "Musta learned it from my pa, he always checked up on everything before he bedded down for the night."

"Elizabeth needs her bag," Daniel explained before the man could ask.

"'Course she does. Women got a whole mess of things they gotta do for getting ready for bed. Never have figured out why they can't just take off their clothes and climb in like a man does.

136

My Minnie has to go through all kinds of preparing just to get ready to go to sleep. Tuckers me out just watching her."

Daniel had never seen a woman prepare for bed but he doubted that he would have the same reaction. He knew that watching Elizabeth ready herself for bed—his bed—would be the most visually stimulating thing he could ever experience. His senses would heighten with each piece of clothing she removed; count the pins as she pulled them from her hair and wait breathlessly for the moment when the glorious mass would tumble down her back, waiting until he could bury his face in its silkiness, wrap his hands in its softness, watching as she slowly approached the bed and offered herself to him with love, her desire matching his.

As if to remind himself that his thoughts were pure fantasy, his headache momentarily intensified. It could never be. Neither Elizabeth nor any other woman would ever be his wife. He had nothing to offer a woman . . . except his eventual madness. He lived daily with that threat, he couldn't ask the woman he loved to share that agony with him. He couldn't bear to give her children that she would be forced to raise alone or to watch the love fade from her face as his madness progressed to the point where he would have to be destroyed in order to protect the very people he loved.

Loneliness nibbled at his soul with the delicacy of a hummingbird sipping nectar from a summer flower. The choice was his, his destiny was preordained, his life would be solitary because the alternative was unthinkable.

The travois had been removed from the horse but its contents were still carefully tied together. Elizabeth listened to Harry's cheerful chatter and the rumble of Daniel's much deeper voice as she tried to free her bag. The wet leather had begun to dry and the knots had tightened. In her nervousness her fingers were too clumsy and she sighed with frustration.

Aware of her slightest nuance, Daniel walked over to the travois and soon had the thongs untied, pulling the bag free without dislodging the other bundles.

"It's too cold out here for you." He pulled the quilt up beneath her chin. "Take the lantern and go on back to the cabin. I'll be there soon."

Grabbing at the chance to be alone, Elizabeth took the bag from him and picked up the lantern. She rushed from the barn before he could change his mind and insist on walking her back.

Elizabeth didn't notice the stars or the moon or the whispers of the night. She hurried back to the cabin, closing the door firmly behind her. She didn't know how long she would have but she intended to be fully dressed before Daniel could return. It would be difficult enough to sleep beside him with the many layers of clothes separating them, it would be impossible with only her thin nightdress as a barrier to her naked body.

Opening her bag, she pulled out a clean dress. Since she had no others, she would have to let her petticoats dry overnight and put them on in the morning but she intended to dress as if she were ready to leave instead of readying for bed.

Untying the ribbon beneath her breasts, she pulled the dress over her head. The ruffle at the hem was caked with mud but she hoped she could brush most of it out after it had dried. She found that each of her three petticoats had suffered the same fate, the normally pristine white cotton was brown with dirt.

Listening frantically for any sound that might indicate Daniel's return, she unlaced her shoes and kicked free of them, rolling her damp stockings down her legs. Clean stockings, dug from the bottom of the bag, provided a welcoming warmth as she fixed them snugly in place. Tempted to unlace her corset for comfort, Elizabeth forced herself to slide her clean dress over her head. It would be a wrinkled mess by morning, but that couldn't be prevented. The current style was a low neckline and high waist, both gathered by ribbons woven through the fabric. She tied the ribbons at the waistline and tugged at the neck. She had worn the dress many times but it had never before seemed to be this low. It seemed to her that far too much of her bosom was exposed.

Finally giving up on her dress, Elizabeth climbed into the far side of the bed and pulled the quilts up to her chin. Nervous tension should have kept her awake. Knowing that she was going to spend the night in the same bed with a man who was nearly a stranger should have kept her eyes wide open.

But she hadn't considered her tired body as she sank into the softness of the bed. She sighed with pleasure. It was heavenly! Like floating on a cloud, she decided as she snuggled into the warmth.

She fought to stay awake until Daniel's return but the feather mattress was far too inviting. She stared at the light of the lantern as her eyes drifted closed.

Daniel talked with Harry until he was afraid that his delay was becoming obvious. He finally walked back with the man, saying good night as he slowly opened the cabin door.

The light from the lantern illuminated the room, making it easy for him to see Elizabeth on the far side of the bed. The colorful quilt was pulled up beneath her chin and one hand curled against her cheek.

He couldn't help but wonder what her preparations for bed had been. When he saw the dress she had worn that day and her petticoats spread out to dry he began to wonder what she was wearing for sleep. The thought of her dressed in a thin nightdress was almost more than he could bear and he knew that would be enough to keep him awake all night. But he feared where his thoughts would wander and even more, if he was strong enough to resist what his body would demand.

As if she knew his dilemma, Elizabeth turned, her arm coming out of the blanket. He saw the ruffled sleeve of her dress and almost sighed with relief.

Daniel sat on the edge of the bed and unlaced his knee-high moccasins. Letting them drop to the floor, he settled back against the wall, the hard logs providing little comfort, but even more important, inviting little sleep. The cold night air soon invaded his clothing but he did nothing to alleviate the situation.

When the silence was broken by the door quietly opening, Daniel reached for the knife at his hip. John's worried face appeared from the darkness, the lantern light showing his frown as he looked around the room.

"Something wrong, John?" Daniel asked quietly, his voice a deep rumble of sound.

His expression was filled with distrust as he looked at Daniel sitting on the very edge of the bed, on top of the quilts, his back against the wall. His gaze moved to Elizabeth, snuggled beneath the quilts, her eyes closed in sleep.

"She don't know what a man can do to her," John stated firmly, carefully keeping his voice low.

"And you do?"

John nodded, blinking fiercely. "I was real little but I'll never forget what some men did to my ma."

Daniel wanted to reach out to the child but knew that his touch wouldn't be welcomed. "I won't hurt her, John."

"She's a nice lady. She don't deserve nothing bad happening to her."

"You have my word. I will do nothing to bring her harm." John studied Daniel's dark gaze and finally nodded. "Go on back to bed, son. It'll be a long day tomorrow."

The door shut quietly behind the child and Daniel turned his gaze toward the light flickering against the wall. He remembered from his childhood when sleep was far away and he found pictures in the ever-changing patterns; a bear, a wolf or maybe a rabbit. Usually he fell asleep before the light went out, only to wake in the morning and discover that someone had come in and blown out the flame.

As the room grew cold, he watched avidly until the lantern sputtered dry. As darkness settled around him, the chill invaded his bones. Daniel was forced to slide beneath the quilts. The gentle sound of Elizabeth's soft breathing was the last thing he heard.

Elizabeth opened her eyes, wondering what sound had invaded her sleep, bringing her wide awake. The warmth beneath the quilt felt so good and she realized that most of it was being supplied by her companion. In their sleep the softness of the bed had forced them toward each other until only inches separated them.

She soon discovered that it was impossible to move away since his heavier weight pulled the mattress down on his side. Squirming enough so that they didn't touch, she closed her eyes and started to drift asleep.

"Light . . . no, fire . . ." Daniel's mumbled

words quickly brought her awake. "Stop . . . who? Please?"

"Daniel," Elizabeth whispered softly. "Wake up, you're having a dream."

"Stop . . . stop . . ." A moan of near agony rumbled through the room.

Reaching out, she gently stroked his cheek. "Wake up."

"No! No!"

Elizabeth moved closer to the sleeping man and caressed his face. She pulled back abruptly when her hand encountered wetness on his cheeks. What dream could be so devastating that it would make him cry? What torture was his nightmare making him relive?

"Run? Run . . . no, stop . . . fire . . ."

"Daniel, hush." With no thought to impropriety, Elizabeth slipped her arm under his head and cradled him against her breasts. His tears were warm against her flesh as she held him. "No more dreams," she murmured. "Sleep."

He snuggled against her softness, a sigh whispering warmly across her skin. Soon his even breathing told her that he was asleep, no longer bothered by the nightmare.

With Daniel cradled against her chest and her cheek resting against the top of her head, Elizabeth closed her eyes and drifted asleep.

Daniel slowly opened his eyes. Daylight was creeping in around the closed shutters. He felt wonderfully relaxed, the tension that had been his companion was gone. The headache was still there but he was surprised that it was no worse. He was startled when he realized that he had not had the dreams as he had expected. In fact his sleep had been uninterrupted and he felt refreshed and relaxed.

He rubbed his cheek against the soft pillow beneath his head and became aware that he was nestled against Elizabeth. Without moving his head he let his gaze roam and his breath caught in his throat at the lovely sight just inches from his eyes.

It was obvious that sometime during the night he had snuggled up to her and she had wrapped her arm around him. The ribbon that held the neck of her dress closed had come loose and the material had slipped down, revealing a softly round breast and a pink nipple hardened by the chilled air. Spellbound, he stared at the bud and the knowledge that he could easily take it into his mouth and taste her sweetness soon had him growing hard with desire.

He could not remember ever wanting anything as much as he wanted to sample her; to let his tongue lick the puckered flesh; to suckle the waiting nub. He knew he should turn away, get up and leave the room before she woke, and was embarrassed by her unwitting display. But the innocence, the sensuousness of it kept him riveted in place.

So this was part of the intimacy shared with a wife, he thought sadly. To waken in the early morning light when the rest of the world still slept and share a quiet time together. To touch and be touched, love and be loved, to know that you were the center of her universe . . . and she was your reason for living.

He had never touched the softness of a woman's body, shared that moment of passion when time stood still and two became one. He had never tasted the sweetness of silky flesh or felt himself sink into the warm nest designed by nature to accept and caress a man.

The longing that he thought he'd learned to accept encompassed him, a need to just once, feel the intimacy of physical love with a woman. Not just any woman, but this woman.

Elizabeth.

Elizabeth Jane.

She had taken homeless, unwanted children to her heart and made them hers as surely as if they had been born from her body. Her love would be a thing of beauty, rock solid, diamond bright. A forever kind of thing.

But he knew once would never be enough. Just feeling the silky warmth beneath his cheek made him long for more. Seeing the puckered nipple inches from his face filled him with a desire such as he had never known. He would forever feel the need to rest his head against her breast and wonder if he had been a fool not to sample her sweetness. He knew he would not be satisfied with only making love to her once. He would need her again and again, for the rest of his life or until insanity robbed him of even that pleasure.

And it would create a child. A child who could inherit the curse Daniel now struggled with. He couldn't, wouldn't, do that to his child, so he would never do anything that might create that child. When desire had ridden heavily on his massive shoulders, he had overcome it by remembering that he could pass on this madness.

But never before had there been Elizabeth.

Reluctantly, Daniel pulled the quilt firmly to her chin, taking care that he didn't rub against her breast. He might be guilty of staring but he wouldn't allow himself to touch.

With a sigh of regret for all the things that could never be, he rolled from the bed, grabbed his moccasins and quietly opened the door. Hopefully, she would never know what she had shared with him. But he would remember it the rest of his life.

Her breast, bared to his sight, had been the most beautiful thing he'd ever seen.

He closed the door, loneliness his only companion.

Ten

The noise outside Elizabeth's window woke her from a heavy sleep. She smiled as she heard Jenny Sue bellow for her cat and Belinda's soft voice trying to quiet the child. Stretching contentedly, she realized that she was alone.

Rolling over, Elizabeth searched for signs of Daniel but his rifle and even the lantern were gone. She would have thought she'd slept by herself if not for the memories of the nightmares that had disturbed his sleep and hers.

Frowning, she wondered what horrible thing in his past could bring such dreams to his present that would make him cry from the agony. She thought of the tears on his cheeks and the anguish in his voice. She remembered how he had quieted when she soothed him, obvious even in his sleep that he turned to her for comfort.

"Me eat!" Jenny Sue's bellow interrupted Elizabeth's thoughts.

"We'll eat as soon as we're done out back," Belinda replied quietly. "Now come on."

The day had begun. With a sigh, Elizabeth threw back the covers and slid her legs over the edge of the bed. A hiss of dismay crossed her lips when she discovered that her dress had slipped above her knees during the night. When she stood and shook it down she realized that the ribbon at her neck hung free and her breast was completely exposed. Her cheeks flamed red as she hastily retied the ribbon.

What if the quilt hadn't covered her? What if Daniel had witnessed her wanton display? Mortified, she stood for long minutes with her face buried in her hands. She couldn't believe that she had deliberately dressed modestly for bed and yet would have given the most casual viewer an unrestricted display of her limbs . . . and breast!

At least she had been alone when she woke, Elizabeth thought with relief. If the situation should ever rise again that she had no choice but to share a bed with Daniel she would remember to tie the ribbons in a knot! She wasn't sure what she could do about her skirts, but she'd think of something.

Elizabeth quickly straightened the bed and tidied the room. After slipping on her petticoats and stepping into her shoes, she rolled her dress from the day before and put it in the bag.

Carrying her bag, she turned at the door to look again that nothing had been left behind and that the room was as neat as she'd found it. Satisfied, she closed the door behind her and walked over to the other cabin.

It was as noisy in the room as the other one had been quiet. The children were up, the quilts neatly folded and stacked on a bench. Each child stood at the table and eagerly ate the thick oatmeal and warm tea provided by their beaming hostess.

They greeted Elizabeth with smiles and tales of happenings during the night—Jenny Sue had needed to use the outhouse, Wilson had kicked Benjamin so hard it still hurt, Belinda snored. It was a picture of a happy, contented family ready to start a new day.

"I feel guilty that they caused you any problems last night," Elizabeth apologized to Minnie.

"Pssah, weren't no trouble atall," she replied. "Why, Belinda insisted on taking her little sister outside and I slept through everythin' else. I didn't miss hardly no sleep atall. And it were a pure pleasure to wake up to such happy voices."

She smiled lovingly at the children. "It sure will be quiet in here after y'all leave. It don't take no time to get accustomed to having little ones around."

Daniel and Harry returned from the barn and Elizabeth blushed rosily. She glanced at Daniel from beneath lowered lashes but was relieved to discover that he was treating her no differently than usual.

"We'll be leaving as soon as you're ready. Looks like the sky is clearing and we've the promise of a warm day." He saw her bag sitting by the door. "If you don't need anything else out of this, I'll tie it back on the travois."

"I'm finished with it," Elizabeth said softly. "I'll be outside in just a few minutes."

With a brief nod, Daniel headed back outside. As he pulled the door closed behind him he sighed with relief. He had worried that their first meeting after their night together would be awkward and that she would read the desire in his face. Her warm greeting satisfied him that the memory was his alone and he was glad she was spared the embarrassment.

Elizabeth accepted a package of food from Minnie and hugged the woman briefly. Promises were made to stop in if they were ever back this way and Daniel gave directions to his home in Kentucky if the couple ever ventured west.

The children, even John, accepted a hug and kiss from Minnie and then the caravan was again on its way.

Most of the time they followed the meandering course of a river rather than the heavily traveled public highway. Since the trail paralleled the river they were rarely far from it and frequently heard the noises made by other travelers. More than once, when the voices were masculine and their language far from suitable for a lady's ears, Elizabeth was glad Daniel hadn't taken the trail.

By late afternoon her feet hurt, she was tired of dodging branches and limbs and climbing over dead-fall. She was hungry and wanted desperately to dangle her feet in the cool waters of the river. Since none of the children complained, she bit the inside of her cheek to keep herself from protesting each new step she took.

As the sun lowered in the sky, Daniel began looking for a place to stop for the night. The trail and the river had separated several miles back and were now more than a mile apart. He knew that it would soon begin to reduce that separation and decided to stop before they came together again. At this point there was less of a chance that someone would venture off the trail in search of water. Their camp should be safer from uninvited guests.

They entered a fairly large clearing where the bank sloped gently down to the river. In a season of rain this area would flood, but for now it made a perfect place to stop for the night.

"We'll stop here," Daniel announced. "Boys, gather firewood, Belinda take your sister and Jenny Sue behind the bushes and Elizabeth—" he turned and looked at her, noticing for the first time that she was limping—"What did you do to your foot?"

"I think I have a blister or two," she replied, then mumbled to herself, "or ten."

Daniel's expression grew forbidding. "Go soak your feet in the river while we set up camp. I'll look at them while supper cooks."

"You will not look at my feet!"

"Elizabeth, your maidenly modesty is out of place here. I've seen bare feet before."

"Not mine!" she interrupted.

No, not your feet, Daniel thought to himself,

but I've laid with head on your bare breast and watched your tender nipple pucker with cold. I've smelled the sweetness of silky flesh and longed to taste your secret splendors. I've desired you as I've never desired another and I've walked away because I know there can be nothing between us. I am a man condemned to hell on earth and you are an angel sent to add to torment.

"Do as I say!"

Elizabeth jumped at the harshness in his voice and hurried toward the river. The expression on his face brooked no argument, in fact it sent a stab of fear racing to her heart.

Feeling somewhat guilty because everyone else was working and she was doing nothing, Elizabeth limped over to the river and looked for somewhere to sit. After peeking to be sure she was being ignored, she slipped off her shoes and rolled down her stockings, carefully tucking them into the toes of her shoes. The cold water felt delicious on her aching feet and with a sigh she closed her eyes, listening to the voices of the children and the gentle swirling of the river.

Time passed in a haze of contentment and she jumped guiltily when Daniel walked up behind her. Without asking for her consent or approval, he reached for one of her feet. He held it so that she couldn't pull free, his grasp gentle yet firm. Color turned her cheeks rosy as he pushed her dress up to midcalf and examined her foot.

"It's . . . it's the other one that has the blisters," she stuttered.

"Another few miles and this one would have had them, too," he commented, pointing to reddened spots at her ankle. He lowered that foot and raised the other, his breath whistling through his teeth when he saw the blisters. Some of them had burst, the skin rubbed raw until it was ready to bleed."

"Why didn't you say something?"

"I didn't want to complain."

"Didn't want to complain?" he asked. "So you walked until your foot is bloody and now tomorrow you won't be able to walk at all!"

He abruptly dropped her foot and rose to his impressive height. "Woman, around here we'd say that was just plain stupid. When you're hurt you speak up."

"I was raised not to complain." Elizabeth modestly lowered her skirt until it nearly touched the water.

"There is a difference between needless complaints and speaking up when something is wrong." Daniel put his hands on his hips. "I hope before the end of this trip you'll know the difference. I'd hate like hell to get a few arrows in my back because you didn't want to complain about the Indians following us!"

"Mr. LeClerc, you are being rather ludicrous. There is a vast difference between attacking Indians and a few blisters on my feet."

"There sure is, Mistress Spurlin." Daniel bent until his face was only inches from hers. "The Indians would kill quickly, but blisters like these can get infected and the poisons will take weeks to spread through your body. You'd suffer like one of Lucifer's disciples before the end."

Elizabeth lowered her gaze, not because she was hurt by Daniel's scolding, as he assumed, but rather because she would take the greatest delight in asking this man exactly who he thought he was! She was an adult, responsible for five children. It was not his place to treat her like one of those children. She had made her own way in the world since she was sixteen years old, with not one person ever complaining about her deportment!

Looking at her downturned face, Daniel felt guilty for his outburst. Of course she hadn't complained. Alone, she had brought five children from Virginia. When a promised job had been given to someone else she'd moved on, looking for another place to live. The place she'd found had been less than desirable but she'd done her best to make it into a home.

She hadn't complained when she'd been kicked out of that new home through no fault of her own. She'd walked through snow, slipped and slid in ankle-deep mud and been drenched to the skin . . . but she hadn't complained, not once. She was a city lady who had adapted remarkably well to the wilderness. Earlier he'd been proud that she didn't complain and now he was irritated with her for that very same reason.

He rubbed at his head, realizing that the pain had increased as the day passed. "Sit here and soak your feet for a while longer. I've got some salve that'll make them feel better."

Watching him walk away, Elizabeth felt an overpowering urge to get up and follow him, just to prove that he couldn't tell her what to do. Knowing that it would be childish, she sighed and dropped her feet back into the water. Now was not the time to confront him. They were at his mercy, and if she didn't like the way he did things there really wasn't much she could do about it except to keep quiet.

But once they reached the settlement . . . that was a different story!

Daniel soon returned and knelt down in front of her. He raised her blistered foot and settled it on his thigh. Elizabeth blushed at the intimate contact and turned her head so that he wasn't aware of her embarrassment.

"This is going to burn a little," he warned as he held her foot firmly in place and began to rub on a yellow paste.

"A little!" Tears sprang to her eyes as the ointment inflamed her tender skin. "Oh, stop, Daniel! Please!" she begged.

"I'm sorry, *ain jel ee*, it can't be helped. I have to make sure the broken blisters are clean." He rubbed as gently as he could then rinsed it in the cold water.

He raised her foot from the stream and cradled it in his warm hands. "You are much too lovely to spend the rest of your life with only one foot because we didn't take proper care." Bending, he placed a soft kiss at her ankle. "I would rather cut my heart out than to bring you pain, *ain jel ee.*"

The tears dried on her cheeks at the tenderness in his eyes and the gentleness of his voice. His soft kiss had brought a different kind of burning to her body, one she wasn't ready yet to explore.

"What is *ain jel ee?*" she asked quietly.

"It is Shawnee, roughly translated it means angel." His dark gaze traveled from her tear-streaked face to her storm gray eyes to her golden hair sparkling in the sun. There was a fire burning in his obsidian eyes when they again met hers. *"Ain jel ee,* I must break the blisters on your other foot so that the salve can do its job." He reached for his knife and touched the point to one of the tender places. "I am sorry."

Elizabeth looked downriver as he administered to her other foot, biting the inside of her cheeks at the burning pain, unaware of the tears sliding down her face.

Angel, he had called her angel, she repeated over and over to herself as she fought to remain quiet. This giant of a man, so gentle and caring, had called her angel. Never in her life had she been given a nickname and in the short time she had known him he had called her several different ones. But the one that she liked best, the one that warmed her heart, had been in a language so foreign she'd never have guessed its meaning.

Angel.

"It is done, Ellie." Daniel reached up and

wiped the tears away. "Next time it won't hurt nearly as much."

"Next time?"

"We will do this every evening until your feet have healed." He smiled as she shook her head. "It does no good to argue with me, I am bigger than you."

Before she could comment, Daniel stood and lifted her, holding her tightly against his massive chest. Elizabeth gasped and wrapped her arms around his neck.

"I've told you before that I'm too heavy for you to carry."

"Heavy?" Daniel threw back his head and roared with laughter, his white teeth sparkling in the sunlight and his red hair burning with a fire of its own. "I have a winter coat at home that is heavier than you!"

"Aren't you exaggerating just a little? If it was as heavy as me you'd never be able to wear it."

"On the contrary, I wear it when the winter wind is turning everything it touches to ice. It is made from the skin of a grizzly bear and lined with rabbit fur. I can only wear it in the coldest weather."

The children came running up as Daniel carried her back into camp, worry etched on their faces. He lowered her onto a blanket, taking care that her feet didn't touch the dirt.

"Elizabeth has blisters on her feet from walking today," Daniel stated. "Does anyone else?"

The children shook their heads as their necks craned for a peek.

"Can I see?" Wilson asked, his eyes wide with curiosity.

"It's only a couple of blisters," Elizabeth replied, but seeing the disappointment on their faces when it became obvious that she wasn't going to let them look, she raised her skirt a couple of inches and exposed her feet.

"You must tell us if you get hurt in any way," Daniel told the children. "I have ointment and medicines that will make them better."

"Indian medicines?" Benjamin asked eagerly.

"Some of them, yes. Some of them are things my maman uses and some are from the apothecary."

"Gor, real Injun medicines?" Wilson's voice held a note of wonder.

Daniel ruffled the child's hair and turned to check on their evening meal. Elizabeth tucked her legs beneath her, wrapping her skirt around her bare feet. Feeling somewhat like a spoiled princess, she let everyone wait on her. When supper was finished and everything cleaned up, Daniel helped the children get their beds ready. Because it was turning colder as the night progressed, the three boys shared blankets as did the three girls.

Listening to their childish voices as they argued briefly over who had to sleep in the middle or who saw the first star, Elizabeth squirmed on her blanket.

"If you will settle down, I'll tell you a story."

Daniel sat beside the fire and worked on a piece of soft leather. After cutting it to the size he desired he began to bore holes with the sharp point of his knife. When everyone was quiet he began to speak.

"When we get to the settlement you will meet a man the Shawnee call Bear Who Walks Alone. He is a big man, bigger than me, with hair the color of a raven's wing and burning black eyes.

"When he was just a young man, a bear attacked the Indian village. Someone he loved very, very much was killed and Bear Who Walks Alone went in search of the animal."

Elizabeth was as enthralled as the children as Daniel wove his story. She gasped when he told of the terrible battle between the grizzly bear and the man, moaned at the extensive injuries inflicted by powerful claws. She hurt for him when she heard of the pain he suffered because of his injuries and how he would have died without the nursing skills of the old grandmother. She was as surprised as the children that a man could fight a bear with only a knife and come out the winner.

"He has terrible scars from that fight but he wears them with pride. They mark one side of his face and most of his body." Daniel began to lace the two pieces of leather together, telling his story in such a way that his listeners waited impatiently each time he paused to gather his thoughts. "Little children have been known to run in terror from him because he looks so ferocious and even adults have turned their faces away, believing that the devil has marked him for some sin."

"Gor, I don't want to meet him."

"He is a good man, Wilson. I think you'll see that for yourself and discover that you don't even see his scars once you get to know him."

"You're making this up," Benjamin accused. "No one can fight a grizzly bear with only a knife! That ole bear woulda tore him to shreds."

"It did, as you will see." Daniel set aside his work and reached for another piece of leather.

"You don't really know a man like that!"

"Ah, but I do." He looked at his avid audience, his black eyes burning with pride. "His name is Luc LeClerc. He is my father."

"You have a father?" Elaine's childish voice was filled with disbelief.

Daniel smiled, remembering when he was young enough to doubt that someone had parents. "Yes, *petit chat,* I have a father and a mother, several brothers and a little sister just about your age."

All of the children, except for John, asked question after question about his family. Finally, when the others quieted, the boy raised his voice.

"Seems to me that there's already a bunch of people living there. They ain't gonna be happy about taking in six more kids."

"Their hearts are as big as their home, John," Daniel stated quietly. "They will welcome you without thought."

Daniel continued to work at his project while

160

the children whispered quietly among themselves until their voices drifted off as sleep took over.

Elizabeth wiggled uncomfortably on her blanket. She needed a few minutes of privacy and didn't know how to explain it to Daniel, other than just blurting it out, which she couldn't do.

"I want to carry you back down to the river and wash your feet again." Daniel put the leather aside and rose, picking her up as easily as he would pick up one of the children.

Putting her arms around his shoulders, confident in his strength, she settled comfortably against his chest. "Do you think . . . I mean, could I . . . ah, would you . . ." Her embarrassment made her stutter uncontrollably.

Realizing her problem, Daniel smiled. "We'll find a private place where your feet won't get too dirty before I wash them."

"Thank you," she whispered, her face burning.

"You're welcome."

Daniel carried her to a spot upriver and gently lowered her feet to the ground. "Yell when you are finished and I will come get you," he instructed as he turned to walk away.

"That's not necessary, I can—"

He stopped and turned back toward her. "You will ask for my help or I will make sure you don't walk."

"And how will you do that?" Elizabeth stood with her hands on her hips, determined that she would win this battle.

"Quite simple," he replied. "I won't leave you alone."

Five words and she admitted defeat. "I'll yell."

"I thought you would." She didn't miss his grin as he moved out of sight.

When she was finished, Elizabeth called for him. She suspected that he hadn't moved far because he returned so quickly. Picking her up again, he carried her to the rock at the edge of the river.

"Just let your feet dangle in the water for a while. It will help soothe them."

"It's cold!" Elizabeth moaned as she lowered her feet into the river. They sat companionably side by side, listening to the swirling of the water and the whispers of the night creatures. "Why did you tell the children about your father?"

Daniel leaned back and stared into the night sky. "When you first see him, his scars are terrifying. Adults look away and politely try to ignore them but little children haven't learned that art. I didn't want these kids to judge him by his scars first and his actions later. I wanted them to be prepared so that they can quickly forget the scars and discover the man."

"Are they really that bad?"

"Yes, *ain jel ee,* they are really that bad, but he has learned to live with them and allows people the necessary time to adjust to them. They have always been there for me but when I've been away for any length of time they always startle me when I return."

Daniel climbed from the rock and knelt at her feet. Pushing her skirt out of the way, he began to rub the salve into the blisters. Elizabeth clenched her teeth at the burning pain.

"I thought you said it wouldn't hurt as much."

"I lied," he replied with a grin. "I didn't want to drag you over here kicking and screaming. It would have disturbed the little ones' sleep."

"I'll never trust you again!"

"Yes you will," he said confidently. "You just won't trust my medicines."

"That, too!"

Daniel was meticulous in his care. When her feet were cleaned to his satisfaction, he picked her up and carried her back to camp.

"This is a great way to travel, I could get spoiled," Elizabeth commented as she nestled against him.

"It would be a treat to spoil you," Daniel whispered. "I think you are one who has had very little spoiling."

His mouth was only inches from hers and Elizabeth felt his warm breath on her cheek. As his head lowered toward hers she shivered in anticipation, wondering if his kiss would be soft and gentle or brutally hard.

Daniel felt the quiver run through her body and pulled his head away. "You are cold. Let's get you covered up before you become sick."

Disappointment was a silent companion for each of them as he placed her back on her blanket. He found a couple more blankets for her and carefully draped them over her.

"Sleep, it's been a long day," he said as he added more wood to the fire and lowered himself to the ground. He picked up the leather pieces and began to work again.

"Aren't you going to go to sleep?" she asked from her warm nest.

Daniel rubbed his aching head and knew that sleep was a luxury he couldn't afford.

"In a while, when I know everything is all right."

"But you must be tired, too."

"Sleep, *ain jel ee.*" His voice was a gentle whisper through the darkness. "Do not worry about me."

"But someone must," she murmured as she closed her eyes.

Daniel watched as she relaxed in sleep. He let himself remember their one night together, knowing it could never happen again. He thought of her turning her face up to his kiss, welcoming his touch, desiring him as much as he did her and a moan came deep from his chest.

Sorrow filled his soul and loneliness etched pain on his heart.

Eleven

"Wake up, *ain jel ee.*" Daniel pushed the sleep-tossed hair back from her face while tucking the blanket up around her shoulders.

"Hmm, not time." Squinting open her eyes, she found that it was barely light enough to see him, she moaned, snuggling deeper into the warmth.

Daniel grinned at her little-girl voice. "Not only is it time to wake up, but I want to bathe your feet and apply some more salve."

"No! It's too cold, I'll freeze!" The thought of putting her feet into the water chased away the remnants of sleep.

Daniel stood and walked over to the fire where breakfast was already cooking. He lifted a pot from near the flames and tested that the water wasn't too hot. Grabbing the salve he carried it back to Elizabeth and knelt down. He pulled the blankets up enough to expose her feet but not enough to chill her.

"I knew you wouldn't like the cold, so I warmed some water for you."

She signed with contentment as he gently washed the blisters, grimacing at the pain but discovering that it wasn't nearly as bad as it had been the night before. His hands never ventured above her ankles, but Elizabeth had to fight her feelings of embarrassment at so personal a touch. Only a painted woman let a man other than her husband touch her. And she wasn't sure that even a husband took the liberties Daniel was taking with her.

When he was done, he handed her bag to her. "Find a clean pair of stockings."

"I'll need my shoes," she commented as she struggled to sit up, keeping the blankets firmly around her.

"You won't be wearing your shoes for several days."

"Daniel, I can hardly be expected to walk for miles each day in my stocking feet." She tried to keep her voice at a whisper, not wanting to disturb the sleeping children.

"You won't be walking, either."

Elizabeth dug into her bag and pulled out a clean pair of stockings. "What am I supposed to do, ride on the travois while the little ones walk?"

Daniel left, to return moments later. "I made these for you." He handed her a pair of moccasins, dark brown in color and velvet soft.

Taking them, she turned questioning eyes toward him. "You must have stayed up most of the night. Did you sleep at all?"

"I don't need as much sleep as most people." He stood and walked back to the fire.

Slipping her feet into the moccasins, Elizabeth was surprised to discover that they were a near-perfect fit. She laced them to midcalf then wiggled her toes experimentally. Standing, she took several steps, marveling at their comfort, until she stepped on a rock. She grimaced with pain as she hobbled a couple of steps.

"I didn't have anything to make a hard sole out of so you'll have to watch your step." Daniel knelt at the fire, stirring the food so that it wouldn't burn while keeping an eye on her.

"They feel wonderful! How did you know my size?"

"When I washed your feet last night I measured them against my hand."

"Thank you, Daniel, it was very thoughtful of you of do this for me."

"I couldn't very well let you get blisters on top of your blisters."

Elizabeth ventured down to the river, careful to avoid rocks and sticks. The morning air was cold, but it seemed to her to be warmer than the day before. She stopped at the edge of the water, watching as a mist swirled eerily just above the surface. She shivered, pulling the blanket firmly around her shoulders as a sense of foreboding webbed its way through her.

There was no reason for her to harbor a feeling of doom, the children were healthy and happy, Daniel was a perfect guide. And yet, as she watched the swirling mist, her thoughts became melancholy and she knew, with a certainty, that something was going to happen . . . something that would affect all of them.

Wanting to shake off her despondency, Elizabeth picked up a couple of stones and tried skipping them across the water. Maybe because they weren't the right shape or were too heavy or maybe for a dozen other reasons, but all of them fell into the water with a splash and drifted to the bottom of the river.

She turned her back to the gloomy sight and looked toward camp. Daniel stood alone, a solitary figure wrapped in a coat that made him appear larger than life. He was a big man, head and shoulders above most, but suddenly she had an almost irresistible urge to take him into her arms and comfort him, protect him. It was ludicrous, the top of her head only reached his shoulder but she felt an urgency to reach out and surround him, an undeniable need to protect him as a mother would protect her child.

The children were just beginning to stir, their heads bobbing up from beneath blankets. Young voices, still hazy with sleep rang through the clearing, but she had a fleeting impression of a man alone. A man who stayed on the fringes, never quite a part of the circle.

He should be part of a family, she thought as she watched him reach out to fluff Benjamin's sleep-tossed hair. He was certainly old enough to have fathered several children and she couldn't imagine any woman refusing to share her life with him. He would be a wonderful husband and an adoring father. But again she had the sensation that Daniel was alone. Even when surrounded by people, he was always alone.

And lonely?

She knew with unquestionable conviction that the man with the booming voice and flaming red hair was lonely to the very depths of his being.

Forcing herself to shake off thoughts that had no substantiation, Elizabeth walked back toward camp. The children were up and about by the time she returned. Breakfast was quickly eaten and everything, including the little girls, was repacked on the travois. Hoping to find that her earlier impressions were pure fantasy, she watched Daniel closely as he moved about the camp. He talked with the children, ruffling an unruly head of hair and giving a bit of advice. He was gentle. He was kind and thoughtful.

He never once smiled, and his black eyes seemed to glow with an inner torment. He frequently rubbed his forehead as if it were giving him pain, and often stared into the distance at something unseen by anyone else. Elizabeth could not shake an overwhelming surety that she was right.

When everything and everyone was loaded onto the travois she began to hope that he had changed his mind and decided to let her walk. As long as she watched her step the moccasins would be comfortable. A couple of sharp rocks and she'd have more problems than a few blisters.

Moving to her accustomed place, she waited for the caravan to begin on its way. Daniel's approach warned her that he hadn't changed his mind, or forgotten.

"You ride, Mistress Spurlin." He motioned for her, patting the rump of his horse.

"I'm perfectly capable of walking, Mr. LeClerc, thanks to these fine moccasins you made for me." She held up her foot and wiggled her toes as if to remind him of them.

"You ride."

"Thank you, but no, I'll walk."

"Ellie, I'm not in the mood to argue. You're wasting time, get over here."

She knew from his tone of voice that his patience was running thin. Elizabeth slowly moved to his side. "Daniel, I don't like horses. Remember?"

Grabbing her waist, he threw her into the saddle before she could protest further. "Straddle him, Ellie. You'll feel safer and be more comfortable."

"I don't like this!" she muttered through clenched teeth, trying to put her leg over the horse and maintain her balance. Modesty be damned, she thought when her dress rose almost to her knees. Staying firmly on the horse was vastly more important than covering her legs!

"You'll have to let your legs hang over the travois poles," Daniel explained as he shortened the stirrups. "It probably won't be comfortable, but the leggings on your moccasins will protect your skin."

"I want to go home," she protested quietly, tears sparkling in the early morning sun.

"We are going home, *ain jel ee.*" He pulled her skirt down, tucking it carefully beneath her leg. His big hand rested on her thigh. "We have a long way to travel before we get there."

"I like it right here. There's plenty of water and enough trees to build a huge cabin. We'll just stay here."

Daniel didn't bother to argue. "I'll walk beside you for a while. That way, if you fall I'll be here to catch you."

She looked down at the ground. It seemed a million miles away. "What if I fall in the other direction?"

"I'll grab your skirt."

"What a comforting thought . . . I'll hit the ground but my skirt will be safe."

"You'll soon get used to it."

"Falling?"

"Riding."

By the fourth day of riding, Elizabeth was more than ready to walk again. She had gotten accustomed to the animal, had even made friends with the large beast, but she was tired of swaying back and forth, tired of the poles chafing her legs, tired of her backside aching from the many places the saddle rubbed. She felt as if she had more blisters on her bottom than she'd ever had on her feet. Because she sat up so high, she had to constantly look out for low-hanging branches. One had nearly unseated her the first day and if not for Daniel's quick reaction she would have fallen from the horse.

Due both to riding and to Daniel's tender care, her feet were nearly healed. He insisted on bathing them each morning and again each evening. At first she had protested, stating firmly that she could do it herself. She might as well have argued with a tree, she would have gotten further. Daniel simply did what he wanted to do, and since he was the size of a mountain there was little she could do to change his mind.

It soon became a pleasure for both of them. In the morning before the children woke or after they had settled down for the night, Elizabeth and Daniel spent those minutes together. Sometimes they talked—of the events of the day or what to expect the next day. Sometimes they were quiet, listening to the sounds around them

And as each day passed, she felt a bond, almost an empathy, grow stronger between them.

Lost in her thoughts, Elizabeth did not realize that the horse had come to a halt until Daniel walked up beside her. He carefully lowered her to the ground but didn't move away. He motioned for John to join them.

"We still have enough daylight to cross the river and set up camp on the other side." Daniel rubbed at the ache in his head. As he had known it would, the pain was growing stronger with each passing mile and they were still several days from the settlement.

"There's a place up ahead where we can be ferried across, but I don't trust the men who run it." He turned to John and placed a hand on the boy's shoulder. "Keep your eyes open and that slingshot ready. Elizabeth, keep the other children with you, near the horse."

"Do you expect trouble?" Her worried gaze fixed on the lines of stress beside his eyes.

With a nod, Daniel pulled his rifle free of its decorative sheath. Not telling her that she would probably be the cause of that trouble, he turned and walked up the trail, motioning for them to follow.

The two men who ran the ferry sat outside their decrepit shack, watery, red-rimmed eyes turned to look at Daniel. A jug was placed out of sight as he approached.

Daniel remembered three men from his earlier journey this way. In spite of his throbbing head, he used every bit of his Shawnee-trained senses to locate the other man. He didn't relax when a slight movement behind the shack give him his answer. In fact, he became more alert when the man did not make his presence known.

"We need a lift across the river."

"You and who else?" one of the men asked.

The question needed no answer as Elizabeth and the children came into view. Without removing his eyes from the men in front of him,

Daniel noticed that Elizabeth now led the horse, and that the children, except for John, were gathered around the travois. John was nowhere in sight and he wondered briefly where the boy had gone.

"Why now that be a right purty family you got there." One of the men stood, hitching his pants up around his waist, his eyes glued to Elizabeth. "Right purty."

Daniel made no overtly menacing movements, but to Elizabeth his very stance was threatening. The rifle, pointed toward the ground, was cradled on his arm. His eyes were narrowed, but remained fixed on the men in front of him.

"Well now, why don't you good people set a spell. We ain't figuring on crossing the river again today. We'll be plumb pleased fer you to stay the night and we'll take you over tomorry."

"We'll go now."

The other man rose to his feet. "I don't figure you heard none of what my partner were saying. We ain't gonna take you over tonight." His gaze rested first on Elizabeth then traveled to Belinda. "I swanee, tomorry'll be plenty soon enough to take you across. It's been a long time since we've had us some company."

"Behind you!" John's voice rang through the clearing even as a rock whistled past Daniel's head. Without taking time to aim, Daniel fired at one of the men who was reaching for his own rifle and threw his knife with deadly accuracy at the other one. Turning even before the knife

174

reached its goal, he swung a mighty fist at the man approaching from his back.

Elizabeth's eyes widened with shock at the speed in which the entire event had happened. It was over almost before she had realized it had begun. Three men lay on the ground. She looked at Daniel and found that he wasn't affected in any way, in fact he wasn't even breathing hard.

John stepped out of the woods, his slingshot prepared for another attack. "They dead?"

"I didn't aim to kill," Daniel stated as he checked on his victims.

"Should have."

"No, John. I won't kill someone unless there is no other choice." All three of the men moaned when Daniel pushed against them with his foot. "They're going to be hurting pretty bad for a while, but they'll live."

He turned toward the boy. "Your warning probably saved my life. He was coming at me with a knife." Daniel had heard the man's approach and knew the outcome would have been the same even without John's warning, but he wanted him to know that his quick actions were appreciated. It wasn't exactly a lie, and it would go a long way in improving the boy's self-confidence.

"Everyone all right?" he asked Elizabeth. At her nod, he walked toward the flatboat tied up at the shore. It was rickety but looked sturdy enough to get them across the river. It would have to be poled across using long poles that pushed against the river bottom. It worked better when two men, one on each side of the raft, poled together, but Daniel was the only one with the strength to do it.

Elizabeth watched as Daniel casually moved away from the carnage. In a blink of an eye she had seen him change from the gentle man she had come to know to a deadly killer. He spared no concern for the three men he had brought down, checking only to be sure that they were no longer a threat. She had suspected that Daniel could erupt into a frenzy of fury if antagonized but there had been no anger in his face, he had calmly done what was necessary to protect them and then moved on. She wondered if it would have been more acceptable to her if he had struck in a fit of rage. Somehow, the calm, calculated attack seemed unnatural . . . almost savage.

Elizabeth and the children moved up to the river's edge. Daniel tied a cloth over the horse's eyes and walked the animal carefully onto the raft. Untying the travois from the animal, he lowered it to the raft. He instructed the children to sit as far away from the animal as possible. If the horse panicked he didn't want one of them thrown into the river.

"What can I do to help?" Elizabeth asked quietly, hoping she was hiding the fear she felt, fear of both crossing the river and of the man who was leading them further and further into the wilderness.

"I want you and John up front." Daniel watched

the flow of the river. The current seemed strongest in the middle of the river. "If the current threatens to overtake us, you two may have to grab a pole and help keep us on course."

John scrambled to the front of the raft, but Elizabeth watched Daniel. "Was this,"—she nodded her head toward the men behind them,—"really necessary? Was there no other way to stop them?"

Daniel felt her apprehension. "I am one man with seven people to protect, seven precious people. I couldn't bargain with them, what they wanted was beyond question. They made the first move, I finished it."

Knowing the answer, she still forced herself to ask the question. "What did they want?"

"You."

Elizabeth closed her eyes and breathed deeply, as she felt her fear of him evaporate. He had handled the situation in the only way he could and she was grateful that he had been the victor. "Are you all right?"

"I'm fine." He studied the warm gray eyes staring at him and carefully lowered his voice. "If the horse panics, stay away from him. Don't try to keep him on the raft." He gently caressed her cheek, noticing a light layer of freckles on her nose. "He can be replaced. You can't."

Elizabeth turned her face into his hand, lightly kissing his palm. Color exploded in her cheeks at the boldness of her action and she pulled away from him, hurrying to take her place on the ferry.

Daniel closed his hand around the burning touch. A picture of her hair wrapped around him, their naked bodies joined together, flashed briefly in his mind. Desire coiled tightly around him and he shook his head to rid himself of his sudden flight of fancy.

His head throbbed rhythmically, reminding him that he could love her only in his imagination.

Pushing them away from shore, Daniel quickly moved to the front of the flatboat. It rocked alarmingly as he moved along one side from the front to the rear and then back again, each time digging the pole into the river bottom. The children quickly adjusted to the swaying, their voices ringing with laughter as water splashed onto them.

As the strong current in the middle grabbed at the tiny craft, Daniel tried his strength against it, struggling to keep them from flowing downriver. The horse shook his head several times but stood firmly, trying to adjust to the movement. After what seemed an eternity to Elizabeth, the raft approached the other shore. She sighed with relief when she felt them drag bottom.

It happened even as the sigh left her lips. The horse, maybe sensing that firm ground was near or perhaps just deciding that enough was enough, suddenly sprang off the raft. The weight of the animal made the boat tilt precariously and Elizabeth grabbed for something to hold on to as she slid into the water. Childish laughter of moments before turned to whimpers of fear as the children fought to maintain a hold.

As the horse's weight left the raft it rocked back into place and Elizabeth heard one of the children scream in panic. She tried to identify the voice—was it Wilson? Benjamin?—as she pulled herself back onto the wooden slats.

Unaware of the cold breeze blowing over her wet clothes, Elizabeth glimpsed one of the children splashing helplessly as the current moved him downriver. She didn't know if any of them could swim and her heart seemed to stop as Daniel dove smoothly into the water, his strong strokes quickly bringing him to Wilson. When the boy was in Daniel's firm grasp she turned to check on the others.

Belinda had a cut on her chin that dripped blood on her wet dress and both of the little girls sat on the travois crying softly, Jenny Sue clutching a wet, bedraggled cat to her chest. Benjamin's anxiety for his brother turned to visible relief when Daniel reached the child. John was . . . Elizabeth's heart began to proud.

"Where's John?" she asked, her mind refusing to accept what her eyes were telling her. "Where's John!"

Twelve

"Where's John?" Elizabeth's voice rose in panic as she searched the riverbank. Not seeing him there, she put a hand above her eyes to shade them from the lowering sun and frantically scrutinized the rippling surface.

"Oh, my God, where is he?" She put her hands over her mouth to hold back the scream she could feel wanting to burst free. She was afraid that once she started screaming she wouldn't be able to stop.

Standing chest-deep in the water, Daniel put Wilson onto the flatboat and then shoved the raft firmly onto shore. He turned and scanned the river, searching for a glimpse of the child.

Suddenly, Daniel exploded into the water, swimming with all of his strength. It seemed to her that he was aiming for a log floating lazily on the current. When he reached the log and rolled it over she was horrified to see that it was John . . . John, who had been floating facedown in the water.

An icy stillness descended on Elizabeth as she watched Daniel pull the child toward shore. When his feet could reach the bottom he stood and carried the lifeless body in his arms.

Tears cascaded down Elizabeth's cheeks as she looked at the little boy who had always tried so hard to be tough. She thought of the many scars covering his back and the embarrassment he'd tried to hide when she'd discovered them. The only thing tough about the child had been the life he'd been forced to live.

Once on shore, Daniel wrapped his arm around John's waist and held the boy upside down. The body hung limply, arms dangling, fingertips touching the dirt. With an open palm he repeatedly slapped the child's back.

"Come on, boy, breathe," he hissed between clenched teeth. "Don't die on me, son. Dammit, breathe!"

"Daniel, enough," Elizabeth whispered. "He's gone."

"No, he's not! I would have seen it if he was meant to die." He continued to slap the small back, occasionally shaking the child. "I didn't see it, Elizabeth! He's got to live! Breathe, dammit! Breathe!"

The other children stood watching, tears of sorrow and fear silvering their cheeks.

"Daniel, it's over." Elizabeth placed a hand on his straining arm. "Let him go."

"No!" His voice was a snarl of rage contorting his face to a savage mask. In a burst of wild fury, Daniel shook the boy. "Breathe!"

In the silence that followed, John coughed. It was weak, barely audible, but it was heard by those who so badly wanted to hear it.

"Breathe, John," Daniel coaxed, his voice a combination of plea and demand, once more shaking the child.

John's cough became stronger and as Daniel finally lowered him to the ground he began to vomit the river water that filled his lungs and stomach. Over and over again the boy coughed and choked. It was the sweetest sounds they'd ever heard.

When he was breathing again, Daniel knelt beside him and gathered John into his arms. He cradled the boy against his chest, his breathing as shattered as John's.

Tears ran freely down John's face and he clung to the man as tightly as Daniel clung to him; the child needing the strength of the man, the man needing the innocence of the child.

Daniel stroked the small head against his chest, his eyes closed in silent prayer, while John found unknown security in the firm heartbeat beneath his ear. There was no need for words from either of them as a bond that would last a lifetime was forged between man and boy.

"Thank God," Elizabeth whispered as she knelt beside them. John turned from Daniel and willingly, almost eagerly, accepted her embrace. She repeatedly kissed his head, running her hands over him to reassure herself that he was alive.

Daniel held his hand over his eyes, his head

pounding unmercifully. The heart-wrenching fear for John had caused his headache to increase threefold. In the last week he'd had less than eight hours of sleep and exhaustion pressed down on him, making it an effort for him to stand.

Tonight, he knew, he would sleep. And he would dream.

Finally staggering to his feet, Daniel walked toward the quietly grazing horse and untied the rag from its eyes.

"If I didn't need you so desperately I'd skin you," he muttered to the animal. Every movement was a struggle almost beyond his ability as he walked the horse back down to the river and retied the travois.

"We aren't going far. The little ones can walk, John needs to ride." Daniel picked up the boy and laid him gently on the canvas. Catching the reins in his hand he led the group away from the scene of near death.

The subdued group moved far enough away from the river so that it was no longer in sight. At the first decent-sized clearing, Daniel halted. Everyone was wet and shivering with cold by the time a fire was lit. Elizabeth dug out dry clothes and helped the children change, her own fingers shaking so badly it was difficult for her to work buttons and laces.

Daniel helped John change, his face darkening with rage when he saw the scars on his back. He knew the marks were left by a whip and that the boy was self-conscious because of them.

"You and my father have much in common."'
There was no hint of anger in his voice. "My
father has never felt shame because of his scars,
nor has he ever tried to hide them. Take pride
in the fact that you survived because of your
strength."

John turned, his eyes once more filled with
tears. Daniel gently gathered the boy to him and
held him as the child cried for all the times he
hadn't cried before.

"I didn't steal enough money for him," John
gasped between sobs. "It hurt so bad . . . I didn't
think he'd ever stop . . . he just kept hitting me
and hitting me . . . tried to run but that just
made him madder . . . don't remember when
he finally stopped . . . remember waking up on
the floor the next morning and my back burning like fire."

Daniel emitted a growl of fury but his embrace was exquisitely tender. "It's over, John,
it's all over. Never again will anyone mistreat
you or they'll answer to me. And if for some
reason I'm not around, I promise they'll answer
to my father or one of my brothers. You're part
of our family now and we don't let anyone hurt
our family."

John rubbed his nose across the back of his
hand, sniffing loudly. "What if they don't like
me?"

Daniel's heart broke a little bit more at the
uncertainty in his voice. "What's not to like?
You're a brave, intelligent, good-looking boy. I
liked you from the first, so will they."

"I'm bad."

"No, John, you're not bad. You like to get into mischief once in a while like any boy your age, but that doesn't make you bad. My maman spent the first half of my life switching my legs with a hickory stick because I couldn't stay out of trouble. That's the way boys and mothers are. Boys find trouble and mothers help them see the difference between right and wrong, because they love their sons and want them to grow up strong."

John couldn't imagine anyone, least of all a woman, switching this man's legs. In fact, he had trouble imagining Daniel as a boy.

"It's been a long day for all of us. Let's go get some supper." Daniel stood, placing a comforting hand on John's shoulder. Together they walked toward the fire, where Elizabeth had gathered the other children. The look of love on her face shone through the tears rimming her eyes. They had all heard John's tale and the children, still subdued from the near drowning, crowded around the boy.

"You're my brother now," Benjamin said firmly. "Ain't nobody gonna hurt you without me knowing."

"Mine, too," chimed in Wilson.

"Mine, too," Belinda and Elaine added.

Jenny Sue slowly approached the older boy. "You can hold my kitty," she said solemnly, offering the cat to him. When John, tears forming in his eyes, buried his face in the warm, damp fur, she seemed to reconsider. "Only till supper, my kitty!"

Elizabeth, her heart bursting with the pain, wanted to find something as soft and warm as the cat to snuggle against to help absorb some of her agony. Her gaze moved to Daniel, his black eyes burning with the dual torments of pain and rage. Without thought she took the few necessary steps that put her into his arms.

She had come home.

Her arms wrapped tightly around his waist, her head just beneath his chin. Daniel rested his cheek against the top of her head, his arms cradling her against his hard body. His throbbing head needlessly reminded him that his nightmare was far from over, but for just a few minutes he gloried in the comfort of her in his arms.

"Me hungry!" Jenny Sue wailed.

Elizabeth reluctantly pulled away from Daniel, but a twinkle lit her eyes. "Life, for Jenny Sue at least, is centered around mealtime. Let's get them fed, I think everyone needs a full stomach and a good night's sleep."

Stars twinkled gently overhead and the night music drifted softly around them. The children, exhausted from the events of the day, slept quietly in their beds.

Sensing Daniel's agitated restlessness, Elizabeth stood up from the log she'd been sitting on, her cape around her shoulders for warmth, and offered her hand to him. "Walk with me to the river?"

Daniel took her hand in his, not questioning the comfort that simple touch brought to him. They were silent as they walked the short distance back to the scene of near disaster.

The moonlight glittered on the water, turning it to rippling sheets of silver. The raft was still resting on the shore where Daniel had pushed it. With a shove of his foot he sent it back into the water where it caught the current and drifted lazily downstream.

"My parents were never married," Elizabeth began quietly, watching the raft cut through the moonlight. "My mother went off somewhere until after my birth, she gave me to my father to raise. He wanted me until he married when I was seven. His new wife didn't want his bastard daughter around so I was shipped off to a boarding school. It was a very elegant school where I was trained to become the perfect mistress for some man of wealth.

"I couldn't see spending my life at some man's whim, so when I was old enough I took a position as a teacher at the school. When the headmistress died and the school closed, my father found me the position as governess for Belinda, and later Elaine. They, too, are bastard daughters."

Daniel was quiet and she appreciated his silence. It made it easier for her to tell him the facts, simply, without embarrassment.

"When their father died a few months ago his widow sold the house we lived in and kicked us out without a dime. My father had made it eminently clear that his obligation to me was finished, he had a wife and two legitimate children to provide for. I had no choice but to take the two little girls and find employment."

Elizabeth thought of the fear that had encased her when she had been left on her own with only the two girls and a small purse of money. "I had the promise of a job teaching school in Cincinnati. That's where I found Benjamin and Wilson. They ran into me as I entered a mercantile, making it possible for the shopkeeper to catch them. He was going to turn them in for thievery, but when I agreed to pay for the stolen merchandise and promised to take them out of town he agreed. They were stealing because they were hungry.

"John's father sent him to us. The purpose was to rob us of anything of value. I guess a woman and four children looked like easy pickings. John, for whatever reason, decided to stay with us." Looking toward him to see how he had accepted her story, her voice drifted off.

"Ellie . . ." He was so proud of her bravery to accept, without question, the care of five children who had been abandoned by uncaring parents. She had not asked for his sympathy, had told her story in a matter-of-fact way.

Could he do the same? Or would he sound like the raving lunatic he was destined to become.

He knew there was every possibility that he wouldn't be able to see her and the children safely to the settlement and he had to find a way to prepare her in case it happened.

But how do you tell someone that you're going crazy, he wondered. She had already been through so much, how could he make her understand that he wanted to see her safe, had intended to see her settled, but that something more powerful, something unseen by anyone but him, could force him to abandon them in the wilderness.

His family were the only ones who knew of his affliction and they found it difficult to understand. And they loved him, unconditionally. How could he explain it to this woman?

Anger at the unjustness of life rippled through him. Here was someone he could spend the rest of his life loving, but the rest of his life was going to be shadowed in the promise of insanity.

"Sometimes it's easier to just come out and say what needs to be said." Elizabeth's voice was softly understanding. "Something has been bothering you for days. Tell me, I'll try to understand."

He looked at the moonlight caressing her face, at her warm eyes that seemed to look at him with love. He knew it was his imagination, his overwhelming need for her, but for just a few minutes it was good to think that she could love him.

"I'm going mad, Ellie." Daniel turned from her before he could see the love turn to fear and distrust. His deep voice rumbled through the darkness. "Since I was a small boy I've seen things that others can't see. I . . . I know when something . . . bad is going to happen."

"Is that what you meant when you said you'd have seen if John was going to die?" she asked quietly.

Startled, he looked at her. "I said that?"

Elizabeth nodded. "After you'd carried him out of the river, when you were shaking him and I tried to get you to stop, you turned and said that he wasn't dead, you knew because you would have seen it."

Closing his eyes and rubbing at his head, Daniel sighed. "The people I see are almost always strangers. I've only dreamed about someone I knew a few times but the events never happened to them."

"Why?"

"I don't know, they just haven't." Daniel looked into the distance. "I found Jenny Sue because of the visions. Somehow I knew exactly where to look for her and what I'd find when I got there. I've never found anyone alive before. They're always dead. Always!

"It starts with a headache and within a few days I begin to dream. I see bits and pieces at first but finally I see the entire event. Night after night I live through the deaths, the horrible, agonizing deaths of strangers, sometimes whole families. Finally, when the agony has consumed me, I'm forced to go to wherever it happens."

His voice drifted into nothingness. "I'm always too late . . . always."

190

"It's happening to you now," she added gently.

"The headache began back at the cabin. I was hoping I could get you to the settlement before it got too bad, but now I don't know, I just don't know.

"I can't explain the pain to you. I'm consumed by it until the world around me is nothing more than a red haze. I'm aware of other people, of things happening, but I can't focus on anything but the nightmare I'm living through. I become someone deranged by visions only I can see.

"Each time it happens it's a little bit worse than the time before."

"Do you know when it's going to happen this time?"

"From the very beginning I'm aware of the general direction I need to take. By the time it's at its worst I just follow where my senses lead me, I'm incapable of doing anything else."

"Then go," Elizabeth urged quietly. "We'll be all right."

"It's not time yet and I'm not about to leave you and the children alone out here." He raised his hands pleadingly to her. "I want you to understand that I'll do my best to get you to the settlement or at least to somewhere you'll be safe. But by the time we get there I won't be the man you know, Ellie I'll be a stranger, one pushing madness. I don't want to frighten you or the children, but there's no other choice but to go on."

Taking his hand in hers, Elizabeth raised it to her lips. "You could never frighten me, Daniel. I can't believe that what happens to you is insanity, but even if it is, you'd never do anything to hurt one of us."

"You don't understand," he caressed her cheek. "I could hurt you and not even realize it until days later. When the visions take over, I don't see anything else!"

"We'll take our chances Daniel." She rubbed her cheek against his hand, wondering why she didn't feel fear after the things he'd told her. Maybe she'd already experienced so many other things that this was just one more. Or maybe, deep inside, she knew that Daniel could never hurt her.

Or maybe she was as crazy as he claimed to be.

Daniel's hand slid from her cheek to the back of her head. With a few deft movements he pulled the pins free that held her hair in a chignon at her nape and watched as it cascaded to her hips. Wrapping the soft strands around his fingers, he pulled her closer, until she rested against him.

Elizabeth watched with fascination as his head lowered to hers. She watched his eyes close when his mouth gently touched her lips. Her eyes drifted shut, to absorb the feel of his lips, the taste of him.

His mouth was warm and gentle and firm, moving softly back and forth across hers. Startled, she jumped when his tongue caressed her lips, but his hand tangled in her hair kept her mouth beneath his. Over and over again his tongue teased her lips. Finally, Elizabeth parted her mouth and with a sigh, Daniel accepted her invitation.

Her knees became shakier with each intimate invasion until only Daniel's arm around her waist supported her. A burning need for something unknown grew with his touch. He released the ribbon closing of the cape and watched it slither to the ground. His hand gently pulled her hair away from her neck and his lips moved to the tender skin. He suckled lightly, tasting her neck, her jaw, the tip of her ear.

Elizabeth turned her head to give him freer access, her hands clinging to his shoulders. He followed the neckline of her dress with his fingers, lightly touching the slope of her breasts. When he encountered the ribbon that tied it closed, he pulled it loose, widening the neckline with a gentle tug.

Daniel stepped back, pulling her arms down from his shoulders. He watched with fascination as the dress slid to her elbows before coming to a stop. Her breasts, pushed up by the corset and covered only by the thin corset cover, invited his touch. Firmly rounded, he could see the puckered centers as his fingers slipped over the warm skin. When they encountered fabric rather than flesh, he found the ribbon to release the corset cover.

Daniel bent, wrapped his arms beneath her bottom and lifted Elizabeth. Embarrassment flooded her cheeks that her breasts were in perfect alignment with his face. Putting her hands on his shoulders as if to push away, her breath caught in her throat when he buried his face between them.

His beard-roughened cheeks rubbed the tender flesh, as his mouth tasted their sweetness. Moving ever closer to the waiting nubs, Daniel relished his way from one to the other.

"Daniel, stop . . ."

His face moved away from her breasts, his burning gaze meeting hers. "You are so beautiful," he murmured, his tongue flickering out at last to tease her nipple.

"I can never make you mine, Ellie. Let me have this much, when the madness finally consumes me, let me have this to cling to."

His lips found her waiting nipple and he began to suckle, pulling the peak deeply into his mouth. Cradling his head in her arms, Elizabeth felt the sensation down to her toes. He moved from one breast to the other until she thought she'd go mad with the need for more.

Slowly, reluctantly, when he knew he could go no further without total consummation, Daniel lowered her to the ground. He steadied her until her legs stopped shaking, gently retying the ribbons and pulling her dress back into place.

Elizabeth wondered if her own eyes were as glazed with desire as were Daniel's. His seemed to burn with an inner fire that could cinder whatever they touched.

"I have never known such beauty," Daniel

stated quietly, his big hand shaking against her cheek. "The memory of your sweetness will give me a harbor of sanity when lunacy threatens."

"Oh, Daniel," she whispered softly, "you can't—"

"Hush, *ain jel ee*." His fingertips rested against her trembling lips. "I have fought it for years, now you must accept it. Before too much longer I will slip over the edge.

"I must be destroyed."

Thirteen

The sun had yet to rise but one by one the stars blinked out as the darkness of night turned to the gray of dawn. Elizabeth sighed with relief that the long, endless night was finally over. Longing to chase away the nightmares of the day, she'd found only quick snatches of sleep, interrupted by dreams worse than the events had been. Again and again she'd lived through John's lifeless body being carried onto the riverbank, but in her dreams it was too late to save him. Repeatedly, she watched the three men attacking Daniel but they became the victors, she and the children their prize. In slow motion she'd felt the raft start to tilt, the children's screams of terror waking her.

Finally, deciding that no sleep was preferable to the continuous nightmares, Elizabeth had leaned against a tree and waited for dawn. But even then she hadn't found the peace she sought. Her body tingled in a strangely delicious, scary way each time she thought of Daniel's hands and lips tenderly caressing her.

It had been wrong.

It had been wonderful.

She shouldn't have let him kiss her, let alone touch her, in such an familiar manner. And she certainly shouldn't have enjoyed it.

But she had.

Not only had she enjoyed it but she had encouraged him to continue. She was innocent of the intimacies between a man and a woman but she knew enough to know where his caresses were leading. She should have made him stop after the first kiss. Her only regret was that he had stopped.

Daniel . . .

He had disappeared not long after bringing her back to camp. She knew instinctively that he hadn't gone far, that the slightest noise would bring him to her side, but necessity for privacy had outweighed his need to stay with them.

Kneeling beside her, he had touched her cheek, her hair. She knew he had thought she slept when he whispered the words in Shawnee, words that she longed to know. His deep voice had resonated with an emotion so honest it could only be love, but so filled with pain it tore at her heart.

With barely a murmur of sound he had left camp, and buried beneath her mound of blankets, Elizabeth had cried for him; and herself.

His fears became hers. His loneliness wrapped around her with a desolation that was absolute.

The sun breaking the horizon did nothing to dispel the feeling of hopelessness. Forcing herself to rise, Elizabeth added wood to the fire and watched as it grew from a few glowing embers to a sparkling blaze. The children began to stir as she prepared their breakfast. A new day had begun.

One day closer to the end of life for the man she was beginning to love.

Daniel returned to camp, a couple of skinned rabbits in his hand.

" 'Morning," he greeted solemnly, kneeling beside the fire and staking the carcasses over it.

"Are you all right?" Elizabeth asked quietly.

His nod was a simple answer for anyone who had overheard the exchange, but in his eyes she read a thousand other answers. "We'll let the rabbits cook before we break camp, then we won't have to stop for a noon meal."

Without words, she understood. He intended to move faster, stopping less often and for shorter durations. It was a race against time, a race no one could win.

Putting one foot in front of the other, Daniel led the caravan closer to his wilderness home. His head throbbed unmercifully, making each step a form of torture.

It had been three days since he'd last slept. Three days since the nightmare had unfolded in its entirety. He knew now that it involved a fire that destroys a barn, several animals and the two small children who try to save their pets.

Sweat beaded his forehead as he remembered the dream; the heat of the fire; the screams of a mother watching helplessly as her children perish; the smell of burning flesh.

Soon, possibly tonight, he'd be forced to sleep again. And once more he would see the destruction of innocent lives.

"Daniel?" Elizabeth's soft voice broke through his waking nightmare. He turned to her, his eyes showing his pain. "It's time to stop. The children are tired and it's nearly dark."

He looked around, startled to discover that night was rapidly approaching. The children stood quietly behind him, their exhaustion visible in their slumped shoulders.

For the last five days he had forced them to travel an impossible number of miles, but they had never complained. The older boys had taken on the responsibility of gathering firewood and setting up camp. Belinda watched diligently over the little girls, helping them to bed and getting them dressed each morning. They no longer squabbled among themselves, as children are wont to do. Sensing that now was a time for cooperation, they reacted with maturity far beyond their tender years.

Elizabeth was aware, as Daniel was not, that the children had taken on the responsibilities to give her time to watch over him. They all watched over him.

She had tried to explain to them what was happening to him. It was difficult for her to make them understand something that she couldn't really understand. But they accepted her without question.

Daniel looked around him for the first time and discovered that Elizabeth had carefully chosen the place for them to stop. It was a small clearing with water nearby.

"It's a good place," he commented with a nod of his head. "We'll stop."

"We don't have much to eat." Elizabeth hated to add to his burdens but he was the only one capable of hunting.

"I'll go." Unsheathing his rifle, he turned and walked down the trail.

"Think I'll go along with him," John said quietly. " 'Bout time he gave me some lessons in hunting . . . or whatever."

"Thank you, John. Stay with him." Elizabeth hugged the boy quickly then sent him on his way before Daniel could get out of sight. Since the accident at the river John accepted her embraces almost as freely as the other children.

"Me tired," Jenny Sue whimpered. "Wanna go home."

"I know, sweetheart, me, too." Elizabeth picked up the little girl, finding comfort in the tiny body in her arms. "We'll be home soon and there will be all kinds of new people to meet, new friends to make."

"Want Dan'l."

Hugging her tightly, Elizabeth carried her to a log where she sat down with the child on her lap. Of all the children, Jenny Sue seemed to be suffering Daniel's preoccupation the most. She had gotten accustomed to sitting on his lap, being carried around on his wide shoulders. She couldn't understand why he didn't do that for her now.

Elizabeth rocked Jenny Sue, humming softly under her breath. She felt guilty for not helping set up camp, but sometimes other things took precedence. For now, reassuring Jenny Sue was more important than gathering leaves for a soft bed or checking for snakes hiding under fallen trees.

Daniel and John brought back a turkey and a couple of smaller birds. The birds were cut into pieces to cook quickly, while the turkey was left whole and staked over the fire to cook more slowly. He had begun to recognize familiar landmarks and estimated that they were within a day and a half of their destination. He hoped the turkey would see them through their final journey.

He wasn't so sure he could.

Keeping his back to the fire in a useless effort to hold off the reality of the visions, Daniel leaned against a tree, staring into the distance, seeing nothing that was genuine, hearing nothing that was real. The nightmare had begun to plague his waking hours.

Elizabeth looked at the man leaning against

the tree. Staring at nothing, he hadn't moved or spoken for well over two hours. It was almost eerie to watch his stillness, to know that he was with them physically but that his mind had drifted to a place none of them could follow. As if sensing that he was on the point of breaking, the children had quietly eaten and were settled into their beds.

"Daniel?" Elizabeth placed her hand on his arm, bringing him back to reality. "Eat."

"I can't." The sight of the meat she held out to him brought bile to the back of his tongue.

"Try."

Her gray eyes were so warm, so worried. For her sake, he took a bite. He had to force himself to swallow, to take another bite. The meat lodged in his throat, his stomach rolled and he wondered how long he could keep it down. After the third piece, he handed it back to her.

Elizabeth smiled encouragingly and wrapped his hand around a tin coffee cup. "The children are tired and will soon be asleep. You go on, we'll be safe."

Startled, he stared at her in disbelief. He had thought he'd been successful in sneaking away from camp each night, returning before anyone woke. "You know?"

"From the first night, at the river. I know you're within sound of us and we've been safe." She reached out and gently cupped his cheek. "I'm sorry that you've had to deal with all us and this vision. I wish we could free you from your responsibility, but we still need you to guide us."

"We're almost there." Daniel unconsciously leaned against her hand, finding comfort from her touch. "We should be home by day after tomorrow."

The cup hung, forgotten, from his hand. She guided it to his lips, urging him to drink. When it was empty, Elizabeth took it from him and squeezed his hand.

"Go," she whispered.

"No, I won't leave you out here alone. I can make it . . . only another day and you'll be close enough to find it on your own if you must. I can make it . . ."

Elizabeth leaned against him, wrapping her arms around his lean waist. She wanted to comfort him as she had Jenny Sue, for he needed reassurance as much as the child.

Feeling her warmth, Daniel looked down at the top of her head. He closed his eyes and breathed the essence that was exclusively hers. Slowly, his arms moved from his sides to wrap around her, holding her closer, tighter, trying to drive away the demons that plagued him.

"Hold me, Ellie," he moaned. "I need your touch."

Moving away from him was the hardest thing Elizabeth had ever done, but sensing that they needed to be away from the children she took his hand in hers and led him to the stream.

"Sit, Daniel."

He sat, pulling her down with him, his nearly

painful grasp holding her tightly on his lap. The bubbling water became part of the chorus in the melody of the night. Creatures rustled beneath the bushes, an owl hooted and far in the distance a lonely whippoorwill called for a mate. The fragrance of spring filled the cool air with the sweetness of flora coming back to life after a long winter's sleep.

Leaning her head against Daniel's chest, Elizabeth wondered how she could help him, if she could help him. For now her presence seemed to be enough, the physical contact bringing its own kind of reassurance.

"Tell me . . ." Her voice was barely a whisper of sound, joining the chorus surrounding them.

"Let me share it with you," she encouraged again when he didn't reply.

Daniel leaned his head against the tree, refusing to close his eyes, sleep waited for him to relax his guard. He would fight it as long as he could, but in the end it would win, as always, and the nightmares would infest the tranquility as surely and as swiftly as locusts attacking a wheat field.

"For as long as I can remember I've had no one I could depend on." She snuggled against him, rubbing her cheek against the softness of his shirt. "If something needed to be done, I did it myself. I never asked anyone for help, struggling along as best I could, even when my best wasn't quite good enough. I guess that's made me rather independent and self-sufficient."

At another time, another place, Daniel would have smiled at her understatement. Never had he met a more self-sufficient or independent woman.

"Of course, there are those who claim that I'm domineering and stubborn. They're entitled to their opinions, but if they took the time to look beneath the surface, they'd see that I'm really just a scared little girl who wonders if she'll ever find someone to trust, someone with wide shoulders to lean on, with strong arms to catch me when I fall. A friend.

"But a part of that trust would have to be sharing; the good times and the bad, the happiness and the sorrow."

"Ellie . . . I can't bring you into my insanity. You're too sweet, too beautiful, to share that burden."

"Did I mention stubborn?" Elizabeth didn't resist the temptation to reach up and kiss the side of his neck.

Relishing the feel of her warm lips against his skin, Daniel closed his eyes. But behind his lids was the vision of devastation, the sound of young voices raised in terror, the sorrow of parental loss.

"A friend, Daniel. I've never had a friend."

He tightened his grip around her until she found it difficult to breathe. "Only children . . ."

"Share it with me, Daniel . . ." she whispered. "Let me be your friend."

He knew it was wrong. She was too sympathetic. Perhaps because of that sympathy or maybe because of the empathy they shared, or maybe the reason didn't matter any longer, for whatever reason, Daniel began to tell her of his vision, the agony a living thing in his voice.

"A fire . . . in a barn . . . horses screaming in panic . . . a litter of kittens with eyes just opened . . . round balls of fur scorching from the intense heat . . ." His teeth clenched with pain. "Two little girls . . . trying to save the kittens."

His fingers dug into her side, but Elizabeth was too lost in the nightmare vision to feel the pain that would leave bruises for several days. A shiver moved through his big body.

"I can feel their terror as if it were my own. The heat on their skin burns my flesh. Their screams . . . oh, my God, Ellie, I can hear their screams . . . over and over and over until . . ."

The sound of the stream bubbling merrily beside them was almost obscene as Elizabeth strained to hear his lowered voice. "Their mother . . . the fire burns too hot . . . too fast. She can't save them but she can hear their screams.

"She's so young . . . aged too soon by life . . . she's alone, Ellie. There's no one with her to share her sorrow, her suffering. There's a field that should be ready for spring planting, but it lays unplowed . . . she stands there . . . alone . . . and listens to her babies . . . dying."

In the silence that followed, Elizabeth could almost hear the little girls screaming, feel the heat of the flames, know the anguish of the mother. Daniel had lived with this feeling day and night for nearly two weeks. She understood why he felt as if insanity waited for him. Surely no one could live repeatedly through visions such as this and expect anything but madness to follow.

"Has it happened yet?" she asked quietly.

"No." His voice held such conviction that she didn't bother to ask him how he knew.

"If you went now, got there in time, could you prevent it from happening?"

She felt his body stiffen, his eyes seemed to burn through the night at things she couldn't see. "I don't know . . ."

"Go, Daniel. Try."

Since the dreams had first begun in his childhood, Daniel had fought them. He had come to realize that he could only fight for so long and then they took over, but he did everything he could to avoid them for as long as possible.

He had never tried to prevent the event the dream foretold from happening.

Torn between a sudden urge to go to that faraway place, to save the lives of two little girls and the need to see Elizabeth and the children to safety, he bit back a groan of despair. He couldn't be in two places at the same time.

His head throbbed remorselessly, reminding him that the end was near.

"Go back to the children, Elizabeth."

"Daniel . . ."

"This isn't open for debate. I'll see you to safety before I do anything else."

"But if—"

"There are no 'but ifs.' " Daniel stood, bringing Elizabeth to her feet at the same time. "Go."

"Daniel, listen to reason—"

"Your reason or mine? I've lived with this . . . this curse all of my life. I know what's coming, what to expect. To you it's new and the answers are simple. Nothing in life is that simple, Elizabeth. There are always choices and sometimes they aren't easily made. But I've made mine. Nothing you say or do will change that."

"If we're as close as you say we are, surely we can get there by ourselves! Just point us in the right direction!"

"Just because we're within a day or so of the settlement doesn't make the dangers any less. If I left you alone you'd be as defenseless as a newborn babe." Daniel looked into the far-off distance, seeing what only he could see. "I have enough to accept right now, if I left you alone and something happened I couldn't live with the double blow of the visions and losing you."

His burning black gaze told her that there would be no more discussion, his decision had been made. Reluctantly, she turned and headed back to camp.

She checked on the children to assure herself that they were safe, tucking up a blanket here, covering an exposed arm or leg there. Only John was awake, his blue eyes dark in the night, silently questioning her. Reassuring him with a soft kiss, Elizabeth settled down in her bed but turned her back to the merrily burning fire. It was too much of a reminder of the killing fury of Daniel's visions.

The night creatures, disturbed by her passage, soon returned to their rustling investigations. A gentle breeze murmured whimsically through the bare branches overhead while the nearly full moon spread ever-changing shadows on the ground. Occasionally one of the children muttered in sleep and in the distance the river bubbled contentedly.

To Elizabeth's heightened senses, the breeze became the sound of a fire raging out of control. The moonlight was the flickering glare of the flame as it hungrily consumed everything it touched.

And the innocently bubbling river became the anguished tears of a mother inconsolable in her grief.

The weather had turned warm and dry, a perfect spring day made to celebrate life. But Elizabeth knew with each footstep she took that Daniel was consumed by his vision of death.

They had traveled hard the day before. The two little girls had fallen asleep on the bumpy travois while the older children had gamely fought to keep up. When darkness made the trail difficult to follow and the children stumbled in fatigue, Daniel stopped and made camp.

Now they were within a few hours of the settlement and Elizabeth had never felt a greater relief or a greater agony. Their journey would be at an end and Daniel would be released to travel to his own destination. But would he find anything other than death and destruction? Was madness waiting?

"Ho! The trail!"

Startled, the weary group stopped in their tracks. Since crossing the river there had been frequent signs of other travelers but they hadn't actually seen anyone.

Daniel aimed the rifle up the trail but kept it pointed toward the ground. He motioned for the others to stay back, catching a glimpse of John as the boy melted into the shadows of the trees.

"Ho!" Daniel called in response.

Elizabeth felt little reason to trust the figure that emerged. Long white hair hung to his shoulders, matching in color the beard that flowed down his chest. A weathered hat of no discernible fashion rode low on his face, hiding all but the alertness in his eyes. His buckskin clothes were dark with age, the long fringe on the sleeves of his shirt shortened in some places and missing in others. He carried his rifle over his left arm, the fingers of his right hand on the trigger.

The old man quickly scanned the woman and children but his gaze never left Daniel for long.

"Tell the boy to come out of the woods. He ain't gonna do no good a'tall with that little ole peashooter he's carryin'."

"He's guarding our backtrail and doing a mighty fine job of it," Daniel stated quietly.

"He's already saved my life once with that pea-shooter. He may not be able to kill you with it but I'll bet dirt to gravy that you'll have a headache for a few hours."

Daniel's gaze moved past him. The old man turned slowly, his attention caught by the good size rock John held ready in the slingshot.

"Saw you slink off but didn't hear you come up behind me," the old man said quietly. "You done that near as good as an Injun. Been taking lessons?"

"Put down your rifle." John's voice broke with nervousness but his hands were steady.

"Wouldn't want to do that boy," the old man replied but his finger moved away from the trigger and his stance relaxed. "Ain't smart for a man to put down his weapon when it's the only thing twix him and the devil. I done lived too long to be that stupid and I ain't overly ready to see what ole Lucifer has in store for me."

He turned slowly, his gaze moving over Daniel, the slight shake of his head making his beard flow in rippling waves. "You're a sight, boy. A woman, six youngens and a vision riding you hard."

The old man finally lowered his rifle and stepped toward the younger man. " 'Bout time you got here," he murmured. "Welcome home, boy."

"Kaleb."

211

Fourteen

Daniel wrapped his arms around Kaleb, tempering his strength to allow for Kaleb's smaller size and greater age. Even though there was no blood relationship between the two men, Kaleb was the only grandfather Daniel had ever known and his love for the old man was obvious to their observers.

"You're a sight for weary eyes," Daniel stated. "If you weren't so ugly you'd be beautiful."

"Been told that before, boy. My Ethel Mae thinks I'm just about the purtiest thing she's ever seen."

"When did she lose her eyesight?"

"Love will do that, boy. Makes even the homeliest man a thing to behold." Kaleb turned his glittering gaze to Daniel. "Them visions seem to be coming awful close together all of a sudden. You left here in the middle of one and come back with 'nother. 'Pears to me that this 'en's ridin' you hard. Must be 'bout at the end."

"It is," Daniel confirmed, rubbing at his throbbing head.

Kaleb knew Daniel as few others did. He had watched the helpless baby grow to an inquisitive boy and then become a man any father, or grandfather, would be proud to claim. It hurt him that there was no way he could take this pain from Daniel's shoulders.

"I'm figuring that you were leadin' this group to the settlement, so let's make our howdy do's, boy, then you can be on your way. I'll see 'em home safe."

Daniel turned and walked the few steps back to join the others. "This is Elizabeth Spurlin and her children." Daniel introduced each child to Kaleb, except for Jenny Sue. She had walked up beside Daniel, the cat clutched firmly against her chest, and wrapped her arm around his leg.

Elizabeth watched the old man greet Daniel but when his sharp gaze turned toward her she had no feeling of reassurance. There was nothing even remotely friendly in his summer sky blue eyes and the look he gave to her and the children seemed to say he found something lacking in them.

"Daniel lied!" Wilson turned accusing eyes toward the man who had entertained them with such wonderful stories of his family.

"Them's mighty big words from a little boy." Kaleb's narrow eyes became mere slits in his battered face. "I helped raise Daniel and I don't take lightly to no man, or boy, calling him a liar."

Wilson's disgruntled gaze slid from Daniel to Kaleb. "He said you was scalped by Injuns." He looked at the gray hair hanging around Kaleb's shoulders. "You ain't been scalped! You got more hair than I do!"

Elizabeth watched as Daniel crossed his arms over his chest, a look of humorous expectation vying with the pain etched across his face. Even then, she wasn't prepared for the shock Kaleb was to deliver.

"Well, boy, guess you're the kind who has to see something before he believes it." Kaleb shifted his weight, letting his long rifle hang from the crook of his arm. "Now, I ain't saying that's all bad, but when a man you know and like tells you something, why 'pears to me that you should take his word without question."

With a flourish, Kaleb reached up and pulled off his battered hat, brutally exposing what it had hidden. The thick, silver hair grew only from ear to ear, around the back of his head. The roughened skin on the top of his head stretched tightly over lumpy scar tissue.

Time had taken its toll, adding a myriad of wrinkles to the loose skin hanging down his forehead and over his eyes. The once red scar crudely circling the top of his head had faded to a dull pink but there could be no mistaking what had happened to this man. Somehow, despite all odds against it, he had survived a scalping.

"Gor!" Wilson whispered, stepping back as

214

the other children moved forward for a closer look.

With a hidden smile seen only by the adults, Kaleb replaced his hat. "Now if you apologize to Daniel for calling him a liar, I might be convinced to tell you a story tonight of how I found my scalp hanging from a war lance and persuaded that Iroquois buck to give it back."

Wilson looked down at his feet, mumbling an apology. He turned eager eyes to Kaleb, hopeful that it was good enough to warrant the story.

"Howdy do, ma'am." Kaleb nodded to Elizabeth and at each of the children in turn, finding the exhaustion in their faces but seeing that they had crowded around the woman. It was obvious to him that they had closed ranks, intending to protect her from unknown harm.

"Who's this little mite?" Kaleb looked down at the little girl hanging on to Daniel.

Kaleb knelt down, his eyes nearly on level with the child. "Mighty nice kitty you got there." He slowly reached out and stroked the cat. "Bet he'd like them big ole rats I got in my barn."

"My kitty!"

"Yep, you can tell that right off." The yellow tiger-striped cat draped flacidly over her arm. The work-worn hand lightly petted the soft fur.

Unexpectedly, Jenny Sue held the cat out to him. "My kitty!" she declared as he took the animal from her.

Elizabeth watched as Kaleb continued to softly stroke the cat and was startled when Jenny Sue held her arms up to the old man.

"Up!" she demanded.

Handing his rifle to Daniel, he picked up the child and slowly rose to his feet. Jenny Sue laid her head against his shoulder, her fingers stroking his beard as he had stroked the cat.

"Still got the touch," Daniel said quietly.

"Women always did like me, even without my hair." Kaleb shifted his burden so that Jenny Sue and the cat both rode on his left arm. "Unload your horse and be on your way, boy. I'll see that these people get to the settlement."

"Elizabeth?" Daniel turned tortured eyes toward her.

The piercing blue gaze stared steadily at her. "Go on, Daniel. We'll be just fine with Mr., ah . . . Mr. . . ."

"Just Kaleb will do, mistress."

"We'll do just fine with Kaleb as our guide." Her voice held more conviction than she truly felt but this would release Daniel from his commitment.

"Take them to Maman," Daniel said as he began to untie the travois from the horse. "I will see them settled when I return."

"Don't you worry none, boy, I'll see that they get there right as rain." Kaleb attempted to set Jenny Sue down on the ground until the little girl whimpered and clung tightly to his beard. "Looks like I'll be a' carryin' this 'en with me."

"She could do with a little spoiling. She's been through a lot in a short time." His gaze turned toward the other children, but came to rest on Elizabeth. "They could all use a lot of extra love."

Elizabeth tried to read the message in his eyes as his dark gaze burned into hers. "Protect them for me until I return, Kaleb. And if I don't come back . . ."

"You'll be back, boy. Hear me?" The old man's voice rose as a flicker of fear raced through him. "You'll be back!"

Daniel's gaze never left Elizabeth as he mounted the horse. With the reins held lightly in his left hand, he cradled the long rifle across his thighs.

She longed to touch him, to feel the strength of his arms, the warmth of his caress. She tried to memorize the fiery sheen of the sunlight glistening through his hair, the compelling depths of his ebony eyes. She wanted to remember every word he'd ever spoken in a voice that vibrated thunder, the nuance of each expression.

She had to remember . . . perhaps for a lifetime.

"Be safe, Daniel," Elizabeth whispered.

Daniel tore his gaze away from her, pulled the horse around and headed back down the trail. Within seconds he was out of their sight, but she didn't move until she could no longer hear the sound of the horse's hooves.

"Come back safely." Elizabeth's voice was only a hint of sound and her eyes closed with anguish as she felt the distance separate them. "Please come back."

Opening her eyes, she looked at the children

217

and saw the apprehension in their faces. Daniel was gone but she still had the responsibility of their young lives to consider.

Clasping her hands in front of herself, Elizabeth turned to Kaleb. "How much further to the settlement?"

"Ain't far, as the crow flies. A good little walk the way we got to go."

"Children, pick up your bundles."

"We can come back for your things," Kaleb offered.

Elizabeth shook her head as she bent and helped sort the bags. "It may not be much, but it's all we have and would be impossible to replace should someone else discover them before we returned. We'll carry them as long as we can, then if necessary we'll hide them and come back later."

"It'll be a long walk carryin' them pokes," he warned.

"Kaleb, we've already had a long walk."

She smiled reassuringly at the children. "We'll take turns carrying the little girls, though I think we may have trouble dislodging Jenny Sue from her current perch." She shrugged her shoulders apologetically at Kaleb. "She has taken a liking to you, I'm afraid."

"I've heard tell that children and animals can sense the truth about a man long before an adult gets around to figuring out the truth." Kaleb's sharp gaze read her wariness. He wasn't sure what this woman meant to Daniel or why he was in the middle of the woods with her and her family, but he would protect her simply because Daniel had asked him to.

"I've heard the same. Maybe Jenny Sue knows something I've yet to learn."

"Maybe so, mistress, maybe so."

"Kaleb, if you'll lead we'll endeavor to keep up. We managed to match Daniel's long stride so following your shorter one will seem like a casual Sunday stroll."

Kaleb shifted Jenny Sue slightly, nodded to John at the back of the group and headed up the trail. He didn't relish the journey. It had taken him a little over three hours to reach this point so he estimated that it would take at least twice that long to return. Six hours would be an eternity with children whining that they were tired and a woman stopping every few minutes to rest because of the load she was carrying.

Several hours later Kaleb's amazement was surpassed only by his respect for Elizabeth and the children. They had trailed behind him without complaint at his pace. When they were within a few miles of the settlement he had insisted that they leave their bundles and had hidden them carefully before Elizabeth agreed. Elizabeth and the older boys had taken turns carrying Elaine and had even insisted that they carry Jenny Sue when it became obvious to them that she was becoming a heavy burden to Kaleb.

Shadows deepened into gloom as the sun began to set. Elizabeth put one foot in front of the other, watching carefully for roots and rocks that waited for the unwary. She had already tripped numerous times and had begun to feel irritated by her own clumsiness. It seemed that they had walked forever and she began to wonder if they'd ever reach their destination.

Her weary gaze watched the silent children. Their pace had slowed considerably and she worried that she was asking too much of them. It was obvious that soon they wouldn't be able to go any further and spending another night on the trail, this time without even a blanket to wrap up in, would be miserable.

"Come on, Wilson, we're almost there," she offered with a smile when the boy lagged behind.

"I ain't gonna walk another step after we get there," he mumbled in reply.

"Am not going to walk another step," Elizabeth corrected automatically.

"You ain't gonna walk either, huh?"

She smiled and ruffled his hair affectionately. "I have to admit that the thought of sitting in a rocking chair and watching the clouds drift by does have its merits."

"How 'bout eating some hot bread with butter runnin' down the sides?" Benjamin asked. "Or jelly! Lots and lots o' jelly!"

"Taking a bath in hot water," Belinda supplied.

"Wif bubbles that tickle my nose!" a wistful Elaine added.

"Ain't takin' no bubble bath! That's girl stuff."

"Cream 'taters!"

"Chol'it cake!"

"Chocolate."

"Yah! Chol'it cake!"

"No shoes!"

"Soft bed!"

"No more rain drippin' on my head when I'm sleepin'!"

"Peppermint sticks!"

"Chol'it cake!"

"You done said that, Elaine," Wilson reminded her.

"So? Me like chol'it cake!"

"What do you want, John?" Elizabeth asked.

John had added nothing to the list of wants, listening quietly from his place at the back of the group. "Only one thing I can think of," the boy finally replied.

"What's that?" she encouraged.

He looked down at the cat hanging flacidly from his arm. "I ain't gonna touch this damn cat for a month!"

"My kitty!" Jenny Sue bellowed over Kaleb's shoulder.

Shaking his head in amazement, Kaleb looked back, sharing a grin with Elizabeth. Even now, the children weren't complaining. They were making a game of listing things any ordinary child would want.

Elizabeth didn't have the heart to correct John's use of profanity as she normally would have. For most of the afternoon, he had carried either the cat or Jenny Sue, and sometimes both, without complaint.

Kaleb gave them no warning as they rounded a curve in the trail and a vista of unexpected beauty opened before them. The land had been cleared of trees and undergrowth, leaving rolling hills of native grass newly green by the coming of spring.

Several horses grazed placidly behind a split rail fence that wound out of sight. Willows, their branches just showing a hint of color, draped gracefully over a merrily bubbling brook.

Sensing that they had reached their destination, the children perked up and even Elizabeth felt a temporary renewal of energy. Following a well-worn-path, they climbed a grassy hill that overlooked their final destination.

The house seemed to welcome them, inviting them to come visit and stay awhile. Smoke drifted lazily out of the chimneys at each end of the huge structure. And a delicious smell of freshly baked bread drifted on the evening breeze.

"Gonna get your wish, boy," Kaleb said needlessly. "Less 'en I'm missin' my guess, Linsey be bakin' bread right now, or maybe that chocolate cake the little ens awantin'."

"Sure hope she don't mind company!" Wilson said cheerfully as he lead the group toward the house.

"I believe Daniel said that this was a settlement?"

"Settlement's on round the bend aways." Kaleb lowered Jenny Sue to the ground and watched as she toddled along behind the older children. As usual, John remained behind. "This is the home of Daniel's parents, Linsey and the Bear."

"Kaleb," Elizabeth reached out and grabbed the old man's arm. "Perhaps you could take us on to the settlement? We can't just barge in on these people."

"Ain't barging in, girl. Daniel said to bring you home. That's what I've done."

"But we are unexpected."

"Lord amercy, Linsey's 'bout the companiest woman I ever met. She ain't happy less she's got someone to worry over. She'll be plumb cheerful to have you and the little ens to fuss about."

He saw the worry, and fear, that crossed her delicate features. "Girl, you dragged six youngens through the woods without worryin' about all the things that coulda happened. Now you're standing there worryin' about facing two of the nicest people God put on this earth. Seems to me you got your worries backward."

"I'm too tired to worry, Kaleb." Elizabeth smiled softly, looking longingly at the waiting house. "If you say we won't be barging in, then let's go on. I think I have just about enough energy left to make it down this hill."

From the distance, Elizabeth heard the sound of a door slamming closed. She saw a big man come to an abrupt halt as he watched the approaching children. For a heart-stopping moment it could have been Daniel and she closed her eyes at the agony of his leaving.

The man on the porch was as big as Daniel,

his shoulders as broad, his head held in the same proud manner. But the dying sun shone on hair as dark as a raven's wing, the black glistening blue rather than the fiery red she longed to see.

"What did you find this time, Kaleb?"

Kaleb and Elizabeth came to a halt behind the children. "Elizabeth, this is Daniel's brother, Kaleb."

"Hello, Elizabeth." The younger Kaleb took her outstretched hand and placed a gentle kiss on it. "Around here I'm called Kal, to avoid confusion."

"It's Mistress Spurlin to you, boy." Kaleb's eyes narrowed. "You can let go of her hand, too."

"But I like holding her hand." Kal's eyes, as black as his hair, so resembled Daniel's that Elizabeth felt the breath catch in her throat. "I haven't held anything nearly as . . . sweet . . . in a long time."

"You won't have a hand to hold anythin' with when Daniel returns," Kaleb warned.

"So that's the way it is." Kal smiled at Elizabeth but didn't relinquish his hold on her hand. "Where is that brother of mine?"

"Followin' another dream."

It was evident in the sudden pressure of Kal's grasp and the flicker of pain in his eyes that he and Daniel shared a bond deeper than just brotherhood.

"Do you think you can let go of her long enough for us to go into the house, Kal? They've walked a long way and would appreciate a hot meal and a soft bed."

"And chol'it cake," Elaine whispered loudly.

Kal smiled, released Elizabeth's hand and turned to the children. "And who is this little darlin'?"

"Me 'Laine. I like chol'it cake!"

"Well come with me 'Laine, and I'll see if we can find something to satisfy that sweet tooth."

Kal took her hand and opened the door, leading the group into a large room that seemed to be filled with equally large people. The happy voices ground to a halt and three pairs of masculine eyes as black as night turned toward Elizabeth and the children.

"What'd you find, now, Kal?" the youngest man asked, his eyes twinkling merrily.

"I have a young lady here who is suffering from a severe case of sweet tooth." He looked down at Elaine and winked broadly. "And since you always know where all of the sweets are hidden, I figure you're the right one to help her out, Mark."

"Looks like something pretty sweet standing behind you." Dark eyes surveyed Elizabeth from head to foot, making a blush rise warmly to her cheeks.

"Ain't you got no manners, boy?" Kaleb blustered, escorting her into the room. "Oughta be ashamed."

Rather than showing remorse, a dark eyebrow slanted wickedly as a gleaming smile slashed across his handsome face. "Introductions seem to be in order."

"Where'd I go wrong? I tried to raise him right," the old man mumbled as he turned to Elizabeth. "This be Mistress Elizabeth Spurlin and her children. Elizabeth, these hellions, who was raised better than they let on, are Daniel's brothers."

"Mark." He pointed to the youngest who had knelt down to talk to Elaine. "James." A shy grin covered his face as he nodded in greeting. "And that one who knows no shame is William."

Will groaned, running a hand through his midnight hair. "Did I hear her lovely name twined with Daniel's? Tell me it isn't so."

"Back off, Brother." Kal grinned, unnecessarily demonstrating that he was every bit as handsome as the younger Will. "Big brother found her first."

"He always did get the best toys," Will grumbled good-naturedly.

Elizabeth stared at Daniel's brothers. Except for the obvious differences in their ages, each was a copy of the other, exceptionally large, exceedingly attractive and filled with enough charm to enchant the most forbidding matron.

"Are you not a little old for toys, Son?" a deep, quiet voice asked from behind her.

Turning, Elizabeth's gaze clashed with one as dark as a moonless night, as gentle as a butterfly's touch.

"Gor! It's the Bear!"

Fifteen

Wilson's whispered exclamation cut through the sudden silence with the purity of ringing crystal. Black eyes twinkled and lips twitched in merriment as the younger men turned toward their sire.

"Sounds like he expects you to eat him for supper," Will commented drolly.

Without removing his gaze from Elizabeth, he responded quietly to his middle son. "Your continued audacity may cost you your dinner."

"Shoulda starved him from birth." Kaleb's muttered remark was ignored by everyone. They all knew that the old man would give his life to protect each of them, and while Daniel was undoubtedly his favorite, he loved all of the men he had helped raise from infancy.

Elizabeth's gaze was caught by the intensity of black eyes in a face so badly scarred it had become a mask of parody to the beauty of the unmarred side. There could be no mistaking that this was Luc LeClerc, Daniel's father. His size and burning eyes had been given to each of his sons but more so to his eldest.

"Mistress, does my countenance so disturb you that it leaves you speechless?" he asked gently.

Elizabeth smiled softly. "I see each of your sons in your face and your coloring. But in your eyes . . . in your eyes I see Daniel."

"And that gives you comfort?"

"Yes," she replied simply.

"Did you really kill a grizzly with just a knife?" Wilson asked, his voice thick with fear and respect.

"Wilson, behave yourself," Elizabeth admonished, never taking her gaze from Luc's. "Forgive him, I fear he is at an age to be fascinated with horror stories."

"After raising Daniel and his brothers there is not much I don't know about little boys and even less that I don't forgive."

"Me 'ungry!" Jenny Sue bellowed from the back of the crowd of children.

"*Mon dieu,* so much noise from one so small."

"I believe it is Jenny Sue's form of self-defense, so that she doesn't get lost in the crowd."

Smiling at Elizabeth, Luc knelt in front of the tiny girl. "Ah, little one, in my house that can not be allowed. I see you have brought a *petite chat* for a visit."

"My kitty!"

He stroked the animal hanging from her arm. "We will find a saucer of milk for your kitty, then we will find something to remove this fierce hunger you feel." He carefully unbuttoned her coat, patiently helping to remove it without dislodging the cat.

Staring wide-eyed at his battered visage, Jenny Sue's lower lip began to tremble, her eyebrows drawing together in a frown and her clear blue eyes showing signs of tears. It had been so long since a new child had been around that Luc had nearly forgotten how truly fearsome he looked. Elizabeth stepped forward as he attempted to ease away before he could frighten her further. They both stopped abruptly when Jenny Sue's hand reached for his face.

"Hurt . . ." Her tiny fingers unknowingly severing a pain so deep that it had lingered for three decades, she stroked the line of scars that had made grown men turn away in revulsion.

"No, little one." Luc's deep voice was huskier than usual. "Your touch has taken away the hurt."

Surprising everyone, she leaned over and placed a sloppy kiss on his cheek. "Make better."

Clearing his throat before he could speak, he softly touched her smooth cheek with the back of his fingers. "Thank you, *ah pel o thah,* your kiss made it much better.

"Me like chol'it cake," Belinda chimed, breaking the spellbound mood, her hand firmly clutching Mark's.

"There'll be no living with him," Will sighed.

"Hope no one witnesses it," James agreed with a sorrowful nod.

"The great Bear, brought to his knees by one tiny little girl!" a smirking Mark added.

Helping Elizabeth remove her cape while Luc glared at his sons, Kal grinned. "What my brothers are trying to say is that, while our father is afraid of nothing, he is woefully unsuited to parenting little girls. He gives them anything, and everything, they want, even when it isn't good for them."

Luc scowled at his sons but it was obvious that they were neither frightened nor intimidated by him. "Little girls, of any age, are to be cherished."

"And spoiled . . . rotten!" Will added with a grin. "Our little sister, Dara, is in danger of becoming the most rotten little girl around."

Luc stood to his full impressive height. "And who is responsible for that? If I should tell her she can not have something, you do your best to get it for her." Will looked sheepish but made no effort to deny the accusation. "And, if not you, then one of your brothers runs to her bidding."

"Are you going to leave our guests standing in the doorway all night while you argue?" a soft voice asked.

Startled by the unexpectedly feminine voice, Elizabeth turned. Tiny and delicate, vibrant red hair just touched with silver, Elizabeth thought her to be one of the most beautiful women she'd ever seen. It was nearly impossible to believe that she was the mother of these massive men.

"An, *ain jel ee.*" Luc held out his hand. "Come

meet our guests, Mistress Spurlin and her children."

"Me 'ungry!" Jenny Sue clutched the little finger of Luc's hand, clearing showing her preference. "Kitty 'ungry!"

"Well, my goodness, let's find you something to eat." Linsey took Elizabeth's arm and led her toward the back of the house. "We'll get down to introductions later. I think that now you are tired and hungry and rather bemused by my family."

"We've walked a long way," Elizabeth agreed. "And the children are sorely in need of food and rest."

"We are in another war with the British, Tecumseh is uniting all of the tribes to try to push the white men out, the French are none too friendly and my son drags you and your children across hundreds of miles of wilderness." Luc shook his head. "I thought I'd taught him better."

"Daniel?" Linsey's hand tightened on Elizabeth's arm. "You've been with Daniel? Where is he? Is he safe?"

"He ain't here." Kaleb's sharp gaze met Linsey's shadowed green eyes. "He's followin' another dream."

"So soon . . ."

Dinner was a boisterously crowded affair, but the warmth of Luc and Linsey could not be doubted. Elizabeth was ordered, gently, to sit and enjoy her meal while the children were attended by the many adults in the room. Elaine sat on Mark's lap, enjoying his undivided attention, while Jenny Sue clung firmly to Luc.

Promising to return the next day with his own large family, Kaleb departed amidst words of gratitude from Elizabeth and pleas from the younger boys for the stories he had yet to tell. And through all of the noise and laughter, the confusion and mayhem, Linsey elegantly handled the duties of hostess.

"Dara will have trouble accepting this." Sitting beside Elizabeth, Kal nodded to Jenny Sue and Elaine snuggled on masculine laps. "She's not accustomed to the competition."

"We don't want to cause any trouble." Elizabeth noticed that Jenny Sue was nodding drowsily on Luc's lap.

"You won't." Kal reached over and squeezed her hands in reassurance. "There is no doubt that my little sister has been spoiled rotten, but once she gets over the shock of sharing her men with the others, I think we'll find that she is as generous as she is pretty.

"She'd be here tonight but Ethel Mae, Kaleb's wife, came over earlier and Dara wanted to spend the night at their cabin."

"We won't be here long." She moved her hands slightly so that his slid away. "We'll have to find someplace to stay and I'll need to look into employment opportunities. We left Indiana so quickly I'm afraid I didn't give much thought to how I'd support the children once we got here."

"What type of employment do you seek?" Luc shifted a sleepy Jenny Sue on his lap.

"I have been very well educated, I read and understand French and Latin, though I do lack the ability to converse freely in either. I'm very quick with numbers and my penmanship has been remarked upon for its clarity. I play the pianoforte, sew passably well and know the correct seating at a formal dinner of foreign dignitaries."

"Well that's a relief!" Will signed, amusement playing across his handsome face. "We have so many dignitaries to dinner!"

"Behave! Did I not teach you better manners?" Linsey scolded.

"You tried, Maman." Jamie grinned at his older brother. "Unfortunately, you failed."

"That's enough out of you, too." Her burning gaze made both of her massive sons squirm in their chairs. "Forgive my sons, I should have beat them when they were little enough for me to do so!"

The chuckles from the four men made Elizabeth decide that Linsey had never beaten any of her children.

"Quite an impressive list of accomplishments, Mistress Spurlin," Luc commented, allowing his wife to chastise their sons.

"Not quite so impressive when you balance it against the things I can not do," she added, truthfully.

"Such as?"

Elizabeth held up her hand and began to count her missing talents off on her fingers. "I can't light a fire, the boys will tell you that we'd have frozen to death if they'd waited on me to get a fire going! I can't chop wood, clean a carcass or hit anything smaller than a barn even when I carefully aim the rifle. I don't know the first thing about planting or harvesting a garden, have never put up anything for the coming winter . . ."

"And she can't cook!" Wilson chimed in.

"It's true," Elizabeth nodded sadly. "I am probably the worst cook ever to create a stew."

Luc threw back his head with a booming roar of laughter and Linsey smiled mischievously.

"Forgive us," Linsey smiled. "We are not laughing at you I believe that Luc and I both share the memory of the first pot of stew I attempted to make."

"It wasn't very good?"

"It was so bad it has become another legend about the great Bear Who Walks Alone. It is said that to survive, he ate the broth made to remove the hide from a grizzly—while it still lived!" Linsey's enchanting laugh filled the room. "It was so bad a great Shawnee warrior promised never to scalp me if I promised not to feed him!"

"I think I'm missing a great story here," Elizabeth said with a smile, feeling amazingly relaxed and at home.

"There will be time, Mistress, to tell you many stories," Luc promised.

"Please, call me Elizabeth."

Linsey looked at the little girls sleeping in Luc's and Mark's laps. "Let's get the children, yours and mine," she emphasized the possessive pronouns, "in bed for the night and we will discuss your future."

"We're being sent to our rooms!" Will stated indignantly.

"No, you are far too old for me to send you to your room." Linsey stood gracefully, smoothing her skirt. "However, I see no need to endure your rudeness. You may go anywhere you like, as long as it's not in the same room with me."

Elizabeth saw that spankings had never been necessary. Linsey still controlled her sons by showing her disappointment in them. Their demeanor became extremely gracious as they tried to wiggle their way back into their mother's good graces.

By the time the children were in bed, Linsey had kissed each of her sons, speaking quietly to them, showing that she was no longer upset.

John, Benjamin and Wilson were given a room to share. The furniture was moved around and an additional bed brought from another part of the house to make the room complete. Elizabeth could tell from the looks on their faces that none of the boys had ever slept anyplace even remotely similar.

"Gor, it's a castle!" Wilson stated in awe.

"Are you sure this is our room?" Benjamin's

eyes were open wide at the magnificent furnishings.

"It is your room for as long as you stay with us." Linsey smiled gently at the boys. "And I hope that stay will be a long, long time."

John, as usual, remained quiet, but the look on his face equaled that of the other two boys.

Luc and Mark carried the sleepy little girls to a room that seemed to be all lace and ribbons. Both Elaine and Belinda were accustomed to frills and quickly accepted the room. Jenny Sue was far more concerned with parting from Luc than appreciating the lovely room that was hers.

"No!" she wailed when Luc attempted to unwrap her arms from around his neck.

"It is time for you to find sleep, little one." Afraid that he would hurt her, Luc carefully pulled one hand free only to have it wind around him as he dislodged the other one.

"Me no seepy!"

Elizabeth couldn't hide a grin at the helpless look on his face when he turned to her. His sons knew him well; he couldn't resist the pleas of one tiny girl.

"Jenny Sue, that's enough." Elizabeth pulled her out of Luc's arms.

"Me no seepy . . ." she whined, tears pooling in her blue eyes.

"Kitty is sleepy. You wouldn't want him to have to sleep by himself and maybe get lonely." Putting the child down, Elizabeth pushed the snarled red hair out of her eyes. As Luc made a quick, silent exit, she began to undress the little girl.

"Kitty?" Jenny Sue rubbed her eyes with her hands and yawned widely, cooperating tiredly as Elizabeth removed her clothes.

Within minutes Elizabeth had all three girls in bed, kissed them good night and blew out the candles. She checked to be sure that the boys were all right, then wandered slowly back down the stairs.

As she descended, she admired the heavily carved banister, stopping frequently to look at a picture hanging on the wall or to lightly touch the Chinese silk wall covering.

Here, in the middle of the wilderness, the house was as grand as any she'd visited in Virginia. The furniture was the latest produced by Hepplewhite, Adams and Duncan Phyfe. Inlaid wood floors, some with oval carpets, glistened with a high shine of polish. Glass hanging lamps, many with colored shades, lighted the rooms. Scenic wall panels, pastel paint or Chinese silk fabric covered each wall.

It was a house worthy of the greatest family in Virginia, and yet it had the feeling of being a home filled with love and happiness.

"You have a lovely home and a delightful family." Elizabeth entered the room where Luc and Linsey waited, a welcoming fire taking the chill off the air.

"Thank you, I appreciate my home but it can't compare to my children. They are the joy of my life, even if there are times I could throttle them." She motioned for Elizabeth to be seated. "I know that you are tired, but if you are like me, you won't truly rest until you know what your future holds."

With a sigh, Elizabeth sat down, lifting her feet to a tapestry-covered footstool. "When I admit that I left Indiana without thought for the future, I know you must think me terribly careless with the lives of those children. Daniel insisted that the decision be made quickly. I knew what we would find couldn't be any worse than what we were leaving."

"My son can be extremely impetuous, but never more so than when he is fighting one of his dreams."

"I didn't understand it then." Elizabeth wrapped her arms around herself as she remembered the pain Daniel had suffered. "I do now."

Luc reached over and pulled Linsey's hand into his. "He'll come home safely, ladies."

"This time, maybe." Linsey's green eyes filled with pain for her son. "But the next time? Or the next?"

Elizabeth felt like an intruder as she watched a world of shared agony pass silently between the couple. With a visible effort, Linsey shook it away and turned to her with a smile.

"For several years I have taught school for the settlement children, not because I wanted to, but because there was no one else. Sometimes, my only students were my own children, however with first Ethel Mae and now you coming here with your families, there are more than a dozen children who need a teacher. Would you be interested in the position?"

She continued before Elizabeth could answer. "The position comes with a cabin. It is small, only two rooms and a loft, but it would be large enough for now and we could always add a room at a later date. There would be little money, but you'll be paid in services and foodstuffs, and who knows, someone might even volunteer to teach you to cook."

Nearly overwhelmed with the offer that was far more than she'd ever expected, Elizabeth had trouble responding. "When do I start?"

"There will be plenty of time after you are rested and the children feel at home. The cabin is in need of a good cleaning before you can move in."

"That is something I can do," Elizabeth replied with a grin. "I've always been good at moving dirt from one spot to another."

"It is settled then. You will live in the cabin and be our teacher."

"Thank you." Tears brimmed her eyes and she hastily blinked them away.

"It is I who thank you," Luc said quietly. "Now I will no long have to share my wife with a horde of children."

"You're selfish, Luc LeClerc." Linsey's eyes glowed as she looked at his beloved countenance.

"With you, *ain jel ee*, always."

Sixteen

Elizabeth sat on the porch of the cabin, the old rocking chair creaking soothingly with the slightest movement of her bare foot. Inside, the children were fast asleep in their beds, secure in their surroundings.

The evening breeze whispered softly through the trees while furtive scurryings here and there momentarily gave away the hiding places of night creatures setting out to investigate the changes made during the day while they had slept.

The new leaves on the trees, a bright green in the glow of the sun, rustled briskly, glistening in the radiance of a full moon. The deep, rich smell of newly turned dirt vied with the fragrance of spring blossoms, making the very act of breathing a joy.

After nearly three weeks of living at the settlement, Elizabeth was almost content. The cabin had quickly become home to her and the children. The three boys claimed the loft as their own, allowing the girls to ascend only by infrequent invitation.

Not to be outdone, the girls kept the door to their bedroom closed at all times, hinting at the mysterious things they kept for their eyes only.

More than once, when everyone was supposed to be doing chores, Elizabeth had caught a boy opening the door to the bedroom or a girl climbing the ladder to the loft.

Arguments rose over whose turn it was to carry in wood or draw water from the well. Tears fell over a slight, real or imagined; laughter flowed freely at each other and themselves. Shared quiet time before bed when they gathered around and listened spellbound to the stories Elizabeth read or that one of their frequent visitors told. The ordinary, everyday things that composed a family, and Elizabeth cherished each and every one of them.

The children were beginning to see each other as sisters and brothers rather than six strangers living together and accepting what they couldn't change

The move into the cabin had been accomplished with a maximum of fuss and a premium of enjoyment. The morning of the move from the house to the cabin, Kaleb had shown up with his wife, Ethel Mae, and her brood of well-mannered, but boisterous, children. If possible, there were too many helping hands since everyone got into the spirit and wanted to do his or her part in readying the cabin for its new occupants.

By midafternoon every nook and cranny had been enthusiastically, if somewhat inexpertly swept, scrubbed or scoured. Furniture was moved from the attics of the house to the cabin and a section of the main room partitioned off to give Elizabeth some privacy.

The news of the activities had spread like wildfire through the settlement and by early afternoon everyone for miles around had arrived with a hamper of food to welcome the new teacher and her family.

These people who had once been strangers from the city newly come to the wilderness remembered the adjustments they had made, the people and possessions they had left behind when they had set out in search of a better life. They arrived at the gathering bearing gifts, whatever they could spare and considered vital to housekeeping; linens, dishes, pots and pans, shovels and a hoe, an ax, a hatchet, and a butchering knife nearly as long as Elizabeth's forearm. She was overwhelmed by their warmth and generosity. The impromptu party had lasted well into the night when the exhausted crowd departed for their own homes.

School had been suspended until spring planting was completed, as it would be again during the harvest season or any other time when the children were needed at home. Elizabeth didn't object since it gave her time to plant her own garden and become more familiar with her neighbors.

She was nearly content . . . except for a growing restlessness at Daniel's continued absence. Then today, without warning, a sense of anticipation had begun to grow.

With a blanket thrown around her shoulders and dressed in a cotton nightdress styled much like her day dresses with a high waist, low rounded neckline and sleeves ending at her elbow, she watched as the ever-changing shadows created fantasy images on the ground. Raising one foot to the seat of the rocker, causing an indecent expanse of bare leg to show, Elizabeth wrapped her arms around her leg and rested her chin against her knee.

She closed her eyes, remembering exactly when the feeling of expectation had settled around her while she'd been hanging a load of wash on the rope strung between two trees. It had come as suddenly as a summer shower bringing with it a warmth to soothe her frozen heart.

It had whispered across her skin, enchanting her with promise, enticing her to wait . . . he was coming home, to her.

Throughout the afternoon, Elizabeth had tried to maintain a normal attitude but by evening the children had begun to look at her strangely. Perhaps she smiled too often, laughed too freely. The fairy tale she had chosen to read at bedtime had been light and silly and she had allowed the children to stay up far later than usual.

But now the moon rose high in the sky and anticipation had grown to a fevered pitch. She

243

could feel his presence as surely as the rough wood beneath her foot. She sensed not only his eagerness but the subdued sorrow that was as much a part of him as was his fiery red hair or substantial strength.

She knew without seeing him or hearing the words, that once again he had arrived too late to prevent tragedy from occurring. But he was whole, in body if not in spirit.

And he was coming home.

"Ellie." The deep rumble of his voice teased her.

Elizabeth tensed, expectation gone, reality too difficult to grasp after all the weeks of waiting. "Will you still be there if I open my eyes or are you only part of my nightly dream?"

"Open your eyes, *ee kwai wah*."

With eyes still closed, she smiled at the Shawnee word sliding smoothly from his lips. "What did you call me?"

How could he explain that the simplest translation of the word was woman, but that it meant so much more. It conveyed the essence of woman; gentle and tender to those she loved but tough to anyone who threatened her loved ones, soft but with an inner strength that would rival forged iron, giving, caring, compassionate.

"It means woman . . . my woman." His booming voice was lowered to a whisper. "Open your eyes, *ee kwai wah*, I'm far too big to disappear like a puff of smoke."

"Daniel . . ." His name was a caress as she

stood, stepping forward. He reached out. "Daniel."

She was in his arms as she had longed to be, his body solid against hers, his breath warm against her cheek.

"You're home . . . you're home . . . you're home," she whispered over and over again.

"I am now." Daniel buried his face in the soft crease of her neck and breathed deeply of the scent he had come to know as her. "God, I've missed you."

"Daniel . . ." Effortlessly, he picked her up and carried her away from the cabin. With her head nestled against his shoulder and her fingers buried into his shirt, Elizabeth didn't question his destination. She would be content to stay in his arms until the end of time.

From the doorway a pair of dark eyes watched as the couple moved out of sight. John knew the identity of the huge man and that Elizabeth was in his arms. When they were lost in the darkness, he went back into the cabin. Checking first to see that the girls were asleep, he quietly climbed the ladder into the loft.

Having a family wasn't bad, he decided as he settled down on his bed. Having others kids to share with was kind of fun, and Elizabeth was a great mother. Having Daniel for a father would just about make the situation perfect. The hint of a smile crossed his face as he drifted back to sleep.

Daniel sat down beneath a giant tree, its branches spreading for hundreds of feet in each direction. A bubbling creek sparkled with diamond brightness beneath the kiss of the moon. He was unaware of other lovers who had found privacy in the same haven, as they searched, sometimes with hopeless desperation, for the answers to their futures.

Settling Elizabeth on his lap, her head snugly beneath his chin, he leaned back and closed his eyes. Almost desperate in his need to be with her he had traveled nearly nonstop for the last three days, resting only when he couldn't force his feet to take another step. Now exhaustion weighed heavily upon his broad shoulders, but he was content . . . he was home, at last, and she was in his arms.

Elizabeth rubbed her cheek against the soft buckskin of his shirt, one arm wrapped around his waist, the other lying against his chest. She listened to the strong rhythm of his heart and felt the tension slowly leave him.

"I helped Martha bury her children." He rubbed his chin on the softness of her hair, remembering the bitter sorrow of the woman who had lost everyone she loved. "Her husband had gone out hunting several months ago and never returned. She was waiting for warmer weather before packing up and moving back to Virginia."

Sensing that he needed to talk, Elizabeth moved her hand to the side of his neck, gently caressing the firm skin, feeling the pulse of life against her palm.

"She gathered up a few personal things and

a couple of items that each child favored then insisted that we burn the cabin. She never said a word or shed a tear as we stood there and watched until it was only glowing embers.

"I wanted to escort her back to her home but she was adamant that I leave her at the nearest settlement. She thanked me for my help." A sound of hopelessness rumbled through his chest. "I got there in time to watch her children die a horrible death and she thanked me for helping!"

"You did what you could," Elizabeth offered gently.

"It wasn't enough!" Daniel leaned his head back against the rough bark of the tree and stared unseeing at the moonlit sky. "All the way back here I kept wondering why it's never enough. It goes around and around in my brain until I want to beg it to stop. I see what's going to happen but I can't stop it!

"Why me, Elizabeth?" He asked pleadingly. "Why me? What have I done to deserve this? I don't want to know the future. I want to be like other men, to plan a life with one woman, raise children with her, live to see my grandchildren come into the world."

His pain tore little pieces from her heart. She had no answers and could do so little to soothe him.

"The hardest thing to accept is that I have no future." It was stated quietly, unequivocally.

"Don't say that!" She sat up, staring at him as a frisson of fear raced through her, widening with each breath she took. "No one can know how long their lives will be, but everyone has a future."

"They aren't facing madness." Daniel's dark gaze lovingly caressed her "It's only a step away, Elizabeth. I've come to know it intimately, like an enemy just a pace behind me. I have faced it, so must you."

"No! I won't accept that!" Tears rimmed her eyes, one silvery drop falling free to glide slowly down her cheek. "I can't."

Pulling her back against his chest, he threaded his fingers through her hair. "I've come home to see that you and the children are settled. I want to be sure that you have everything you need. I can rest in peace if I know that you're provided for."

She sat up so abruptly that his chin banged painfully against her head. "I won't sit here and listen to this."

He cupped his hands around her face so that she couldn't pull free. "By the time I got to Martha I was like a rabid animal. The barn was fully inflamed and the children had stopped screaming. It was too late, they were already gone but I dug into that burning barn with my bare hands. I didn't feel the fire eating at my skin or hear her pleas to stop. I had to get to those children.

"I probably would have dug to my own death if a timber hadn't fallen and knocked me out. Somehow she pulled me far enough away that I didn't burn alive."

"Oh, my God . . ."

"I'm a big man, sweetheart, stronger than most, and when the madness is on me there is no limit to my strength. I could hurt someone, someone I love, and not even realize it for days." His fingers unknowingly dug into her head. "Someday I may have to be destroyed to protect the very people I love most!"

"No!" She fought to be free of him, tears of anguish covering her face. "No, Daniel!"

"Yes, Elizabeth." He pulled her against his chest, his hands incredibly gentle as she struggled to be free.

"I won't let that happen! I won't . . . I won't." Her voice trailed off as tears made speaking impossible. "I can't."

He held her as her tears dampened his shirt. He held her as her heart broke. He held her to stop himself from raging at the injustice of fate, who had given him a woman to love and then taunted him with the knowledge that he wouldn't live long enough to do so.

When her tears had slowed and her sobs no longer shredded her breath, he raised her head. His touch was exquisitely tender as he traced the line of her jaw, the smooth skin of her forehead, the gentle arch of her eyebrows.

"There have been many times when all of us were together, that my parents would seem to become lost in one another, alone in the crowd." His voice was rough with the emotion lodged in his chest. "When I was younger I couldn't understand their absorption with one another;

how a simple touch could take them away from us. Time and again, Maman would put her hand on Bear's chest and they'd share this something special that excluded the rest of us.

"His temper is legend but she has never shown the slightest fear. I have seen her stop his raging anger with the simplicity of a smile or the lightest of touches . . . I never understood." His big hand trembled slightly as he memorized the slope of her cheek. "Now I know."

"Daniel . . ."

"Touching you gives me strength. With you in my arms I find a peace unlike any I've ever known."

His gaze followed the moon-streaked silver traces of her tears. Slowly, he leaned over and tasted her sorrow, the salty sweetness lingering against his lips.

Elizabeth closed her eyes, feeling his touch with every fiber of her being. As softly as the first flakes of snow that barely touch as they drift past, his kiss lingered long after his lips had moved on.

Trusting him, knowing he needed to touch her as much as she needed to be touched by him, she leaned back against his arm, giving him unhindered access. His lips followed the slope of her cheek to the velvet skin of her neck. He lingered to taste, to learn . . . to remember.

Knowing he shouldn't but helpless to stop, he allowed his fingers to make a path of their own, from the slant of her shoulder to the surprisingly muscular firmness of her arm to the slender strength of her delicate fingers.

The movement of his hand over her caused the blanket to slip from her shoulders. The moonlight caressed the silky flesh, creating intriguing shadows where the nightdress hid the slope of her breasts.

"You are more beautiful to me than the promise of tomorrow," Daniel whispered. "I want to lock you in a silk-padded room so that nothing can harm you. I want to give you every treasure the world has to offer. But I'm so selfish that I don't want to share your smile or even the sound of your voice with another. I want to be the center of your world, your every thought to be of me."

Elizabeth laid her hand against his cheek. "I don't need to be protected or spoiled with gifts. All I need is you."

In the dark night she could see his black eyes glow with an obsidian fire. His head lowered, blocking out the moonglow as his lips met hers, producing a warmth and a light stronger than a thousand suns.

Teasing himself as much as her, he nibbled at her lips, lingering to sample the shape and texture of her mouth, tantalizing them both with the promise of more.

He had been the first man, the only man, to kiss her. She remembered the taste of him and wanted to taste again. Suddenly impatient with his gentleness, Elizabeth forced his head down to hers. Her tongue parted his lips, invading the warmth of his mouth. His startled moan of surprise at the unexpected assault gave her the courage to continue.

Remaining still, Daniel allowed her to investigate his mouth. With eyes closed to better savor the gentle touch of her soft lips and tongue against his, he forced a tight rein on the growing desire beginning to rage through him.

Remembering the time beside the river when he had kissed her, Elizabeth tried to imitate the bold thrusting action of his tongue. Her hand was against his beard-roughened cheek and her breasts unknowingly rubbed against his chest, their puckered peaks hardening with unfamiliar need.

She felt his tongue meet hers at the same time that his hand came up between their bodies, the back of his arm rubbing against her aching breast. Unaware of his fingers pulling free the ribbon at her neckline, Elizabeth was startled to feel the cool night air on her flesh. That feeling was quickly lost when his hand covered her breast, rubbing back and forth over her nipple until it was pebble hard and aching for something more.

Elizabeth raised her arm and wrapped it around his neck, placing her breast more firmly into his hand. She moaned with dissatisfaction when he continued to lightly glide over the raised peak.

"What do you want, *ee kwai wah?*"

"More." She kissed the side of his face, fol-

252

lowing the line of his jaw, the tiny tough hair tickling her lips.

"More, what?" His voice was husky with suppressed passion.

"I don't know!" she moaned in frustration. "Just more!"

"More of this?" he asked, his fingers gently pulling at her nipple.

"Yes . . ."

"More of this?" His head lowered to her neck, biting lightly, then soothing with his tongue.

"Yes . . ."

"Or this?" He kissed and suckled his way down the slope of her breast until his rough cheek rubbed against the waiting bud.

Elizabeth moaned at the sensuous sting of the teasing prickle. She was vaguely aware of being picked up and lowered to the ground, the blanket protecting her from the dirt and leaves. Daniel leaned over, spreading open the bodice of her nightdress to bare her breasts to his view.

In the moonlight, his hands appeared dark against the whiteness of her skin and she watched his apparent fascination with the part of her made so differently from his own body.

"So soft . . . so incredibly soft." He cupped her with his hands, his thumbs rubbing over the peaks. "I have never felt anything even half so soft."

A shiver of anticipation raced through her as he lowered his head and lightly kissed the underslope of each breast. The teasing of his thumbs was replaced by the fluid glide of his fingers; touching but not lingering as they traced back and forth over the excited flesh.

Daniel released the ribbon beneath her breasts and slowly pushed the thin fabric down her body until, caught beneath her, it stopped low on her hips. With long, lingering strokes that moved from the lower slope of her breasts down to the spot where the cloth still guarded her, he marveled at the feminine beauty.

She seemed to burn everywhere he touched and after a few short minutes Elizabeth no longer attempted to hold back the moans of pleasure. Each time his hands returned from their exploration of her body he would deliciously investigate the incline of her breasts; shaping them, studying them. His breathing was almost as ragged as hers, his hands trembling as he learned her.

"I want to touch you." Shyness made bold by passion threaded through her voice as she reached for him.

"No, sweetheart." A smile she couldn't see creased his lips. "That wouldn't be wise."

"Why? You're touching and kissing me. Why can't I do the same to you?"

"This must stop before it goes too far." He plucked at her nipple, delighting in her response. "I should stop now before it's too late."

"No, you shouldn't." Elizabeth arched her back, unknowingly inviting him to further the caress.

"I should." Daniel lowered his head, nuzzled her belly, his lips gentle on her tender flesh. "But

I won't. Maybe, as long as you don't touch me, I can control this so that we don't go too far."

"How far is that, Daniel? I already feel that I'm floating above the ground."

"I shouldn't be touching you at all, sweet Ellie. That's a husband's privilege." He savored the velvet softness of her abdomen, his hands caressing her delicate ribs as he teased his way up her body.

As his mouth teased her breasts, Elizabeth buried her hands in his thick red hair. Kissing, biting, licking, he learned every inch of the rounded flesh, taking care not to hurt her and always coming agonizing close, but never touching, the throbbing centers.

"Is this making love?" she asked, her voice broken by moans of desire.

"Ah, sweet, sweet woman." Resting on one elbow, Daniel leaned against her, allowing her to feel his weight but keeping his aroused flesh from her. "Making love is each time I see your smile or hear your laugh; watching you play with one of the children or kiss them good night. Being with you early in the morning before the sun has kissed the dew from the leaves or late at night when everyone is asleep but us."

"But I thought making love was . . . was . . . you know . . ."

He smiled tenderly at her obvious embarrassment. "Are you trying to say that making love is when a man worships a woman's body with his own? When they are joined together and two become one?"

She nodded her head, the vision of his body becoming a part of hers making speech impossible.

"That is only part of it. Making love is a touch, a smile, a loving gesture. It is so much more than physical."

"Make love to me, Daniel," she whispered, mesmerized by his voice.

"I can't." He bent and lapped at her waiting nipple, smiling at her quick gasp. "Not in the way you mean. It is a husband's right to expect his wife to come to him as a virgin. I won't deny your future husband that right."

"There will never be another man!" she stated adamantly.

"You are so young with so much life ahead of you." He brushed the hair back from her forehead and bent for another taste of her satiny skin. "I've already taken more than I should, far more than I've ever shared with another. I won't take your maidenhead, it is far too precious a gift."

"It is mine and I can do with it what I wish!"

He smiled sadly at her argumentative tone of voice. "Yes, it is yours. No, I won't take it."

To stop the disagreement, but mostly because he could no longer resist, he lowered his head to her breast, suckling strongly on her nipple. Elizabeth forgot the argument, forgot to breathe. The feeling of his mouth around her nipple made everything else disappear.

His hand journeyed back down her body, touching, caressing. When he encountered the barrier of cloth, he stopped, momentarily. His own desire was a throbbing reminder of the danger of continuing and the reason to continue.

Carefully, Daniel slid his fingers beneath the cloth. Discovering the curly hair that guarded the entrance to her, he slowly found the silky dampness waiting for his touch.

Elizabeth jumped when his fingers found the feminine core of her and a moan of passion lodged in her throat as he suckled her breast and began to rhythmically stroke her. The world spun away until there was only him, his strength, his gentleness. Gone was the fear of tomorrow, the constant reminder of madness, as passion never before experienced brought its own form of insanity.

"Daniel, what's happening to me?" she moaned as pressure built to a breaking point.

Watching her reach for the stars, listening to her sounds of pleasure, Daniel felt his own passion threatening to overwhelm his control. He had never touched a woman as intimately as this, had never heard her moans of passion or felt the warmth of her desire.

He had never loved as he loved her.

"Daniel . . . Daniel!" His name was lost as his mouth covered hers as she found the release she hadn't known existed.

"I love you, Elizabeth Jane," he whispered, his voice breaking. "As God is my witness, I love you."

Seventeen

Kneeling at the edge of the garden, Elizabeth dug her hand into the rich, black dirt, watching as it drifted through her fingers. An unknown sense of satisfaction filled her as she looked at the tiny green shoots poking their heads above the ground. The garden had been tilled by Mark and Will but she and the children had planted every seed themselves.

She looked at the rows of corn, envisioning the many ears they would produce and wondering exactly what she would have to do to preserve it. Ethel Mae's reassurance that she would help when the time came didn't do much to relieve Elizabeth's concern. She had never preserved food and it seemed a giant mystery to her that something put in a jar in August would be edible in February.

Spring planting was nearly finished and school was scheduled to restart in a few days. Elizabeth welcomed the idea, knowing that keeping up with a roomful of children would keep her mind occupied. The physical labor of planting the garden or doing the many necessary chores around the cabin gave her entirely too much time to think. Thoughts that almost always centered around Daniel.

Since the night of his return she had seen very little of him; an occasional glance in the distance as he worked in the fields with the other men and once when he had come to the cabin.

Even then he hadn't come to see her. He had come to claim Jenny Sue. Elizabeth had fought the idea since the child had become a part of her adopted family. Daniel had watched her playing with the other children and had agreed to leave her there.

Since then he had carefully stayed away. The children saw him when they visited with Bear and Linsey but the infrequent times she had been to the house he was always absent.

The empathy that had developed between them on the journey west had strengthened and she was always aware that he was near.

Close but so faraway.

"What are you doin', girl?" Ethel Mae walked up behind Elizabeth, startling her from her thoughts.

"Just looking at my garden and wondering how I'd ever produce anything worth eating." Elizabeth stood, shaking the dirt from her skirt, wishing she could shake the sadness from her mind as easily.

"I came to see why you ain't over at the barn

raising." Ethel Mae was a big, raw-boned woman with golden blond hair and warm blue eyes that would melt with love each time she looked at Kaleb. To her, he had hung the sun and moon and all the stars.

Elizabeth chuckled at the question. "I thought the smartest thing I could do was stay away. I don't know the first thing about raising a barn and I'm sure I'd be a considerable hindrance."

"Well, child, I do declare." Ethel Mae put her hands on her wide hips. "Ain't nobody ever told you 'bout a barn raising? The men folk do all the building. Us women folk do the fetchin', make the vittles and have us a grand ole time gossiping. It's as much a party as it is work. And tonight we'll hold us a hoedown in the new barn."

"Hoedown?"

"Dance, child." Her eyes narrowed. "You do dance?"

"I can't cook, build fires or plow but, yes, I dance."

"Well, whatja waitin' for? Ever'one thought maybe you was ailing and sent me over here to check on you. All your youngens is over there but you ain't. Nearly ever'one else in the settlement is there and those who ain't yet will be soon. Shake a leg, missy, we be amissin' some of the best gossip."

"How do you know we'll miss the best gossip?"

" 'Cause when a body ain't there that's the one that be gossiped about. I figure by now

260

they're really gettin' goin' good on me and you!"

Elizabeth chuckled, her mood lifted by the irrepressible good humor of Kaleb's wife. "How does one dress for a barn raising?"

Ethel Mae didn't have the heart to tell Elizabeth that her worst dress was better than nearly everyone else's Sunday best. "Wash that splat of dirt off your cheek, girl, grab a clean apron and you'll do just fine."

Elizabeth looked at Ethel Mae's serviceable, sparkling white apron. "I'm afraid that none of my aprons is very utilitarian."

"Utili what? You sure do use some fancy words!"

"It means that all of my aprons are made with lace and bows. They are intended solely for the purpose of uselessly sitting around a morning room and looking pretty. Not one of them is meant to be worn for work."

"Well then we'll just stop by my place and get you one of mine. They've all seen their share of work and then some. Come winter we'll make you up a bunch of workin' ones so you can keep your others for pretties."

"I don't want to put you to any trouble."

"Ain't no bother, we'll be walkin' right past there and I'll just step inside for a minute."

Elizabeth tidied her hair, tried to shake the worst of the wrinkles from her dress and washed the dirt from her face, then joined Ethel Mae on the well-worn path toward the settlement.

"You bein' a teacher and all, do you think you

could learn me some of them fancy words of yours?" Ethel Mae asked, her voice unusually hesitant. "I know I don't speak real good sometimes."

Elizabeth stopped and looked at the woman. "Oh, Ethel Mae, I think you speak exceptionally well." She took a work-roughened hand in hers. "You speak from the heart, your words filled with love. No one could ever say anything more eloquently."

"Eloquently?"

"Special," she smiled softly. "As special as only you are, Ethel Mae."

"I'm eloquently?" A look of pride filled the face that showed each of its forty years of life.

"Very, very much."

"Eloquently. I think I like that."

From his place high on the roof of the barn, Daniel spotted Elizabeth long before she arrived at the clearing. He stopped working, watching the gentle sway of her skirt as she approached. The sun beamed down on her uncovered head, turning her hair to gold.

He was unaware that everyone was watching him watching her, smiles of satisfaction and nods of approval passing between them. They all liked and respected Daniel and were pleased that he had found someone they also liked and respected.

He had thought she wouldn't come. Nearly everyone else, including her children, was there

262

so he had decided that she was intentionally avoiding the barn raising because she knew he'd be there.

A painful longing ripped through him when he heard her laugh float up on the breeze. God, how he missed her. Staying away from her, wanting her with every breath he took, had torn away a part of his soul, leaving only a bloody vacuum of space in its place.

Daniel saw Kal walk over to meet her and nearly fell from his place on the roof when he saw her stumble. He forced himself to bite back a snarl of rage when Kal reached out to steady her, leaving his arm casually around her shoulders.

"Are you going to sit there mooning over your woman all day or do you intend to help us finish this barn?" Will asked, a grin hidden behind a frown.

"She isn't my woman." Daniel forced himself to turn away but the memory of Kal's arm around Elizabeth remained burned into his mind. He grabbed a board and moved it into place.

"Could have fooled me." Will watched his older brother slam a nail into the thick board. "You look at her like you're staking a claim and she looks at you like you're the only man in the world."

"She isn't my woman!" Unbridled anger at what he couldn't have gave him the strength to sink a nail into the board with one stroke.

"You don't have to kill it," Will ventured daringly, motioning to the board. "It's already been cut down to size."

"Close your mouth or I might just cut you down to size, little brother," Daniel uncharacteristically snarled.

There was barely an inch difference in size between the two men and Will adored his older brother but like brothers the world over, couldn't resist teasing him. He knew when he had pushed too far. He figured one more comment would just about be enough.

Picking up a board, Will nailed it in place. "So, you gonna just sit back and watch Kal cozy up to her?"

It was enough.

Daniel's eyes burned with unbridled fury as he looked at his younger brother. His hands folded into fists and he brought them down with a killing fury on the board he had just nailed into place. It split into two pieces, saved from falling to the ground far below by the nails embedded in each end.

Will whistled beneath his breath, wise enough to know when to stop pushing.

Elizabeth stumbled when she saw Daniel on the top of the new structure. Outlined by the clear blue sky, his hair burning with the glow of the sun, she had no doubt that it was he who walked around up there as if he had no concern for the fact that only birds could fly.

"Need to keep your eyes on our dirt around

here," Kal chuckled as he steadied her. "It has a way of jumping out and tripping the unwary."

"Daniel's up there." She couldn't take her eyes off him as he moved gracefully around the half-finished structure. "If he falls . . ."

"He isn't going to fall." Kal put his arm around her shoulders and turned to watch his older brother. "We've been climbing trees since we were big enough to reach the lowest limb. His time with the Shawnee wasn't wasted, he moves with the surefootedness of an Indian."

"But if he falls . . ."

"He ain't gonna fall, honey child." Ethel Mae wrapped her arm around Elizabeth and led her toward the trees where several woman sat happily chatting.

Boards had been placed on saw horses to create tables. Covered with brightly patterned cloth, there appeared to be enough food to feed several armies. The covers that kept away bugs and inquisitive little fingers did nothing to hinder the delicious smells that drifted out, grabbing the senses and making mouths water.

The owner of the nearly constructed barn had butchered a cow several days earlier in preparation for the feast and it now roasted over a glowing fire, the hissing and popping of the fat as it dripped adding to the hunger-causing smells. Cakes, pies and cookies had their own table, carefully watched over by youngsters with a sweet tooth.

Mothers kept an eagle eye out for tiny hands reaching furtively for an early dessert while reminding husbands, just as eager for a taste, that they needed to set a good example for their children.

"I didn't bring anything." Elizabeth raised horrified eyes to Ethel Mae when she realized that the picnic was a community affair.

Ethel Rae patted the younger woman's hand. "Why, girl, you weren't aknowin' about our ways, you bein' new and all. Next time you can bring somethin' but this time you just sit back and enjoy."

Elizabeth couldn't help but grin when she thought of her culinary abilities. "I'd probably be more welcome if I continue to come empty-handed. You've never tasted my cooking."

"It'll get better. Why with all those youngens to feed you're bound to get plenty of practice."

Elizabeth was greeted warmly by all of the women and a place was made for her in the shade on a quilt. She knew most of the woman by name but was content to sit and listen to their gentle gossip without taking part in the conversation.

While Will kept a constant supply of boards ready for Daniel to nail into place, he had plenty of opportunity to keep an eye on Elizabeth. He watched as she was welcomed to the gathering and admired the graceful way she settled to the ground, her skirt settling around her like a colorful cloud.

It appeared to him that the single men, including his own brothers, suddenly found more reason to approach the women, singling Elizabeth out for more than her share of attention.

Elizabeth nodded, smiled, laughed, whatever reaction was called for at the appropriate moment, while her eyes strayed constantly to the familiar shape on top of the barn. It seemed to her that he worked harder and faster than any of the other men, his hammer a ringing blur in the clear spring air.

She sensed his fatigue, his growing impatience, his anger. In fact, as time went on, his anger seemed to be growing apace with the complaints of hunger from the children.

When more men began milling around the tables than working on the barn, someone declared it to be time to eat. The gregarious confusion that followed was unlike anything Elizabeth had ever seen. Plates and cups were found, each person generously serving himself. Children, with eyes larger than their stomachs, filled their plates to overflowing. Told that they would have to eat everything they took or they wouldn't get dessert, they eagerly began to stuff themselves.

Elizabeth was amazed at how quickly the food disappeared. Bowls and pots that had been filled to overflowing quickly emptied.

"If you don't hurry there won't be anything left," Kal stated.

"I've never seen food disappear so quickly."

"It's hungry work putting up a barn."

"But it was so much food!" With a smile she noticed that her own children had found plates and were eating as eagerly as everyone else. "My children haven't been so well fed in their lives. They certainly are enjoying the change from my usual—over-cooked, under-cooked, burnt, raw—meals. "

Kal's grin lit up his face, needlessly reminding her that all of the LeClerc men were unusually handsome. "I seriously doubt that your cooking is that bad."

"Drop in for dinner some night," she invited casually. "You'll find that anything edible wasn't cooked by me."

"I may just do that." Kal's grin disappeared, replaced by a look far too serious for the conversation.

Suddenly uncomfortable, Elizabeth moved away from him. Her gaze drifted toward the barn where the ringing of Daniel's hammer could be heard above all of the other noises.

"Won't he come?" she asked quietly.

Kal shrugged and grabbed a plate. "Said he wanted to finish up there first."

"But the food will be gone and he won't get anything."

Filling his own plate, Kal reluctantly admitted to himself that any interest he might have in her was futile. She had eyes only for his oldest brother.

"He won't starve." He carefully watched the worry in her eyes. "His appetite hasn't been too good lately anyway."

"What do you mean? Has he been sick?" Her

voice lowered in concern. "Is it another head-ache?"

"With Brother Daniel you don't know until he tells you. He keeps things to himself."

"Kal, is he sick?" The apprehension in her voice spoke her feelings as loudly as a ringing bell.

"Not physically, Elizabeth." Saying nothing more, Kal filled his plate and moved away from her.

Elizabeth watched the swing of the hammer, hearing it seconds later. Without conscious thought, she generously filled a plate. No one said a word when she took a second plate and was the first person to approach the dessert ta-ble. She was unaware of curious eyes watching the gentle sway of her skirt as she moved away from the crowd, headed toward the barn.

"Boy's been caught and he don't even know it yet," Kaleb chuckled, his eye twinkling merrily beneath his wrinkled brow.

"He knows," Bear stated quietly. "And he'll do everything in his power to protect her even if it hurts himself."

"Daniel?"

Elizabeth's voice drifted up to him on the roof, startling him from his thoughts.

"What are you doing here?"

"You were going to miss out." She held the plates up for his inspection.

Her invitation was almost more than he could

resist. Time alone with her even with the watchful gaze from the group gathered beneath the trees, was a gift to be treasured beyond all else.

Time . . . something he didn't have to spare.

"Leave it down there somewhere. I'm about finished here."

"I'll wait." Elizabeth moved to a tree not faraway that provided some shade and gave her a good view of the roof. "You don't have to wait. Go back to the others."

"Daniel . . . I haven't seen you or talked to you since the night you came back. I thought some time alone . . . I mean, it would be nice to talk . . . or just sit quietly . . . or . . ."

"Ellie . . ." Daniel looked down at her bent head, his determination wavering.

"Please, Daniel. Just for a few minutes?"

He put down the hammer and sat with his elbows on his bent knees. "From up here you can see nearly to forever. The tops of the trees are bowing to the breeze and the clouds seems just out of reach. You can sit here and forget that tomorrow might bring rain or more troubles than a man can handle. You can sit here and think that maybe, just maybe, a few of your dreams might come true."

He tilted his head back and looked at the fluffy clouds floating past, letting his thoughts drift, forcing his torment out of reach.

"Skirts aren't made for climbing."

Elizabeth's voice was much closer and Daniel felt a knob of fear lodge in his throat when he turned his head to find her on the ladder.

"What in God's green earth do you think you're doing, woman?"

"You wouldn't come down so I decided to come up." Elizabeth climbed the last couple of rungs, refusing to look down, refusing to think of how high up she was, refusing to take her gaze from him.

"Get down . . . NOW!" His voice roared through the clearing, catching the attention of several of the diners.

Her hand came up and he saw that she was carefully balancing one of the plates. "I could use a little help."

"Mon Dieu!" Daniel's face paled as he slipped and slid in his rush to reach her before she could fall.

Elizabeth waited patiently, her skirt hiked up over one arm, her hand firmly clutching the plate of food. Belying her casual attitude, the fingers of her other hand were wrapped tightly around the rung of the ladder, her knuckles turning white from the pressure.

"Have you lost your mind?" He took the plate from her, grabbing her arm to hold her securely in place.

"Don't spill that!" Elizabeth watched the food slide to one side. "That is your dinner and you're going to eat it. I don't care if it's on the plate or on the roof."

He sat the plate down on some boards, ignoring the fact that the food threatened to tumble off. Her other hand was grabbed and she was effortlessly pulled onto the roof. Daniel's hands came to rest on her shoulders, the force of his grasp telling her louder than words of the anger he was fighting back.

"Well if you're going to shake me, get it over with." She casually smoothed her skirt into proper place. "But please remember that it is a long way down and I can't fly."

"You should have thought of that before you came up."

"It's all your fault."

"My fault?" He couldn't remember ever being as angry before in his life. Or as scared. When he'd seen her head pop up over the edge of the roof he had felt his heart lurch with fear.

"It's entirely your fault. If you had come down I wouldn't have come up."

"I would have come down."

"When? The day after tomorrow? I didn't want to wait that long."

"Sometimes I think you don't have the common sense the good Lord gave a grape."

"Shows how much you know." She lifted her head haughtily. "The grape knows to hang on to the vine until it's ripe and I knew to hang on to the ladder until you reached me."

The tone of his voice told her that what he said next wasn't complimentary and that she should be relieved that he spoke in Shawnee. When he finally stopped she looked up at him, batting her eyelashes in an exaggeratedly flirtatious manner.

"Since I'm hungry and I know you must be, too, it would be a shame to let all of that food go to waste. Why don't we sit down? Surely you can yell at me just as easily while we eat?"

Reaching into the pockets of the voluptuous apron Ethel Mae had insisted she wear, Elizabeth pulled out two spoons, two napkins and a cork-stopped bottle of something she'd found at the end of one of the tables.

"I'm not sure what it contains," she said at his questioning look, "but it looked drinkable."

Daniel took the bottle from her, removed the cork and leaned back his head. The raw, undiluted homemade whiskey lived up to its reputation of white lightning as it burned its way down his throat, taking his breath and making his eyes water.

"Goodness!" Her eyes widened at his reaction.

"Your turn." Daniel held the bottle out to her.

"Ah . . . no, thank you. I'm not thirsty just yet."

"Chicken?" His eyes twinkled, challenging her as surely as any words.

"Of course not! I just don't want any at this time."

He said nothing, simply holding the flask out. Elizabeth may not have grown up with brothers and sisters who taunted each other into reckless feats, but she knew a dare when one was offered.

She sighed and reached for the bottle. "After I take a drink can we sit down and eat?"

Daniel nodded, his hands moving down to her waist. She should have accepted that action as a caution. She should have remembered his own reaction.

She shouldn't have accepted his dare.

The liquid hardly touched her tongue before she knew she was in trouble.

Her lips began to burn and her tongue curled. Tears flowed freely as the liquid fire made its way down to her stomach. She tried to gasp for breath but nothing could get past the horrible flame of the homemade brew. She felt light-headed while her face grew red in reaction. She knew she had made a grave error in judgment long before her teeth began to tingle.

"Breathe, Ellie." Daniel grinned broadly.

"Wha . . . what . . . is that . . . stuff . . . ?"

"I'd take a guess that you've found a bottle of Kaleb's best homebrew."

"Best!" she moaned, still fighting for breath. "God save me . . . from his worst!"

Everyone heard Daniel's laughter rumble like thunder through the clearing.

Eighteen

Elizabeth quickly discovered that there was more security in sitting than standing on the high-pitched roof. So, following Daniel's example, she folded her legs and carefully tucked her skirt beneath her to keep it from blowing in the wind.

"Something to drink?" Daniel offered her the whiskey flask, grinning at her shudder and delicate refusal. But she noticed, rather smugly, that he, too, refrained from further sampling of the liquid.

"I wasn't more than eight or ten when I was taught how to sit in a tree for hours without moving, an arrow cocked in my bow, waiting for a buck to saunter by. Hawk and I would see who could sit still the longest. I'd choose one tree while he'd chose another where we could keep an eye on each other, just to make sure there wasn't any cheating." A gentle smile crossed his face. "I was so much bigger than him that it wasn't long before my legs would start to cramp and I'd have to change positions. He'd always give me this smug look that seemed to say that he was a better Indian than I was."

"Correct me if I'm wrong, but he is the Indian."

"Sure he is, but try to tell a ten-year-old that heredity counts."

She watched contentedly as he bit into the last biscuit. The plate was nearly empty and she'd seen to it that he'd eaten his share and most of hers.

"You had a wonderful childhood. I wasn't allowed to climb trees or swim in the river or do any of the things I'd see the other kids doing. I had to behave, at all times, as was fitting for a young lady."

"Boring?"

"Incredibly! How much nicer to learn how to have fun." She turned sparkling eyes to him. "It's not too late. You could teach me how to climb trees or swim or use a bow and arrow."

Daniel looked at the bubbling excitement shining in her eyes, at the way the sun glistened through her hair turning the strands to pure gold. He thought that if he looked hard enough he could see the little girl who had sat dutifully working her needlepoint while her eyes turned with longing to the world outside her window.

"I can't, Elizabeth." His voice vibrated with regret.

"Why not?"

"It's been such a long time since I've had any reason to play, I don't think I remember how."

"I'm sure it'll all come back to you! Besides, I've seen you playing with the children."

Daniel stood, picked up the nearly empty plate and sailed it off the roof with a violent flick of his wrist. "It's time I got back to work. This break has stretched far longer than usual and I think it's because no one wants to come back over here and disturb us. At this rate we'll never get this barn finished."

"I can help." At his raised eyebrow she searched her mind for something useful that she could do. "I could hand you boards or nails, or something."

"You can go back down and visit with the ladies."

"Once again I get to sit and watch everyone else have fun." Her lower lip pouted, making it an almost irresistible enticement to the man who needed no further temptations. She was already hard enough for him to resist.

"Down, Elizabeth." Daniel pointed to the ladder, hoping he could convince her to leave before he threw caution to the wind, taking her into his arms and kissing her like she'd never been kissed before . . . or would be ever again.

Looking at the ladder and then at the ground far below, she wondered if she'd made a horrible mistake in climbing up here in the first place. But if she hadn't she suspected that Daniel would never have come down.

"Why haven't you come to see me?" Her voice was soft, without accusation. It was a question she hadn't planned to ask, once voiced there was nothing to do but wait for his answer.

"I've been busy." Daniel stared off into the distance, suddenly almost a stranger rather than the friend who had shared his food and stories of the past with her just minutes earlier.

"Not too busy to play with the children or to help build this barn."

"No."

"Just too busy to see me?"

"Yes."

It hurt, really hurt, to have him admit it in a single word. Maybe if she could have detected the slightest regret or apology in his voice it wouldn't have cut so deeply.

"Daniel . . ." Biting back tears, refusing to cry, Elizabeth looked out over the treetops.

"Ellie, go back to the others."

"Don't do this to us, Daniel."

"There is no *us,* there never has been, never will be." Beneath his cotton shirt, Daniel's muscles bunched and strained, threatening to tear the seams as he fought to keep from taking her into his embrace. "This conversation has come to an end, Elizabeth."

"Hey, you two," Kal called up to the pair on the roof. "Are you going to sit there all day or can we get back to work?"

Without looking at Daniel, she stood and walked the few steps to the ladder, lowering her foot to the first rung. Somehow, whether from unfamiliarity with descending ladders or perhaps from the tears that clouded her vision,

Elizabeth slipped. Before she could do more than gasp, Daniel was there, grabbing her arms, pulling her to the security of his strong body.

"Are you all right?" His voice was shaking nearly as much as the arms that held her painfully tight against him.

"I am now." Elizabeth leaned her head against his chest, finding comfort in the steady pounding of his heart.

"It was a foolish thing to do!" His voice grew in volume but his arms didn't loosen their hold.

"I didn't slip on purpose."

"You shouldn't have come up here in the first place!"

"You wouldn't have come down!" Elizabeth stepped away from him, hands on her hips, chin thrust forward. They were nearly yelling at each other, providing entertainment for the spectators below.

"You're right. I didn't want to come down or have supper with you. I didn't want to see you, talk to you or be anywhere near you!" He grabbed her hand when she reached for the ladder.

"Let me go!" Elizabeth snarled between gritted teeth. "I'm perfectly capable of getting down by myself."

"I doubt it!" Without showing signs of effort, he swung her into his arms and stepped onto the first rung. Kal steadied the ladder as Daniel carried her to the ground.

"Are you all right?" The concern in Kal's voice was her undoing. Keeping her eyes turned from him, she fought to maintain a normal voice.

"I think I'll go on home. . . . I need to change my dress." Holding up her skirt she showed him a tear in the fabric.

Without further word to either brother, Elizabeth headed back toward her cabin.

"Why didn't you just push her off the roof and get it over with?" Kal snarled at Daniel.

"She slipped, I had nothing to do with it." Daniel watched her until she was out of sight.

"I'm not talking about the ladder, you fool. You did a good job of breaking her heart. The woman's in love with you!" He grabbed Daniel's arm, forcing his brother to look at him. The pain in Daniel's eyes matched the glimpse of agony he'd seen in Elizabeth's gaze.

"And you're in love with her," Hal stated quietly, the anger leaving his voice.

"Leave it alone, Kal." Daniel reached for the ladder and began to ascend.

"Why, Daniel? Why are you doing this to her? To yourself? She'd make any man a wonderful wife."

Daniel climbed steadily up the ladder, the annoying ache at the back of his head the only answer he needed.

From the solitude of her cabin, Elizabeth heard music drift merrily through the night air, filling it with jubilation and joyful noise. She had not returned to the picnic after changing her dress and now the music made her self-imposed isolation unbearably lonely, she wanted to beg them to stop. How could they enjoy themselves when her own heart was broken beyond repair?

Kal arrived at the cabin soon after dark. "The party waits for no man, or woman."

"Thank you, Kal, but I think I'll just stay here."

"And do what? Pout? Lick your wounds? Don't look at this as an invitation you can refuse, Elizabeth. Think of it more as an order."

"I don't want to go."

"I'm aware of that, but you will, even if I have to throw you over my shoulder and carry you kicking and screaming all the way."

"Is that a threat?" Elizabeth looked at his wide shoulders and knew he had the strength to do just what he said.

"A promise."

"I won't have a good time," she warned unnecessarily.

"You might be surprised."

Dignity intact, unaware that everyone knew about the scene on the roof, she followed the trail to the barn, her feet leaden, her heart wrapped in a shroud of mourning.

Elizabeth discovered that a hoedown was a party unlike any she'd ever attended. Music from a fiddle, harmonica and banjo filled the new barn with happy sounds while feet stamped and hands clapped to the rhythms. The young, and young at heart, threw themselves into the celebration.

Leaning against a roof support, she was a reluctant observer. The dancers moved in a series of completely unfamiliar steps, bobbing and weaving first one way and then another.

"Dance with me?"

Elizabeth blinked, realizing that she had been mesmerized by the dancing figures. Kal stood before her, his hand outstretched in invitation.

"Thank you, but I don't know the steps," she declined.

"No problem, I'll be your teacher."

Gasping as pain riddled through her body, she tried to forget that only hours earlier she had asked Daniel to be her teacher.

"No," she mumbled. She didn't want to be an observer or a participant. She didn't even want to be here. All she wanted was to go somewhere and try to find a way to mend her tattered heart.

Without giving her a further chance to refuse, he grabbed her hand and pulled her to the center of the floor.

"I'm getting pretty tired of you pushing and pulling me wherever you want me to go," she hissed through her teeth.

"Then we're even, because I'm getting tired of you looking like a kicked dog. If my brother doesn't want you then cut line and let him drag off into the woods alone. There are plenty of other men who would like to have the opportunity to court you but have stayed away because they thought Daniel had a prior claim."

"Who? You?" she asked, her voice filled with sarcasm.

"It's a start, Elizabeth." He smiled grimly. "Who knows, give it a chance and you might discover I'm not so bad after all."

He placed her hands on his shoulders, putting his own on her waist, showed her the basic movements and then swung her into the dance, using his strength to move her around the floor like a puppet on a string.

When one song was finished another began almost before the final notes faded away. Elizabeth found herself partnered by each of Daniel's brothers and several other men. Knowing she wasn't being given a choice, she did her best to smile and pretend that she was enjoying herself. She'd never before known that she was such a good actress.

From the sheltered darkness of the trees, Daniel watched. He hadn't planned to come but found himself drawn there almost against his will. His eyes followed only Elizabeth. He watched Kal lead her onto the floor and gritted his teeth when Kal's hands rested on her waist. His stomach tightened when she tripped and Kal's hands slid up to the sides of her breasts.

Tension grew as he watched one man after another, men he knew well and considered friends, put their hands on her and lead her through the dances. He found that he couldn't stand even his own father touching her.

He couldn't force himself to leave or to make his presence known. He could only stand there, watching her dance, seeing her smile and wondering why she wasn't hurting as badly as he.

When Kal came to claim his third dance, something in Daniel snapped. A killing fury took control and he gave no thought to the fact that his intended victim was his own brother. He could no longer watch another man touch Elizabeth.

One by one the couples saw his approach and cautiously moved out of his way. The look on his face warning even a fool that he was a man to be reckoned with.

Kal noticed Daniel's approach and deliberately kept Elizabeth's back to him. He had suspected that Daniel had been watching and wondered how long it would take his brother to explode. It had taken longer than he'd expected but by the expression of his face, Kal knew that the time had come.

"Get . . . your . . . hands . . . off . . . her!" A snarl curved Daniel's face into a mask of rage.

Startled by the sound of his voice, Elizabeth began to turn to look at Daniel but was stopped by an almost imperceptible shake of Kal's head. The music ground to a halt as all eyes focused on the brothers in the center of the floor.

"Why?" Kal knew he was pushing too far and only hoped that Daniel remembered that they were brothers before it was too late.

"She's mine!"

Burning black eyes, a legacy from their sire, locked in a battle that neither man was willing to lose. Protectively, Kal moved Elizabeth behind him, putting himself between her and Daniel.

"Earlier this afternoon you said you didn't want her. In fact you announced that you never wanted to see her again and she was free." His voice drifted lazily through the tense silence. "So, if she's free, I'm thinking of staking a claim."

"Don't push me, Brother!"

Kal had the common sense to feel a sliver of fear race up his spine. He'd never heard Daniel sound so menacing and knew he walked a thin line. He was as strong as his brother but Daniel had the added strength of rage.

"This is getting out of hand," Luc stated, starting to move to separate his sons. Linsey's hand, gentle on his arm, stopped him before he could take a step.

"Wait, Kal knows what he's doing." She tried to sound confident, but the fear in her eyes gave it away.

"I hope to God you're right," Luc sighed, forcing himself to stand calmly beside her.

"Me, too," she mumbled, holding his hand tightly for support.

Kal folded his arms across his chest, knowing he left himself wide open for attack. "Have you changed your mind, Daniel? Is she free or not?

"Get out of my way, Kaleb."

"Why?"

"She's mine."

"Why?" Kal pushed, watching Daniel's hands

ball into white knuckled fists. "Tell me why I should."

"I . . . love . . . her!"

Kal heard Elizabeth's startled gasp and a smile fluttered over his mouth as he stepped aside. He felt the slither of sweat roll down his back and admitted to himself that he had been closer to death than at any other time in his life. Daniel would have gone through him or anyone else to get to the woman he'd finally admitted to loving.

Seeing no one but Elizabeth, offering her no choice, Daniel picked her up and cradled her against his chest. Turning, he carried her from the barn and into the gentleness of the night.

A poignantly beguiling melody from the harmonica followed them into the darkness, urging them to create memories, to cherish these moments in time.

"Mon Dieu," Luc whispered with a sigh, "I'm glad I didn't have to step between that. I'm not sure anyone could have stopped Daniel."

"Elizabeth could have." Linsey leaned against her husband, equally as glad that the confrontation was over.

"I'm not sure even she could have done anything."

"My Bear," she hugged him tightly, "do you not know that with a word she could have brought him to his knees. My biggest fear was that she would reject him. He could have recovered from physical hurts but he'd never have recovered from her rejection."

286

Luc watched them disappear from sight. "I think it would be wise if we invite her children to spend the night with us." A wicked smile played across his scarred visage.

"I think it would serve our pigheaded son a bit of justice if we sent them home in an hour or so."

"His stubbornness comes from his mother's side of the family," Luc commented casually. "But we'll still take the children home with us."

"My side of the family? When have I ever been anything but cooperative and willing to please?" Linsey asked.

His own black eyes burned with an inner fire only she could spark. "We will discuss this cooperativeness and desire to please, later . . . at home . . . in the privacy of our bedroom."

Words were unnecessary as Daniel carried her down the path toward her cabin. Each had an awareness of the other's emotions. Elizabeth knew that Daniel's rage had dissipated the moment she was in his arms. He felt her despondency vanish with his touch.

Their emotions had been replaced with an urgency to explore the growing desire that enveloped them in a veil of passion.

Daniel opened the door of the dark cabin, kicking it firmly closed behind them as he carried her to the bed in the corner.

Lowering her to her feet, he cradled her face between his hands. The bright light of a full moon filtered through the unshuttered windows. "This is wrong and I've tried to resist. I'm tired, Ellie, so very tired of turning my back on the very thing I need desperately. God help us, Elizabeth Jane, but I love you."

Her only response was a soft kiss placed in the palm of his hand and the melting love that shone from her eyes.

"Tell me to leave. I'll bring you only pain and anguish. I don't think I can bear to watch you suffer when madness takes control of me."

"Make the world go away, Daniel," she whispered softly. "If only for tonight, make everything go away but us. I love you so much."

Stepping back, he tugged his shirt from his pants, loosening the laces and unbuttoning the single button at each wrist. With a graceful, purely masculine movement, he pulled it over his head, dropping it to the floor.

Elizabeth gasped at the muscles straining over firm flesh, the light coating of hair the same color as that on his head. Unclothed, his shoulders were incredibly wide, his arms bulging with strength.Fascinated, she watched the play of shadows over his skin as he reached for the laces tying the neckline of her dress.

Unconcerned that he was carefully removing her own clothes, Elizabeth couldn't resist touching, startled by the warmth of his skin beneath her hand, marveling at the hardness of flesh so unlike her own.

She felt her dress billow at her ankles, followed by her petticoat. He knelt to untie the garters that supported her stockings, gently lifting first one foot and then the other to remove them.

When she was covered only by her lace-trimmed, thigh-length chemise, Daniel exhaled the breath he had been unconscious of holding. Still kneeling, he wrapped his arms around her legs, burying his face in the softness of her stomach.

"Tonight there is only us. No promises for tomorrow, no thoughts of the future." Elizabeth ran her hands through his thick hair. "We won't think of anything but each other and the pleasures we find in this bed."

"Ellie, it's wrong, I know it, but I need you so badly."

"I'm yours, Daniel. For now, forever, until time has come to an end, I am yours."

Releasing her, he stood, taking her hands in his and raising them to his lips. "I've never done this before, Ellie," he stated quietly. "I've never joined my body to a woman's, never made love. I don't want to hurt you because of clumsiness."

Any fear she had felt at the unknown disappeared with his admission. He was as scared, perhaps even more so, than she. "You won't hurt me, Daniel."

"I'll have to, if I'm to make you mine." He lightly caressed the soft skin of her neck. "The first time for a woman is always painful."

"Then we'll make love a second time and a third until any memories of pain disappear. I'm yours, Daniel. Make us one."

He carefully lifted the chemise over her head and took her into his arms. As if she were so fragile she might break, he lowered her to the center of the bed. His own knee-high moccasins and pants quickly joined the pile of clothing on the floor.

He lay beside her, his big hand shaking with need and desire as he touched her. Stroking a softness like none he had even known, he learned the slopes and textures of her body. He worshiped her with his touch, tasted her with his lips, cherished her with his words.

When he covered her with his large body and two became one, he felt her pain, shared her ecstasy. They journeyed beyond tomorrow, beyond forever, beyond eternity.

The world continued to turn, the shadowed darkness of night once more giving way to the bright light of day, as they found again and again the sanctuary of peace in each other's arms.

Nineteen

The rosy glow of predawn lightened the room enough for Daniel to watch Elizabeth sleep. She lay on her back, one hand on her stomach, the other curled beneath her chin. Her hair was spread across the pillows in a glorious golden disarray. He picked up one of the curls and twined it gently around his fingers, inhaling its familiar fragrance.

Memories of their night of shared love filled him with something close to peace. He would forever cherish the moment when they had become one. Even when madness staked its final claim, Daniel knew that it was one memory that would still be his.

He fought back the guilt that poked with razor-sharp fingers beneath the surface of his thoughts. If he allowed it, he knew he'd wallow in enough guilt to satisfy the most stringent moralist.

Later there would be plenty of time for regret. Now there was only time enough for a last, lingering moment to cherish. Watching the gentle rise and fall of her chest, he wondered if he should wake her and tell her he was leaving, that he had to slip out of the cabin before it became too light and someone chanced to see him. A grim smile crossed his face; he doubted that there was anyone in the settlement who wasn't aware of where he'd spent his night.

Deciding that she needed more sleep, Lord knew he'd given her very little chance to rest during their night of loving, Daniel rose from the bed and bent to retrieve his clothes.

There was something enticing about the pile of clothing haphazardly tumbled together on the floor; his familiar masculine trappings mixed with her fascinatingly feminine clothing. He picked up her dress, doubting that the tiny waist would fit over his thigh. The delicate straps of the silky chemise clung lovingly to his fingers. Surely the woman whose body fit into this tiny garment couldn't be the same woman who had cradled his massive body against hers. The same woman who had taken him into her with sensual ease, never hinting that his size was more than a welcomed weight.

Reluctantly, Daniel hung her clothing on a hook by the bed and dressed quietly. As he left the cabin he discovered that closing the door behind him was the hardest thing he'd ever done. A certainty grew that there would be far too few remaining mornings when he could watch her sleep.

The annoying ache in his head taunted him cruelly with each step he took away from her.

Elizabeth woke and knew that she was alone. Stretching, she smiled at the delicious aches in her body. She reached for the pillow that still held the imprint of Daniel's head and hugged it to her, breathing deeply of his scent. He had been a wonderfully considerate lover, his lack of experience in no way hindering their mutual discovery of pleasure.

Outside the window a bird sang happily and on the honeysuckle-scented breeze the ringing of the church bell told everyone that services would start in an hour.

Rising, Elizabeth wrapped up warmly and went to wake the children so that they wouldn't be late for church. She discovered first that the girls' beds were empty and a quick scan of the loft told her the boys hadn't slept at home either. She felt a twinge of guilt that she had completely forgotten about them the night before. Obviously, someone else had taken over her responsibilities.

Elizabeth bathed and dressed, taking extra care with her appearance. She hoped that Daniel would be at church and she wanted to look nice for him. With her lace and feather bonnet tipped at just the right angle, she pulled the door closed behind her.

Feeling almost like she could float to church, her step was light and jaunty. She stopped and picked a handful of wildflowers growing beside the path, discovering that their bright yellow centers perfectly matched the color of her gown. As she passed the newly constructed barn it dawned on her that everyone would probably know, or suspect, that she and Daniel had spent the night together.

She raised her chin. She wasn't ashamed of what they had shared. It wasn't wrong and no one would make her feel that it was anything less than beautiful. If someone was narrow-minded enough to suggest that it was evil then she'd just tell them, politely of course, to mind their own business.

The light of battle that had entered her eyes faded to one of love as she approached the church building and found Daniel waiting at the steps. The smile of appreciation on his face more than made up for the extra time she'd taken with her appearance.

"You're beautiful," he whispered huskily, taking her hand in his and bringing it to his lips.

"Good morning." A look of such intense love covered her face that Daniel's knees threatened to buckle.

"May I accompany you into church, sweet-heart?"

"I'd rather you accompany me back to my cabin," her voice lowered seductively.

"Later." He bent and lightly kissed her pouting lips.

"On the steps of the church, no less. You've turned me into a wanton!"

"Such a delicious, delightful wanton."

"Let's go in before we forget where we are

and completely embarrass ourselves." Elizabeth leaned down to place her bouquet of flowers on the ground.

"Take them," Daniel wrapped her arm through his. "They match your dress. But aren't nearly as pretty as you."

Elizabeth smiled, leaned her head briefly against his shoulder and walked proudly beside him into the church.

As they walked up the center aisle, all eyes of the congregation turned toward them. Elizabeth was too interested in the reaction of Daniel's family to notice those that looked at her with scorn. Her children were sitting with his family and they joined the large group that took up two complete pews.

Finding herself seated next to Linsey, Elizabeth smiled hesitantly at Daniel's mother. Linsey smiled warmly in return and Elizabeth had to bite back a sigh of relief. If anyone intended to criticize her actions, Elizabeth had no doubt that the fiery redhead beside her would be one of the first.

With her hand firmly grasped in Daniel's, Elizabeth had trouble concentrating on the service. A firm believer in God and the words of the Bible, she normally listened attentively. But never before had the distraction been so blatant. She wasn't at all shameful that the thick, dark hair covering Daniel's hand was so much more fascinating than the preacher's words. Or that the hardness of his shoulder pressed against hers needlessly reminded her of the firmness of his flesh beneath her hands.

Surrounded by Daniel and his equally large brothers, Elizabeth stood to sing the final hymn. When the congregation slowly drifted down the aisle to leave she was blissfully unaware of the censorious glances that looked first at her then at her hand held firmly in his.

She may have missed the expressions but Daniel and his family did not. Closing ranks, they moved protectively, waiting for anyone brave enough, or foolish enough, to voice an opinion. Linsey placed her hand on Elizabeth's shoulder, her green eyes blazing a warning that it was she rather than her large husband and sons they should be concerned about offending.

By the time it was their turn to leave the pew, Daniel was in a rage that knew no bounds. Trying to keep his anger from Elizabeth, he waited for the opportunity to expend the building fury on some hapless head.

"Daniel." The preacher's face was filled with concern when he extended his hand. "I believe we should have a talk, son."

The man's face blanched when Daniel's grip gave testimony to his tightly reined emotions. "Don't come where you're not invited, Preacher."

Putting his arm around a confused Elizabeth, Daniel urged her away from the church.

"Daniel, what is it?" Her smooth brow wrinkled in confusion.

"Nothing, sweetheart." He smiled warmly down at her. "Wanna learn how to climb a tree?"

"Luc, Linsey," the preacher greeted carefully. "I hope you'll talk with your son."

"I talk with all of my sons quite frequently, sir." Linsey's soft voice did nothing to hide the anger glowing in her eyes. "Is there something in particular you have in mind for me to discuss with him?"

"I . . ." He hesitated when he discovered the grim smile drifting over Luc's scarred face, a smile that was far from reassuring. "Daniel is a fine man, we're all very proud of him . . . but, ah . . . what he did was wrong."

"Wrong? What have you seen my son do that is wrong?" Linsey questioned.

"Well, I didn't . . . ah, mean to say, we all know what he did." He felt the sweat rolling down his back and wanted desperately to dab at the moisture beading his upper lip.

"What did he do?" Luc's voice was terrifyingly soft.

Jamie encouraged the children away, while Will, Kal and Mark stood like mountains behind their parents. The preacher had dared to venture where no man with common sense walked, and he wondered if he'd live to see the Sunday dinner his wife was even now putting on the table.

"I don't know her well," he began hesitantly, "but Miss Spurlin seems like a fine woman."

"She is," Linsey confirmed.

"I realize that she has several children that she claims aren't hers—"

"Get to the point, Preacher."

"Yes, well . . . the members of my congregation are naturally concerned about her influence with their children. After all, school starts again tomorrow and she'll be with them for several hours each day. They're afraid that she might be a poor example."

"A poor example of what?"

"Well, ah, that is . . . perhaps her morals aren't quite what they should be." Sweat no longer beaded his brow, it now rolled freely down his face.

"Point out exactly who these people are," Linsey hissed. "I'll be delighted to help them change their minds." Her eyes narrowed. "Perhaps I'll start with your wife. I seem to remember a few years back when she arrived here with a newborn babe, claiming that she was widowed. No one questioned her, maybe I'll be the first to throw a stone in that direction."

His face turned as white as the collar that suddenly seemed chokingly tight. "Now, Linsey, that isn't necessary . . ."

"I've known you for many years, Henry. In fact, when you came here Daniel was nearly a year old and Luc and I weren't married. You baptized him and Hawk on the same day that you married us."

"Times have changed . . ."

"Not as much as people's minds have narrowed." She gave him a look that implied he was something she should wipe off of the bottom of her shoe and turned toward Luc. Her voice thickened with the accent of her youth. "Be atakin' me home, Bear. I nae can bare the repulsive odor I be asmellin'."

Luc and his sons grinned. "Are you sure you wouldn't like to tell him exactly what you think of him and his ancestors, *ain jel ee?* It's been a long time since we've heard your gentle Gaelic brogue."

In spite of her anger, she smiled at her family. It was well known by them that whenever she was angriest, Linsey always broke into Gaelic. The humorous part was that she was repeating words she'd heard during her childhood with her Scottish father but had no idea what she was actually saying.

"It's doubtin' I be that his ancestors would claim him!"

Placing a hand on her husband's arm, with three of her sons as escort, Linsey turned and regally walked toward the horse and buggy parked beneath a tree on the far side of the building. Few of the people who'd shamelessly eavesdropped on the conversation doubted who'd been the victor. Some of them did nothing to hide their grins from the discomfitted preacher, who wondered how close to death or dismemberment he'd really been.

For Elizabeth, the afternoon and evening was a wonderland of enjoyment. The anger she'd sensed in Daniel was replaced by a gentle teasing that left her giddy with happiness. Her smile was so filled with contentment that it was remarked upon by everyone who was around her.

Climbing a tree for the first time was every-

thing, and more than she thought it would be
. . . and considerably easier.

Daniel swung onto the lowest branch and
leaned down, grabbing her hands and easily
pulling her up. Each successive branch was
reached in the same manner until they stood so
high up that she could feel the tree bow with
their combined weight.

Climbing down was equally as easy for Elizabeth. Sitting down, she waited until Daniel had
reached the desired branch, braced himself and
then lifted her down.

"Do you trust me, Ellie?" Daniel stood on the
ground, Elizabeth sat on the lowest branch
which was just above his arm's reach.

"With my life." She smiled warmly down at
him, her legs swinging gently above his head.

"Fall."

"What?"

"I can't reach you, you'll have to fall."

Suddenly the ground and Daniel, seemed an
awfully long way down. "Isn't there another
way?"

"Wouldn't trust him if I were you." Mark
swaggered up to stand beside his brother. "Told
me once that he'd catch me."

"What happened?" Elizabeth was aware of the
gleam in Mark's eyes and had little doubt that
he was inventing the entire story.

"Missed . . . broke my arm in two places."

"Oh, my!"

"And my leg . . . never did heal right, still
aches when it's threatening to rain."

"Oh dear."

"Should have dropped you on your head," Daniel stated. "Maybe it would have given you a little sense."

"A little sense is more dangerous than none at all," Elizabeth informed them, a smile playing across her lips. "Just think of the trouble he'd get into if he only had a little sense."

"You wound me!" Mark put his hand on his heart, his face pulled into a grimace of pain.

"If you don't shut up I'll do more than wound you," Daniel snarled good-naturedly.

"Trust me, sweetheart, I won't drop you." He held his arms up, hoping that his brother's nonsense hadn't frightened her.

Without further hesitation, Elizabeth pushed herself off the branch, landing in his strong embrace.

Holding her tightly, Daniel let her legs slide down, his arms around her waist, her feet dangling a foot from the ground. Memories from the night before rushed at him and he moaned softly at her gentle weight nestled against him.

They never noticed when Mark turned away to give them some privacy. Elizabeth's arms wrapped around his neck as her mouth moved to his. Daniel tried to keep the kiss just a gentle meeting of lips, but with the softness of her mouth against his, he quickly forgot his intentions.

"This could get to be a habit," he moaned, pulling his head forcefully away from hers.

"I hope so!" Elizabeth found contentment

with nuzzling his neck, smiling confidently when she heard his smothered groan.

"Woman, you are dangerous!"

"Me? Good heavens, you pulled me up and down a tree, demanded that I fall off and then you say I'm dangerous!"

Daniel slowly lowered her to the ground, letting her feel the hardness of his passion. Elizabeth's eyes widened with a look of such wanton desire that he bit back a need to howl with frustration.

"If you keep doing this to me every time I look at you I'll soon be unable to stand up straight and I might just as well forget about walking!"

"Find someplace private," she invited quietly, the gleam in her gaze testament to her own need. "Someplace where no one will find us."

"Don't tempt me, sweetheart." Daniel turned away from her, hoping that he'd find a way to regain his composure if he didn't look at her for a few minutes.

"Just the two of us, alone." Elizabeth's voice lowered seductively. "We'll create our own world."

"Woman, you'd tempt a saint to stray from the straight and narrow." Daniel grinned at her over his shoulder as he began to walk slowly, very slowly, back to the house.

The evening meal was a noisy, happy event with everyone sharing their adventures of the day. When Linsey asked Elizabeth about her day,

Elizabeth looked wickedly at Daniel before answering.

"I learned to climb a tree."

Linsey turned censorious eyes to her eldest son. "Isn't that a dangerous activity for a young woman?"

"Oh, there was nothing dangerous." Elizabeth grinned. "After all, St. Daniel wouldn't have let me fall."

Every eye turned toward Daniel who suddenly choked, coughing desperately to catch his breath while Mark gleefully beat his back. Smiling smugly, Elizabeth calmly continued eating. Maybe she hadn't been raised with brothers and sisters, but she knew that it wouldn't take long for her to learn the art of teasing that the Le-Clerc brothers had mastered.

As darkness drew nearer, Elizabeth gathered up her family, insisting that it was time to return to their own home. Daniel escorted them, his arm resting comfortably around her narrow waist.

At the cabin, she sent the children inside, reminding them that school began the next day and that it was time for bed.

"I'll never fall asleep tonight," she whispered, leaning against him. "I'll be so lonely. Every time I close my eyes I'll remember sharing that bed with you."

Daniel wrapped his arms around her, pulling her tightly against him. "I love you, Elizabeth Jane. Never forget that for a minute of your life."

"You can remind me every day . . . and every night."

"I won't be here, sweetheart," he said quietly.

"Hush, don't say that." A shadow of fear feathered down her spine.

"I'll always be with you, my love." He rubbed his cheek against the softness of her hair. "Listen closely and you'll hear my voice in the whisper of the wind when dark claims the light. The snowflakes that kiss your cheeks will be my lips against your skin."

His deep voice was so filled with love and anguish that Elizabeth wanted to beg him to stop. "The heat of the summer sun will be the warmth of my love. I'll be the song of the bird that wakes you in the morning, the calling of the whippoorwill at night. I will walk by your side forever, my hand in yours."

His kiss was a gentle promise. Raising his head, he memorized the face he loved so well. "Good night, sweet love." Turning, he left her standing in the light of the opened doorway.

"You won't escape me easily," she whispered, her voice a promise to the darkness. "I'll fight for you, even if it's against you, until my dying breath."

The next day, Elizabeth found that her only students were her own children and Ethel Mae's. She prayed that there was some reason for confusion about the starting day of school, but when the next day and the next were a repeat of the first she knew that her worst fears had come true. The other ten or so children of the settlement were being kept away.

It didn't help that she saw nothing of Daniel. The school was in the opposite direction of the house so there was no chance of a casual glimpse of him in passing. Each evening, after the children were in bed, Elizabeth sat on the porch hoping that he'd come.

After three days of frustration at school and disappointment at night, her temper was simmering enough that she hoped something would happen to let her vent it before it erupted on one of the children.

The morning of the fourth day she wasn't surprised to be met at the door of the school building by several parents, the preacher heading the group.

"Mistress Spurlin, if we may have a moment of your time, please," he called.

Elizabeth sent the children inside, instructing them to wait quietly while she met the hostile faces staring at her. Folding her hands at her waist, she waited patiently, knowing what was coming.

"Mistress Spurlin, the members of the settlement feel that our children might be better served by another teacher." he stated bluntly.

"You're dismissing me?" she asked needlessly.

"Yes."

"On what grounds?"

A tinge of red colored his cheeks. "I don't think it's necessary to discuss that."

"Oh, but I insist." Elizabeth was relieved to feel the anger bubbling up. She had no doubt that tears would come later, but for now she'd face these self-righteous people with her head up and shoulders back.

"Ain't havin' no hussy around my Wilbur," a woman stated bluntly.

"Ain't no tellin' whatall she be ateachin' in there," another agreed. "Sure ain't things to be learned in no book."

"At the very least they'd have a firmer grasp of the English language," Elizabeth muttered.

"Ladies, please allow me to handle this." The preacher's face dotted with perspiration. "We were delighted to offer you the position of teacher when you first arrived here, but obviously we weren't in full knowledge of your association with Daniel. We don't know what happened last Saturday night between you and Daniel, but we do know that he was seen leaving your cabin at daybreak."

"Would it satisfy your nosy, evil little minds if I told you?" she asked.

"That isn't necessary . . ."

"I'm glad to hear you feel that way since I refuse to satisfy such narrow-minded bigotry."

"All them fancy words don't change what you are!" a woman snarled from the back of the crowd. "A hussy is a hussy!"

"We could stand here all morning exchanging insults, madam, but that would only prove that I'm as deficient in intelligence as my opponent. I refuse to debase myself in such a way."

"What'd she say, preacher?"

"She thinks them fancy words make her better than us."

"Please, ladies." Running his hand through his thinning hair, he looked like a man who would rather be someplace, anyplace, else. "You've made your feelings clear to Mistress Spurlin. Why don't you go on home and let me handle this?"

"We want to hear what ya tell her . . . preacher ain't safe with a woman like her . . . no telling what she'd do to make him promise to let her stay . . ."

"Ladies! Please!"

"Who owns the school?" Elizabeth asked quietly.

"Why . . . I guess it rightfully belongs to Luc LeClerc since the land was titled to him. But that doesn't matter. Decisions like this are always settled by vote."

"And who owns my cabin?"

The preacher was accustomed to a certain amount of respect because of his calling and wasn't too happy that Elizabeth was showing none of the regard he felt was rightfully his. He'd been prepared to handle tears and pleas for reconsideration, he hadn't expected quiet disdain and mild contempt.

"Now, see here, missy, I don't know what you're aiming for, but the settlement has decided to ask you to go," he replied.

"I've heard from the settlement, sir, but until I hear the same words from Luc LeClerc I'll continue to educate the children now in the building. Ethel Mae is concerned that her children not grow up to be ignorant and I think my lessons for today may well settle around the evil of narrow-mindedness."

Elizabeth nodded to the stuttering ladies and turned, walking regally toward the school.

"In all my born days . . . Did you hear her? . . . Luc LeClerc will hear about this. . . . Well, I never!"

"Perhaps you should," Elizabeth called over her shoulder, "you'd definitely benefit from it!"

Twenty

Elizabeth had never realized exactly how long and lonely the dark hours of night could be. While the world slept it wrapped a mantle of privacy around lovers or created an endless interval for uninterrupted thoughts and memories for those alone. Enough time, and more, to remember the events of the day, or a lifetime. Time for sorrows and regrets that could be held at bay during the light of day but grew to startling proportions with the loneliness of night.

The children had long been asleep and the stars filled the sky with shards of diamond brightness. Sleep had been elusive for Elizabeth and after more than an hour of tossing and turning she wrapped a quilt around her shoulders and slipped out to the porch. Sitting on the old rocker with one foot drawn up beneath her, the other thumped spiritedly on the wooden floor.

She felt no regret about loving Daniel; her only sorrow was that someone tried to make something ugly out of something so beautiful.

Maybe her lack of guilt was because of the way she'd been raised, Elizabeth thought as she rocked vigorously. All of the girls at the school had been bastard daughters of wealthy men. It was no secret that they were being educated to become mistresses of other wealthy men.

Their education included subjects like politics, geography and mathematics so that they could converse intelligently. They'd also been taught to hide their knowledge so that they didn't inadvertently discomfort a man who was less educated than themselves.

That Elizabeth had fought against her preordained destiny was nearly unheard of in the twenty years the school had been in existence. She never regretted choosing to go her own way, to become self-sufficient. The life of luxury found as a mistress couldn't begin to offset the degradation of allowing her mind and body to be used at some man's whim; to be a toy purchased for the price of a trinket.

Her body was her own and she had given it to Daniel with joy and love. She wouldn't allow a bunch of busybodies tarnish the memories or drive her out of her home.

The cabin had become her home, she realized, the first real home she'd ever had. And unless Luc LeClerc asked her to leave, she'd stay and watch her children grow up in the security it offered.

She missed Daniel with an intensity that frightened her. She loved him with every fiber of her being and his absence was a constant ache that nothing could soothe.

"Ellie?"

As if her lonely spirit had conjured his, his voice came to her through the darkness. With a cry, Elizabeth stood and dove from the porch, trusting him to catch her. Their lips met with a mutual need of hunger.

"I stayed away as long as I could," he whispered, tasting the sensitive skin of her neck.

"Remind me later to yell at you for doing that." She planted a multitude of tiny kisses on his face.

Daniel sat on the step, cradling her on his lap. "Kaleb and Ethel Mae came to the house tonight."

"Then you've heard about the demand that I leave the settlement." Her voice carried the anger than still brewed just beneath the surface. "I'd take great pleasure in knocking some sense into a few hard heads!"

"Daniel . . ." She gritted her teeth and asked the question most troubling her. "Is your father asking me to leave?"

"No, sweetheart, never that." He pushed the hair back from her face. "He was very vocal about his feelings but asking you to leave wasn't one of them. In fact he stated that you and the children were welcome to live in the cabin for the rest of your lives."

"Thank God." She hadn't realized how deeply she'd worried until the issue was out in the open.

"It's my fault." The anger Daniel had felt when Kaleb had told them about Elizabeth's treatment by the settlement was replaced by guilt.

"That's true," she agreed as she settled more deeply into his embrace. "It's your fault that the children and I traveled here safely from Indiana. And it's your fault that we found the first real home that most of us have ever known. And it's definitely your fault that we felt secure enough to be happy and to plan for tomorrow. There's no way you can avoid taking the blame for our happiness, Daniel LeClerc."

"Elizabeth, this is not the time for levity."

She sat up abruptly. "I can assure you, Daniel, that I don't consider security and contentment as frivolous subjects. Nor do I consider extending gratitude to the person responsible an unnecessary waste of time."

"Ellie, I've ruined your reputation and you sit there politely thanking me."

She grabbed both sides of his head, forcing him to look at her. "You've ruined nothing, Daniel. You've given me contentment and security. For the first time in my life I don't have to worry about tomorrow. I've got food to eat and a roof over my head and friends! You have no idea what it's like to have friends who like me for myself! You've been surrounded by people who love you your entire life. For the first time, ever, I have people who care about me, not because they are paid to, but because they like me."

He was humbled by the sincerity in her voice.

"I carelessly took something that wasn't mine to take and I can't forget that you're the one who'll pay."

"You took nothing!" Elizabeth slid from his lap before he could reach out to stop her. She paced in front of him, anger in every stilted step. "I gave, with love, the only thing that was mine to give. I have no regrets and I refuse to let a few narrow minded people tell me I was wrong."

"But it was wrong, sweetheart," he said softly, his voice vibrating with sorrow. "I can't offer you a tomorrow. There are no tomorrows for me."

"I won't stand here and listen to that, Daniel."

He stood and stepped toward her, his eyes narrowing when she moved back. "You have to listen, Ellie. The dreams are getting closer together, the pain is worse. I sometimes think that the only reason I survived the last one was because I wanted to come home to you."

"You'll always have me to come home to."

"Someday, soon, that may not be enough."

"Have you ever considered that you may be causing the pain?" she asked.

"Me?" An incredulous expression that even the dark couldn't hide covered his face.

"Yes, you. Have you ever tried to follow the dream before the pain got so bad you had no other choice? Have you ever tried to prevent the event from happening?"

That the idea had never occurred to him showed in his sudden stillness. "It wouldn't work."

"How do you know if you've never tried!" She stood with her hands on her hips, in a quandary as to whether she'd rather find something big enough to knock some sense into his head or wrap her arms around him and help chase away his pain.

"You don't understand, Ellie . . ."

"You're right, I don't! I don't understand how you can stand there saying that you're nearing insanity but have never tried something so simple. I don't understand why you're so stubborn that you won't even give it a try." She walked determinedly past him, stopping to pick up the quilt that had slipped from her shoulders in her haste to get to him.

"And I certainly don't understand how I could love a man who is so bullheaded. But there you have it in a nut shell. You're so sure that it won't work that you won't even give it a try.

"I've learned how to laugh and love. And I've learned how to cry. I'll learn how to live without you. It won't be easy, but I'll do it!" She hoped that it was dark enough that he couldn't see the tears rolling down her cheeks. Trying to keep the anguish from her voice, Elizabeth opened the door. "Fight your dreams until madness claims you. I'll come visit you every other Sunday afternoon, as long as you're securely in chains!"

He watched as the door closed behind her. "There won't be any chains, Elizabeth Jane," he whispered. "I won't take the chance that I might harm any of the people I love. When insanity comes, as it surely will, then death will be my release."

Elizabeth heard the bells calling the congregation to Sunday services and wondered how things could have changed so drastically in one never-ending week.

As the children rushed past her in their race to be first at church, she reluctantly followed the path into the settlement, remembering her happiness only last Sunday.

Was it only seven days ago that her life had been perfect, she wondered. She'd had a home of her own, the children who had become her family, a job she liked and Daniel.

She still had the cabin and the children. Even her job as a teacher hadn't ceased, since Ethel Mae still insisted that her children needed a teacher as badly as ever.

She had everything she'd had last Sunday, except for Daniel.

Elizabeth kicked at a rock, watching as it rolled into a bunch of flowers growing beside the trail. She hadn't seen him since the midnight confrontation on the porch. And it seemed that the sun didn't shine as brightly or the moon as softly. In fact, nothing was the same without him.

Raising her chin with determination she vowed that she wouldn't let one man control her life to the point that she could find no happiness without him. It would be like severing a part of her soul to cut him from her life but if that's what it took, then that's what she'd do.

For some reason, that decision didn't bring any relief. Instead she felt a deepening of the emptiness inside her.

As he had been last week, Daniel was waiting for her by the church door. The children clambered noisily up the steps, ignorant of the two adults who stared intently at each other, memorizing for a lifetime the beloved face of the other.

When she reached him, Daniel put a finger beneath her chin and tilted up her head. He placed a gentle kiss on her lips, lingering only long enough to taste her sweetness.

Before she could react, he put her hand on his arm and escorted her up the steps. The congregation was singing the opening hymn but it seemed to her that every eye watched as they walked up the aisle to the LeClerc family pew.

As she sat down, Elizabeth looked quickly at Daniel's mother. Linsey's gentle smile of understanding was nearly her undoing. Fighting back the tears that were just beneath the surface, Elizabeth stared at her hands folded in her lap.

For a second week in a row, she found herself unable to concentrate on the sermon. She stood when necessary and bowed her head when appropriate, all the while praying that the service would soon end. To have Daniel so close and yet so far out of reach was an agony she couldn't accept.

She would sever him from her life, she vowed

as pain clutched at her heart. It would just take a little bit longer than she had thought.

With obvious relief, she stood to sing the final hymn. When the service was over, she waited to follow the others down the aisle, surprised when no one left their pews.

Smiling gently, Daniel looked first at Elizabeth and then at his parents.

"With our blessing," Luc said quietly.

"And our love," Linsey added.

Perplexed, Elizabeth turned questioning eyes toward Daniel.

His black gaze was so filled with love that anyone looking had no doubt about his feelings for the woman beside him. "Before the sight of God, my family and our friends, I ask you to be my wife, Elizabeth Jane." His voice rang loudly enough for even those at the back of the church to hear.

"You want to marry me?" Her voice was so filled with surprised uncertainty that it brought a gentle smile to his face.

"More than anything in the world," he replied firmly.

"But . . . but," she shook her head, looking down at her dress. "I didn't dress for a wedding," she mumbled.

"You look beautiful." Daniel raised her chin. "I love you, Ellie. Marry me?"

"Grab him afore he changes his mind, girl!" Ethel Mae's husky voice advised from the back of the church.

Tears filled her eyes and she found that she

could only nod. She placed her trembling hand in his steady grasp and walked to the front of the church to stand beside the man who was her lover and would soon be her husband.

"Dearly beloved . . ."

As if in a dream, Elizabeth heard the words that would join her forever to the man at her side. The thin gold ring he slid on her finger was warm from his touch.

"With this ring, I thee wed. . . with my body, I thee worship. . ." His voice rang with an emotion so vibrant that no one listening could doubt his pledge.

The hand holding hers trembled so slightly that for a moment she thought she had imagined it. But when her gaze moved up to his she saw a questioning hesitation.

She realized that the preacher was waiting for her to repeat her vows. A smile of blinding radiance creased her face.

"I, Elizabeth Jane Spurlin, take you, Daniel McAdams LeClerc, to be my wedded husband . . ."

". . . I take great pride in pronouncing you man and wife. May God bless you all the days of your lives. You may kiss your bride."

Daniel's head lowered to hers, his eyes blazing with passion. "I love you, Mrs. LeClerc," he whispered as his lips met hers in a kiss filled with promise.

"Yahoo!" a young voice vibrated through the building. "Now I got me a mama and a pa!"

Elizabeth and Daniel turned to look at the child who had just claimed them for parents.

John stood on the pew, his thin body vibrating with excitement.

"I think he approves," Elizabeth whispered, blinking back tears of joy.

With a laugh that shook the rafters, Daniel wrapped his arms around her and turned her in a circle that made her skirts fly out.

"Nice trim ankles," Kal said loudly from his pew, his eyes twinkling merrily.

Daniel set Elizabeth on her feet, keeping his arm firmly around her shoulders and turned toward his brother. "Find other ankles to ogle, Brother."

They were quickly surrounded by well-wishers, everyone wanting to pound Daniel on the back or give the new bride a kiss.

"Love him well," Linsey said, kissing her new daughter-in-law.

"A new daughter to spoil!" Luc took her into his massive arms, kissing her gently on each cheek.

"You wouldn't have come to your senses if it hadn't been for me!" Kal commented as he clasped his arms around Daniel.

"Hey! It was me, last week up on the roof, who made him see the truth," Will claimed.

"You didn't stand face-to-face with him, waiting for him to plow one of those fists in your face!"

"No, I just stood thirty feet above the ground and wondered when he threw me off if it would be as hard as it looked!"

Daniel barely heard his brothers' disagreement as he kept a protective eye on his new wife.

Wife . . . the word hit him with enough strength to make him step back. He had done the one thing he'd sworn never to do, taken a wife. In his haste to protect her from the censure of friends and family he had placed her in a much more difficult position. That of wife to a man facing insanity.

She was so gentle, so sweet, her tender heart filled with such love. She didn't deserve the agony that was as sure to follow as night follows day.

And what if he gave her a child? Surely such intense loving would be fruitful. His gaze moved down to her stomach. What if he'd already done so? What if her slender body already carried the proof of their love? What if his child suffered from the same affliction?

What had he selfishly done to the woman he loved with all of his heart? He had protected her from everything but the one thing she most needed protection from . . . him.

"Daniel?" Kal's voice penetrated Daniel's preoccupation.

"Kal, promise me . . ." he said quietly.

"Anything. . ." The smile left Kal's face as quickly as it had come. He could tell that something was greatly troubling his older brother.

"Protect her. If . . ." His voice faded away. Not if, he thought, but rather when.

Kal wrapped his arms around Daniel's shoulders and pulled him into an embrace. "With my life, Brother. I promise you . . . with my life."

He knew that his family would provide for her, protect her from any possible harm. But who would hold her when she cried in the lonely hours of the night? Who would dry her tears and cherish her smile?

Elizabeth turned to him, her smile a beacon of warmth. Seeing the look of concern on his face, she felt his apprehension as clearly as if it were her own.

She placed a loving hand against his cheek. "We'll live one day at a time, Daniel. One precious day at a time. And we'll build memories, enough to last for a lifetime."

Daniel wrapped his massive arms around her, cradling her with infinite care against his chest. "I love you, Elizabeth Jane." His normally booming voice was whisper soft. "More than anything in this world, I love you."

Cares were momentarily put aside as they were ushered outside the church, where an impromptu party began under the trees. Food seemed to magically appear, as did the fiddle and banjo, as neighbors celebrated the union.

Momentarily separated from Daniel, she watched with gentle indulgence as his brothers gathered around him, teasing him in the way only brothers could tease.

"Elizabeth, I hope you won't feel so badly about the settlement now that you're married," the preacher said, his hand warmly clasping her own.

She wanted to say that she understood and forgave them, but she found that she wasn't that generous. "My feelings haven't changed, Preacher."

She pulled her hand free. "Narrow-minded people forced Daniel into a position he didn't want to take and while I cherish being his wife, I can't forgive them for being the cause."

"They meant well, child," he offered.

"If their intentions were considerate, then God save me from their spite!"

"I never would have guessed what a hard woman you are, Elizabeth."

Her laugh turned many heads in her direction. "You can't see beyond your own nose, Preacher."

She turned and walked away from the baffled man, seeing one person after another smile warmly at her. They were as willing to accept her because she had conformed to their idea of proper behavior as they had been to condemn her because of what they considered improper. Someday she might be able to forgive, but she would never forget.

"Ah, it's time I properly kissed the bride!" Kal roared, startling Elizabeth from her thoughts. Wrapping his arms around her he pulled her into his embrace. His kiss was far from brotherly but before she could protest another pair of strong arms pulled her from him and against another equally strong body.

One after the other, Daniel's brothers kissed their new sister-in-law. Elizabeth's head was spinning when the final pair of arms closed warmly around her. She raised her gaze to the burning fire in her husband's eyes.

"I'm already tired of sharing you but it's far too long until dark," he whispered, his voice made husky by desire.

"Maybe no one would notice if we sneak away?" She, too, longed to be away from here, to be alone with him.

His booming laugh filled the air. "Sweetheart, every pair of eyes in this crowd is on us. We can't breathe without someone making note of it. Do you really think they wouldn't know if we left? Or why? I want to make love to you until neither of us can move, but I'm not sure I want everyone to know that I'm doing it."

Her face flamed with color at his bluntness but she lifted her chin proudly. "I almost don't care. If it weren't for the children or your parents I'd say let them all rot and I'd drag you away with me."

"I think you would," he said with equal amounts of admiration and temptation. "Perhaps it would be better if we danced. That way I can hold you and touch you and no one will object."

Elizabeth deliberately stepped forward until only clothing separated their bodies. "If there is nothing else you'd rather do."

"Wanton," he whispered, his lips lowering to hers. "Wonderfully wanton, and all mine!"

Linsey watched the celebration with the natural mixed feelings of a mother. Her first born had taken a wife. She didn't doubt his love for Elizabeth or hers for him but with lingering sorrow Linsey knew she'd never again be the most important person in his life. It was the way it should be, but she wouldn't have been human, or a mother, if she didn't grieve a little for the past.

She saw Kaleb sitting on a bench, a look of such worry on his face that she found herself walking toward him. Sitting down beside him, she leaned against his comfortable shoulder. This was the man who had saved her life so long ago. He was as much a part of her family as her own sons were.

"What's troubling you, Kaleb?" she asked gently.

"Ethel Mae." The old man sighed deeply, rubbing at his wrinkled brow.

Linsey looked toward the woman, watching as she danced with one of her children. "She looks just fine to me."

"She's breeding!" he said on a hiss of breath. "I told her she was getting fat and she just laughed at me and told me that she's breeding!"

"Kaleb, that's wonderful!" She knew how the old man loved children and had always regretted not having any of his own.

"Wonderful!" He sat up, looking at her as if she'd lost her mind. "What in God's green valley is wonderful about it? I'm an old man, girl. I'll be sixty afore he's born. I ain't gonna live long enough to even see how tall he'll get!"

Linsey's summer green eyes grew hazy. The

precognition that haunted her eldest son was not as dominant in her, but at unexpected times she knew what was to be.

"You'll live to bounce her first child on your lap, Kaleb," she said quietly.

"Her? Don't tell me that." Kaleb stood up, his agitation too great for him to be still. "Ethel Mae done told me that it's a girl she's carryin' and that we were gonna name it Mary Belle. I can't believe you're tellin' me the same thing!"

"Mary Belle," Linsey softly repeated the child's name. She remembered Kaleb's first wife, Mary, whom he had adored and who had died too young. "What a wonderful way for her to tell you how much she loves you."

Linsey had never seen Kaleb's gaze so filled with love as she did when he looked at Ethel Mae. "Mary woulda liked her girl."

Taking his leathery hand into her own, Linsey squeezed gently. "You'll be a wonderful father, Kaleb."

"It scares me, just plain scares me."

"Why? You've been around children for years. I've never seen you hesitate or balk at the worst chore."

"But that was different. They wasn't mine."

Linsey looked at her own children, her feeling of love for them nearly overwhelming. "I know. When they're your own you have no protection from your own emotions. When they're happy, you're happy. When they hurt, you hurt. You want to wrap them in silk and keep them from harm. You watch them grow up, knowing the pain that awaits them and wanting desperately to keep them from experiencing it."

"It weren't right." He shook his head with determination. "It weren't right for her to go and get herself in a family way without lettin' me know first."

"She did it all on her own?" Linsey watched as a blush ran up his cheeks.

"Don't go gettin' sassy on me, girl."

Linsey kissed his wrinkled cheek, love for the old man filling her gaze. "Mary Belle will grow up to be a lovely, charming and spoiled young lady."

"Is that somethin' you're seein'?"

"No, Kaleb, just something I'm knowing. After all, her father has spoiled my children for years. I have no doubt that she will be spoiled rotten!"

"They growed up good, didn't they, girl." His voice softened as he looked at the boys he loved intensely.

Linsey looked toward Daniel, watching as he twirled his new wife in the steps of the country dance. Had it really been twenty-six years ago that Luc's shaking hands had placed their newborn, red-haired son in her arms?

She had been so young, so inexperienced and yet had found herself the mother of not one, but two, tiny babes to nurture. Nathan Morning Hawk was barely four months older than Daniel and she hadn't known the first thing about taking care of children.

Unlike Kaleb, who was one of fourteen children, Linsey had been an only child. She'd never been around babies, didn't know how to feed one end or change the other. It had been Kaleb who had pitched in and taught her about mothering. Kaleb, who was finally healing from the loss of his beloved wife, Mary, had adopted not only her sons, but her. He had been there through the happiness of births, the sorrow of deaths. His strong shoulder had offered comfort, his quick mind offered wisdom.

"They grew up good," she finally replied. "But their lives would have been so different without you. You're as important to them as Luc and I are."

"I'm real proud of them boys." He rubbed his wrinkled face and turned toward her. "Mary Belle? You sure, girl?"

Linsey smiled warmly. "I'm sure, Kaleb."

"Don't know much 'bout raisin' little girls."

"That's why she'll be so spoiled. Just as you, Luc and the boys have spoiled Dara."

"That gal ain't spoiled," he replied defensively. "She's just a mite high-spirited."

"She's spoiled rotten! Admit it!"

"Well . . . mayhap I'll admit it to you, you bein' her mother and all, but ain't nobody else gonna say that 'bout her without hearin' from me."

"Poor Ethel Mae, she doesn't know what's going to happen."

"Too late now for her to be worrin' 'bout it." A smile covered his withered countenance. "I'm gonna be a pa!"

Twenty-one

The fire burned brightly, providing the only light in the room. The nights were still cool enough to welcome the warmth but with summer rapidly approaching that would soon be unnecessary.

The children were tucked into their beds, tired from a day of helping Daniel and their new uncles build the room that was being added onto the cabin. Elizabeth sat on Daniel's lap, her nudity hidden by the blanket wrapped around her. They waited to be sure that the children slept before he'd carry her to the bed and quietly make love to her.

"We'll have our own bedroom tomorrow night," Daniel stated quietly, his fingers threading restlessly through her hair.

Elizabeth suckled on the side of his neck. "We could sleep there tonight. Then we wouldn't have to worry about noise."

Closing his eyes, he turned his head to give her more room to taste him. Her lips on his skin were lighting a fire he kept carefully banked until the darkness of night. Now he was more than ready to let it burn.

"There's no bed . . . no floor . . ."

"Who needs a bed? And it won't be the first time I've slept on the ground."

Daniel found the opening of the blanket, pushing it wide enough for easy access to her breasts. He teased the budding centers, gently pulling and twisting, smiling to himself as she arched her back.

"Now aren't you glad I got you naked?" he said, his voice thickening with desire.

Soon after the children had gone to their beds, Daniel had taken Elizabeth behind the partition and stripped her of her clothes. Afraid to make too much noise that might disturb the children, she had fought him silently, his strength making her protests nearly useless, his devilish smile promising that she wouldn't regret his actions. When she was nude, Daniel wrapped her in a blanket, picked her up and carried her to the chair in front of the fire. For the last hour he had teased and tormented her, his hands finding and pleasuring the intimate places he had come to know so well.

Married nearly a week, they were still discovering the ecstasy of making love; the pleasures of touching and tasting. Their hunger for each other was never satisfied for long, always just beneath the surface, ready to ignite with the slightest touch.

The children had stayed with Luc and Linsey

for the first three days, but now were home. Daniel had found it daunting to try making love to his wife with six children within hearing distance. The bedroom had been started the next day, and would be finished by bedtime tomorrow. Not a moment too soon to Daniel's way of thinking. Only that morning, before the sun had risen, he had been nuzzling Elizabeth's breasts when Jenny Sue had walked in, quietly climbed into bed with them and announced that she was hungry.

The blanket slipped further open as Daniel explored the slopes of her waist and hip. His rough hand brought to life every inch of the skin he explored. Curled on his lap, Elizabeth firmly kept her legs closed, knowing his final destination. A startled gasped left her lips when his head rubbed the back of her thighs, his fingers finding their treasured goal.

"Daniel, the boys," she moaned, trying to dislodge his hand.

"They're asleep, unless you make too much noise and wake them up." He stroked the silky smoothness beneath his fingers.

"They'll see . . ."

"Nothing but your head on my shoulder."

Elizabeth lips found the heavy muscle where his shoulder joined his neck. She sucked strongly, fighting back the moans of delight as he teased her. When she thought she could stand no more, Daniel stood and carried her to the bed.

"Tomorrow we'll have a door to close." He stripped out of his clothes and covered her,

330

groaning as he slid into her waiting warmth. His lips closed over hers, catching their mutual sounds of pleasure.

Relaxed, drifting on the contentment he'd found in loving Elizabeth, the dream slammed into him, the horror catching him unaware, unprepared, not sidestepping sleep. He was awake, he could feel Elizabeth's weight against him, her head resting on his shoulder. He could feel her light breath on his chest and the softness of her hand curled on his stomach.

It had never happened like this before. Awake, his mind was captured by the pictures only he could see.

She could feel the weight of the child low in her belly. The river scared the water swirling and dipping. Couldn't they wait until after the rain to cross? Or find another way over other than the rafts? No, the others were waiting . . . they were the last to cross . . . must, now before dark. She didn't want to go, leave her home, her family. The children were so young, Gerome was four and little Sara barely two. And a new baby on the way.

He poled the raft across . . . young himself, hardly old enough to be the father of two, soon three . . . all their possessions on the raft.

The circular eddy grabbed the raft before he knew it was there. Swirling, twirling . . . she stood . . . had to get to her babies. Screaming . . . help me, oh please help . . . Sara . . . tiny body tossed into the current . . . can't swim . . . screams . . . terror . . .

*fingers grabbing for hold . . . wet wood sliding beneath
her . . . water, everywhere water . . . so cold . . .
can't breathe . . . down, way down . . . so quiet, no
noise . . . darkness . . . no terror . . . such incredible
sorrow . . . babies . . .*

"Daniel! Daniel!" Elizabeth shook him, trying
to snap him from the terror. His blank eyes
turned to her but she knew he was still seeing
his dream.

"They'll all die. . . .He'll try to save her and
the little ones and they'll all die . . . so young,
oh God! They're so young!"

"Daniel, enough!"

"So young . . ."

It dissolved, the visions of a doomed future
fading, leaving the pain of knowledge on his
shattered visage. On her knees beside him,
Elizabeth wrapped her arms around him, pulling him against her bare breasts. She felt the
shudders convulsing through his massive body.
She murmured soothingly, nonsensical words
and sounds.

Her own terror grew as she remembered his
scream waking her from a blissful sleep. She'd
felt the stiffness of his body, the horror of finding that his eyes were open but he wasn't capable
of seeing anything but the dream.

Daniel nuzzled the softness beneath his face.
With none of the preliminary play that usually
led up to lovemaking, he forced her down and
mounted her, joining his body to hers with one
nearly violent stroke.

Elizabeth accepted him, willing to give any

comfort, even that of her own body, if it would ease his pain and terror. His strokes were rough, fierce but never painful, as he fought to wipe out the dream, to bury himself in her until they didn't remember ever being two.

His climax came in a brutal shudder. Collapsing on her, barely able to support his weight so that he didn't smother her, Daniel buried his face in the pillow and waited for the strength to return so that he could move from her.

Elizabeth stroked his back, his shoulders.

"I'm sorry," he murmured.

"You've nothing to be sorry for."

"Did I hurt you?"

"No, Daniel. You could never hurt me."

Groaning, he managed to roll over, taking her with him. With him still sheathed in her, she lay on his hard body, her face buried in his neck.

"I love you, Ellie." He rubbed her back, soothing her hair around her shoulders. "But I didn't know you were there. All I could see was the vision. I could have hurt you and not been aware of it until it was all over."

"You couldn't have hurt me." Lightly kissing his chest, Elizabeth rubbed her cheek against the curly hair that covered it.

A sigh filled his chest, then hissed through his clenched teeth. "It's never happened this way before. I was awake, holding you in my arms and then suddenly I was there watching the raft catch in the eddy, knowing what she was thinking and feeling."

"Go now, Daniel. Don't wait until it's too late, go while there's still time to help them."

He carefully rolled her from him then climbed from the bed. Stepping into his pants, he pulled them up, grabbed his shirt and pulled it on over his head.

Watching as he walked away, she slid from the bed. Hearing the door open, Elizabeth wrapped the quilt around her shoulders and followed him onto the porch.

Daniel felt, more than heard, her presence behind him. The throbbing of his head reminded him needlessly that time was running out. He felt an urge to break something, to wrap his hands around something and use every ounce of his strength to destroy it just as he was being destroyed.

He turned and saw the hurt and pain that etched her lovely face. He was destroying her as surely as the visions were destroying him. He knew he couldn't watch as she died a little more each time another dream came. The time had come, sooner than he'd expected. An overwhelming sorrow filled him as the decision was taken out of his hands.

"I'll finish the room tomorrow." He rubbed at his head, knowing that it was useless to try to ease to pain.

"I've asked Kal to look in on you and make sure you don't need anything. He's a good man, Ellie. You can depend on him to be there if you need him. Maybe someday . . ."

"Why won't you go?" she asked quietly. "Why won't you try?"

"It's too late for me." He turned to her and the pain in his eyes made her catch her breath. "I won't follow this dream, Ellie. I've seen what my life could have been like, loving you, being with you. I can't bear to extend the madness beyond this dream. I want it over so that you can go on with your life."

He pulled her into his arms, his grasp nearly painful. "I love you so much. I can't stand to see the bewilderment on your face when I go through this. You've given me more than I've a right to have, I have to let you go and the only way I can do that is to quit fighting."

"No, oh God, Daniel, no!" The horror of what he was planning to do was more than she could stand. "You can't stop fighting! You can't! If you love me you have to fight with every breath you take. Please, don't do this to us, Daniel. Please . . ."

Her tears wet the front of his shirt, her body shaking with the strength of her sobs. He held her tightly, her pain adding to the agony lancing through his head.

"Please, Daniel, please . . ."

"My parents will always be here for you, as will my brothers. The settlement will accept you again because you bear my name. You'll have a comfortable life here with the children . . ."

"Stop it! Stop it! I won't listen to this!" She pulled herself from his grasp, stepping away from him. "Do you really think I care about a comfortable life if you aren't in it? I don't give a damn if I live in this cabin or in a tent. All I need to make me happy is you and you're giving up!"

"I'm tired, Ellie." His gaze lovingly traced each feature of her beloved face. "It's time to make an end of it."

She swiped at the tears on her face as anger boiled through her. "You can give up if you want to, Daniel LeClerc, but that doesn't mean I will! Go ahead, let insanity claim you. I'll still be your wife. I'll still love you. And by God, I'll fight every day of my life to bring you back to me! I won't let go!"

Her anger shattered him, her pain destroyed him. Wanting desperately to take her back into his arms and promise her forever, Daniel stepped off the porch. He had no choice, he had to free her from the devastation he would bring.

"Listen for the wind, Elizabeth Jane."

The bedroom was finished. Elizabeth stood in the new doorway and stared at the massive bed Luc had made for his son. She wondered if Daniel would ever sleep in it or if it would harbor only her slight weight.

Daniel had returned at first light, the sound of his hammer soon ringing in the air. All day he had worked with a vengeance, his temper so close to the surface that his brothers and the children quickly learned not to approach him.

When the final nail was in place, without a word to her, he had walked away.

Kaleb had arrived soon after dinner. He sat with the children telling them stories that had their mouths open with wonder, rapt attention to every word on their young faces.

Elizabeth smiled gently as she passed them, seeing the concern on the old man's face. Opening the door, she walked onto the porch and leaned her shoulder against one of the support posts.

Where was he? What was he doing? Staring into the dark night, Elizabeth could feel his pain and wanted desperately to hold him in her arms. She bit the inside of her cheek when the thought came to her that she might never again feel his strong body against hers or hear the rumbling whisper of his voice.

The door behind her opened and she knew that Kaleb had finished his storytelling.

"Thank you, Kaleb, I know how much the children enjoyed your stories."

"You got a good bunch of youngens there, Elizabeth." He stopped beside her, his hand resting on her shoulder.

"Where is he, Kaleb?" she asked quietly, surprised at the comfort she felt in his presence, his touch.

"He's out there, girl. Couldn't find him 'lessin he be awantin' to be found. He can fade away like a shadow, but he's out there somewheres."

"He's hurting and he won't let me help." She blinked back the tears that threatened.

"Always was a proud one, that boy. Always thought it was up to him to protect everybody else. Guess now he thinks he's protecting you."

"Who's he protecting me from?" she asked in bewilderment.

"Himself," the old man replied quietly.

Elizabeth wrapped her arms around her waist, trying to hold back the pain. "What a mess."

Kaleb patted her shoulder, offering what comfort he could. "You still got the rest of us, girl. Know it don't make up for not havin' what you want, but you still have the rest of us.

"Thank you, Kaleb." She smiled sadly. "It helps to know you care."

"I care, girl. We all do."

Kaleb stepped off the porch and disappeared into the darkness. When the sound of his footsteps faded, she turned and entered the cabin. The children were ready for bed, but their anxiety was obvious to anyone who took the time to look.

"Is Daniel coming home tonight?" Belinda asked the question they'd all wanted to ask.

"I don't know." Elizabeth wanted to lie, to reassure them, but she knew that honesty was better for everyone, even children too young to understand.

"Will we have to move again?" Wilson dug at the floor with his bare foot. "I like it here."

"No, children, we won't move again. This cabin is our home. You'll live here until you're all grown up and want to move someplace else."

"You promise?"

"Yes, I promise." Elizabeth wrapped her arms around the child and kissed him.

"What if he don't come back?"

"Don't say that!" John jumped up from his place in front of the fire and advanced menacingly toward the younger boy. "He'll be back! Don't you never dare say he won't!"

Elizabeth realized that of all the children, John would suffer Daniel's absence the most. The boy had finally found a man he could love and trust and it would break his heart when Daniel was no longer around. Would it be the final straw to break the child's spirit? Would he ever again place his trust in another person?

"John"—she touched his hair and folded him into her embrace—"He'll come back, if he can. But if for some reason he can't, always remember that he loved you so much that he felt it was better for you that he go away."

"How's it better? He's my pa, he said so. A pa don't leave his kids." His pain was so close to the surface that Elizabeth felt as if she could touch it.

"Someday, maybe you'll understand." She kissed his head, resting her cheek against his soft hair. "Maybe someday we'll all understand."

Elizabeth had put off going to bed as long as she could. She would have slept in the old bed but it and the partition had been removed during the afternoon. Climbing into that big bed without Daniel would be a form of torture she wasn't sure she could endure.

Knowing she couldn't delay any longer, Elizabeth picked up a lamp and walked into the new bedroom. Carefully leaving the door open, she stared at the bed that stretched into the darkness on the far side of the room. It was of massive proportions, specially made to support an equally large body.

Linsey had provided the bedding. Each patch on the quilt was made from cloth saved from worn out or outgrown clothing of each of the boys. It was a priceless treasure, each patch marked with initials in the corner so that it's former wearer was identified.

Reluctantly, Elizabeth removed her clothes, hanging them on the various hooks on the wall. She slipped the cotton nightdress over her head and ventured toward the bed.

Folding back the bedding, she sat on the edge to blow out the lamp. The room was filled with darkness as she lay back and turned on her side to stare out the window. When her eyes became accustomed to the darkness she was able to distinguish the outline of the trees through the window. A whippoorwill called softly and a gentle breeze ruffled the leaves.

Tears rolled silently down her face to be caught in the pillow cover. Loneliness was a cold companion in a bed built to offer sanctuary to two.

Lost in her sorrow, Elizabeth didn't hear his nearly silent steps that led him to her. Consumed by heartbreak, she was unaware of his presence until she felt his arms close tightly around her. She went into his embrace, crying her anguish onto his bare chest.

Like a dream, his lovemaking was gentle, sweet, desperate. She drifted asleep wrapped in the security of his arms.

Like a nightmare, he was gone long before the sun brightened the sky.

Concentrating fiercely, Jenny Sue carefully folded her apron together, holding her prize captured in its center. Walking slowly so that she didn't drop it, she headed for the cabin.

"Mama!" she bellowed, her eyes never leaving the apron. "Come see."

Elizabeth stepped from the cabin, a smile crossing her face, but not touching the sorrow that haunted her gray eyes. Jenny Sue, perhaps because of her age, had been the first to call her Mama. The others, except for John, had soon followed. It never ceased to please her.

"What did you find, sweetheart?" Drying her wet hands on her own apron, she knelt down in front of the little girl.

With the infinite care of a toddler, Jenny Sue opened her apron. "It's all gone!" She turned to look behind her, searching for the thing she'd lost.

"Tell me what you found and I'll help you search." She pushed the scraggly red hair out of the little girl's eyes. Only an hour earlier it had been neatly combed into place. Now it looked as if it had never seen the business end of a brush.

"Me got the sun."

"The sun?"

Jenny Sue nodded, grabbed Elizabeth's hand and tugged her into a small clearing just beyond the cabin. A beam of sunlight broke through the clouds, shining brightly onto the ground.

"Sweetheart, there are some things you just can't catch." She hugged Jenny Sue, kissing her baby soft cheek. "And sometimes you have to let things go because they're happier being free."

Staring off into the distance, Elizabeth thought of Daniel. Every night for nearly a week he had come to her in the darkness. He never spoke, taking her into his arms and loving her with desperation. Her phantom lover, he was always gone when she woke the next morning.

"I'll set you free, Daniel," she whispered. "I love you enough to set you free."

"Mama! Mama!"

The panic in the young voice was enough to send a chill of fear racing through any mother. Grabbing Jenny Sue up in her arms, Elizabeth ran toward the cabin.

Her eyes widened with alarm when John plowed into her, nearly knocking her from her feet. Setting Jenny Sue down, Elizabeth grabbed the boy's shoulders.

"What is it, John? What's wrong?"

"You gotta come . . ." The child's face was

white with horror, his voice coming in gasps. "Mama, you gotta come before it's too late."

Her concern for him was so great that it barely registered that he was calling her Mama. At another time she would have been thrilled, but now she felt his panic and was fighting back her own.

"Come on!" John grabbed her hand and tried to pull her away from the cabin.

"Wait a minute, John." Elizabeth pulled him to a halt.

"No! It'll be too late!"

"Too late for what?"

"He's gonna shoot him!"

"Who, John?" Elizabeth felt her heart begin to pound in her ears as dread raced through her body. "Who's going to shoot whom?"

"The Bear's gonna kill Daniel!"

Twenty-two

Elizabeth stopped midstride and grabbed John's shoulders, forcing him to turn around. Tears washed streaks down the thin cheeks, terror turned his blue eyes glassy.

"John, tell me what's going on," she demanded, giving him a shake.

"We gotta hurry, Mama. Please . . ." he begged. "We'll be too late and it'll be all my fault."

Gently, she pushed his sandy brown hair from his eyes. "What will be your fault?"

"I followed Daniel. He was acting funny and I kinda stayed around to see what he was doing." He rubbed his nose on the back of his hand. "When he saw me he got a real funny look on his face and told me to go get Bear.

"I ran real fast and Bear got his gun and came with me. When we got back he told me to leave, to go home. But I didn't. I hid where they couldn't see me. And Daniel roared like a mountain lion and broke a tree in two with his hands.

344

"He told Bear to shoot him. Said to do it before it was too late."

"Oh, my God." Elizabeth shook her head trying to force back the oblivion that was threatening. Her ears rang and John's young face swam before her eyes.

"We gotta hurry, he's gonna shoot him and it'll be my fault 'cause I got Bear!" Pulling free from her grasp, John turned and sprinted down the path.

Elizabeth picked up her skirt and ran with all her strength. Her breath was coming in gasps as she dodged limbs and branches, barely keeping John in sight. She followed him around a curve that ended in a meadow, her eyes widening at the sight before her.

Knee-high grass undulated soothingly in the gentle breeze. Wildflowers bobbed their colorful heads while deep shadows beckoned from beneath the trees. Birds sang cheerfully and in the distance a child giggled in some unknown delight. It was a peaceful refuge for the weary. It was serenity.

It was insanity.

Daniel stood to one side, a tree clutched between his hands. Shirtless, his muscles bunched in an impossible display of strength as he strained against the log. A feral snarl covered his face and the sound of wood splintering echoed in the silence.

Elizabeth turned her gaze from Daniel's formidable display to the other side of the clearing. Luc LeClerc stood with feet braced apart, his long rifle against his shoulder. Even at the distance that separated them, she could see the tears silvering his cheeks.

The gun was pointed directly at the chest of his oldest son.

"NO! NO!" Elizabeth's screams vibrated through the stillness.

Without thought of her own danger, she ran toward Daniel, placing herself squarely in front of him. Luc lowered the point of his rifle and spoke softly to someone behind him. Stepping around his father, Kal approached his sister-in-law.

"Come on, sweetheart," he coaxed softly. "This is no place for you."

Elizabeth stepped back with each step he took forward. "You're going to kill him!"

She didn't see the pain and tears on Kal's face or notice the agony on Luc's scarred countenance. Behind her, she could hear Daniel's breath rattling noisily through his clenched teeth.

"I won't let you do this. I won't let you shoot him like a rabid dog. He's a man! My God, you're his brother, his own father, and you're going to shoot him down like an animal!"

Kal realized that she was getting closer to Daniel, far too close. Another step or two and Daniel would be able to just reach out and grab her. In his madness his brother had the strength to uproot a small tree and break it in pieces. Her slender body would be as fragile as a twig in Daniel's hands.

"Look at him, Elizabeth," Kal said softly. "Turn around and look at him."

Afraid to take her eyes off of Kal for fear that he'd grab her and then she wouldn't be able to do anything for Daniel, she turned and took a quick look at her husband.

Tears washed his face and his eyes were glazed in pain or rage, or maybe both. Though they looked straight at her, she knew that he didn't see her, couldn't see her. His sweat-slickened chest, arms and hands were covered in his own blood where the rough bark of the tree had cut his flesh.

She turned back to assure herself that Kal hadn't moved, but she couldn't keep her gaze from her husband.

"It's his wish, Elizabeth." Luc's voice drifted to her, saying things she didn't want to hear.

"No! I don't believe that!"

"He's too strong, too powerful, to be controlled in his madness. He's always been afraid that he'd hurt someone he loved."

"How can you?" Dry-eyed, she looked at her father-in-law, her face filled with condemnation. "He's your son, for God's sake. How can you stand there, aim a gun at him and fire? Are you inhuman?"

"Yes, he's my son." Luc raised his head, tears washing unashamedly down his face. "I love him better than my own life. I love him enough to honor his last wish and do as he asked."

His voice lowered until she had to strain to hear it, "And I'll find some way to live with myself later, but I'll never forget. *Mon Dieu*, I'll never forget!"

"What will you tell his mother? That it was an accident?"

His haunted gaze drifted past her, to rest on his son. "She knows."

"Come with me, sweetheart." Kal held his hand out to her. "Let me take you home."

"No!" she snarled, her voice every bit as savage as the man behind her. "You won't do this! As God is my witness, you'll have to go through me to get to him!"

"Elizabeth, go with Kal." Luc's voice was no longer soft. It was the voice that had intimidated lesser opponents for decades. It commanded, demanded, that she obey.

"Go to hell!"

"I'm already there, little one."

Hatred flaring from her stormy eyes, Elizabeth turned from the two men. She looked at Daniel and fought to keep her tears at bay. She felt his pain, his anger, his bewilderment.

"Daniel?" she whispered softly. Slowly she took a step toward him.

"Elizabeth, no!" The voice calling to her could have been Luc's or Kal's, she didn't know, didn't care. Nothing would stop her from saving Daniel and if he killed her in his madness then she'd spend eternity with him in a place better than this one.

"Daniel, put down the log. I won't hurt you. I won't let anyone hurt you."

Two steps more and she could go no further,

her stomach pressed against the log in his hands. Reaching up, she softly stroked his cheek.

"I love you, Daniel LeClerc."

For a few long minutes he didn't respond and she didn't think that he'd heard her. He stared at her, his eyes never losing their glazed expression. Then slowly, he lowered the log, letting it drop beside him.

"Elizabeth, step to the side," Luc commanded.

"No way, you bastard." Her voice, if not her words, were soothingly soft. Her eyes never left Daniel. "If I move you'll kill him."

She rubbed lightly at the tears on Daniel's face, stepping forward until her body leaned against his. Resting her head against his chest, she heard the frantic pounding of his heart.

"My poor Daniel," she whispered. "What have you done to yourself?"

"Elizabeth . . ." His voice was harsh, guttural. His arms moved around her, infinitely tender. "Elizabeth . . ."

He was back from wherever he'd gone. Sanity had returned, if indeed it had ever left.

"Kal, go get a bucket of warm water, a cloth and some soap. Find his shirt. Have someone pack his horse and bring it here." Her voice allowed no discussion. Wrapping her arms around Daniel's wide shoulders, she listened for the sound of his retreating footsteps. From the corner of her eye she saw that Luc still stood with the rifle pointed at them, his finger on the trigger.

"Mr. LeClerc, if you'll put down your gun, I can move back. I won't take a step until it's no longer in your hands."

Against his better judgment, Luc lowered the gun to the ground but he didn't move away from it. Elizabeth looked at Daniel and saw the pain in his face.

"Daniel, you are the most stubborn man I've ever met." Taking his hands in hers, she stepped back. "You almost got yourself killed, you fool."

"Why are you here?" He shook his head then moaned as the pain vibrated down to his feet. "Why didn't you let them finish it?"

"Because I love you, you dummy," she murmured. "I'm beginning to wonder why, but I do!"

"Sit!" She pushed on his shoulder until he sat on the tree he'd pulled from the ground only moments earlier.

Head bent and legs folded in front of him, his arms hung uselessly on his knees. Dejection vibrated from him as strongly as the anger of moments earlier.

"Here's the water, Elizabeth." Kal sat the bucket down beside her but didn't move away. He knew he would be no match for Daniel if the violence returned, but he hoped he could at least save Elizabeth if the need arose.

Elizabeth carefully banked the emotions threatening to overwhelm her. Fear, rage, pity, love, hate; she felt each of them in such abundance that she knew she'd be useless to Daniel if she let even one of them have free rein.

"When this is all over with remind me to hit

you," she said quietly, her voice soothing. Wetting the cloth with the warm water, she gently wiped the sweat from Daniel's face. With infinite care she held the rag against his eyes, wishing she could wash away his agony as easily as she could remove the dirt.

Soaping the cloth, Elizabeth ran it carefully down his neck, dabbing at the abrasions on his chest and arms. When the only evidence left of his rage were the multitude of tiny cuts, she rinsed him with clear water.

"You'll need to put something on these so they don't fester," she said quietly. "We won't do it now, there's no time. But promise me that you'll do it as soon as you can."

"Promise . . . why, Elizabeth?" His voice was filled with bewilderment. He'd been jerked out of his rage and into the gentleness of her touch, the sweetness of her voice.

"I love you." Picking up one of his hands, she washed away the dirt and blood then kissed the calloused palm. "You have given me so much. You're my husband and my lover, I'll protect you with the last breath I breathe."

Her voice was a cool whisper in his feverish mind, soothing the agony, promising peace.

"And you're my friend," she continued as she carefully cleaned his other hand. "I can't let my friend hurt if there's something I can do to prevent it."

Elizabeth cared for her husband with the gentlest of touches, unaware and uncaring of the audience that gathered behind them. Luc still stood beside his rifle, but now Linsey clutched his hand, her eyes glued to Daniel. Will stood to the side, the reins of Daniel's horse clutched in his hand. Mark, Jamie and Kaleb all watched as the woman ministered to the man who had been a raging beast until her calming touch.

And John stood alone, his young face revealing the relief he felt because Elizabeth had averted a tragedy.

Pulling his shirt over his head, Elizabeth dressed him as tenderly as a mother hovering over her newborn babe. She carefully buttoned each cuff and tied the strings closing the front.

When she was finished she knew the time had come that she most dreaded. Turning, she motioned for Will to bring up the horse. Without a word she took the reins from him, scanning the animal to be sure that at least Daniel's rifle had been packed. She saw that the horse had been hastily, but efficiently, readied for it's upcoming journey.

"Daniel?"

Still sitting on the log, he raised confused eyes to her, then to the hand she held out. His big hand closed around hers and she felt the fine trembling in his grasp.

"Follow your dream, Daniel." Her eyes held the color of a brewing summer storm. "Wherever it leads, follow it."

Aged beyond his years, he rose, his gaze never leaving hers. His body seemed slow to follow his commands as he took the reins from her and pulled himself into the saddle.

"I love you, Husband." Her hand rested on his thigh. "Come home to me."

His expressive gaze explicit, his voice of thunder silent, he covered her hand briefly with his own. His grasp was painful and far too short before he rode away.

"Please come home to me," Elizabeth said quietly as she watched him disappear. When even the sound of the pounding hooves were only a memory, she turned to the others who had been witness to the scene.

Linsey cried quietly in Luc's arms, his face still showing the evidence of his own grief. She looked at Kaleb and each of Daniel's brothers. She said nothing, knowing that if she let loose the restraint on her emotions she would appear as insane as Daniel had been. But her eyes said it all, condemning and damning each person in turn.

Slowly, she approached John and pulled him into her arms. His eyes still brimmed with tears and she hugged him fiercely, trying to absorb some of his pain.

"Let's go home, sweetheart," she whispered only loud enough for him to hear.

"He'll be all right?" John begged for reassurance from the woman he knew he could trust.

"I hope so, John."

"He'll be back, won't he?"

Elizabeth's own doubts echoed his. "We'll just have to be patient and wait. He'll come home if he can."

Keeping her arm wrapped around his shoulders, they slowly walked away. Elizabeth wanted to run, to hide, to cry her own tears, scream her own rage at a world gone wrong. But she knew she had to continue to be brave for the child who finally trusted enough to love but loved too dearly.

"Elizabeth."

She never hesitated as she lead John away. Her hatred for the man calling to her almost soared beyond her grasp, but she kept her thoughts on the child who needed her as desperately as Daniel had needed her earlier.

He drifted out of the darkness as silently as his eldest son, moving with the ease of a man accustomed to the night. She had known he would come, that the confrontation between them wouldn't be avoided, couldn't be avoided.

Through the endless afternoon and into the night, she had controlled her emotions for the sake of the children. But seeing him stand in front of her, the icy web she had woven around herself threatened to splinter into countless shards of rage and hate.

He offered his hand. Her brief hesitation was noticed and accepted before she placed her hand in his. Trusting him to guide her safely through the dangers hidden from view, she followed him toward the stream that bubbled merrily behind the cabin.

Beneath the spreading branches of a giant willow, he stopped and released the touch he knew was offensive to her. She was neither intimidated nor reassured by his size, his silence, his reputation. Her own emotions were too close to the surface to be concerned about him. She wrapped her arms around her waist waiting for him to say what he'd brought her out here to say.

"My shaking hands held him when he took his first breath," Luc said quietly. "A father loves all of his children equally, but there is something about each one that makes him special. Linsey gave me Daniel. Daniel gave me Linsey.

"It was my intention to return her to Philadelphia. I wanted to protect her from the harshness of the wilderness, but I hadn't planned on Daniel. When he arrived he showed me that I could not live without either of them. Without her I would not have known all the years of love and happiness."

His voice was soft, lost in the memories of so long ago. "My wife is a stubborn woman. I wasn't given a choice at his birth, I would have run and hid until it was all over, but Linsey forced me to be her midwife, forced me to experience the greatest moment of my life. I've never known such terror or fear . . . until today.

"Today I held my rifle pointed toward my oldest son and I died a little with each breath I took. And I remembered . . . *Mon Dieu* . . . I remembered. My finger was on the trigger and in my mind I heard his first cry, I felt the overwhelming love that filled me with his first breath."

His voice broke and Elizabeth waited until he could continue, knowing her turn would come. "I remembered how he trusted me, that tiny little boy with black eyes so like mine, looked up at me with all the trust in the world, knowing that I would make everything right.

"I remembered all the years of his childhood, the delight of his youth, the pride that he was mine. I held that gun pointed at my son and knew that I would die with him."

"You would have pulled the trigger." It wasn't a question. "If I had arrived a minute or two later, you would have killed your own son."

"Yes." No hesitation, a world of pain filled the single word.

"Why?"

"Because he trusted me."

"To kill him? He trusted you to kill him?"

"When the time was right, yes. He trusted me to end his madness. The visions started when he was only a little boy, but they got much worse as he grew older. He began to fear that they would drive him mad and that he would hurt someone else. He came to me several years ago and asked me to end his suffering should insanity ever claim him."

"And of course you agreed!" she commented disparagingly.

"It wasn't a promise I gave lightly. At first I flatly refused, I even thought of alternative plans should the unthinkable happen. It took a long time for me to accept that he knew what needed to be done far better than I. It was a long time before I finally understood his request."

"Why did he ask you, his own father? Why didn't he ask a stranger or someone who knew him only slightly. Why would he ask the one person who should love him the most?"

"Because he trusted me to keep my word. He trusted my love for him enough to know that I wouldn't let him suffer if it was in my power to prevent it."

"You love him so much that you stood there with a rifle pointed at his chest and would willingly pull the trigger?"

"I love him enough to save him from a bigger grief."

"Excuse me if I seem skeptical but I'm having a little trouble believing this entire conversation!"

Luc reached out to caress her cheek, but Elizabeth stepped away from his touch. "Ah, little one, so much hate bottled up inside you."

"Hate?" Her laugh was filled with derision. "What I feel is far beyond that simple emotion."

"Tell me what you feel, Daughter." Luc knew that she needed to express her pain, to rid herself of the emotions that were causing so much agony. She was so self-contained that he feared they might break her before she could free herself.

"Don't call me that! Don't ever, ever, call me that!"

"We are much alike, Daughter."

"Alike? God save me from being like you!"

"We both love with such intensity that we have to guard our hearts in fear that they might break." He ignored her sound of contempt. "You gave no thought to your own life when you stepped in front of my rifle. Your only goal was to save Daniel. He could have killed you as easily as my rifle but you didn't even think about that."

"I had to stop you!"

"You had to try to save him."

"Of course, he's my husband!"

"He's my son. I had to try to save him, too."

"By killing him?" Elizabeth's voice rose shrilly as his reasoning began to make a twisted kind of sense to her.

"I love him enough to save him from himself. So do you."

"No, not that way! I'd never kill him!"

"Wouldn't you, Elizabeth? Couldn't you?"

She moaned and covered her face with her hands. "No! No! I couldn't."

"You would," he replied quietly. "If the only other choice was unthinkable, you could pull that trigger yourself."

"I hate you!" She raised her head, tears streaming down her face. "Do you hear me? I hate you, and Linsey and Kaleb and Kal and everyone else!"

"Ah, *mon ange,* so much pain."

"I love him. Do you understand how much? When I came into that clearing he was hurting so badly I could feel it and you were standing

358

there with a gun pointed at him. Did you even try to help him?"

"He wouldn't let me near him." Luc wanted so badly to take her into his arms and chase away her agony that he clenched his fists to keep them at his side. "I tried, but I don't think he even knew who I was. Every time I got close to him he'd take a swing at me with that tree."

"He knew me! He didn't try to hurt me!"

Luc didn't reply. He waited for her to continue. "He let me touch him and hold him, let me wash away the blood . . ."

Her voice drifted into silence as realization filled her. "He knew . . . he knew I was there . . . He wanted you to shoot him but not in front of me . . . My God, he was protecting me from the truth. . . ."

"He loves you," Luc stated quietly. "Enough to grab on to his remaining sanity and fight to come back."

"He knew what you were going to do . . ." Tears closed her throat until all she could do was moan.

Carefully, giving her ample opportunity to reject him, Luc enclosed her in his massive arms. Pulling her tightly against him, he rocked her back and forth, holding her as she cried.

"Will he be all right?" she asked, her voice breaking. "Will he come back to me or have I forced him to suffer alone, without anyone who loves him and understands? Have I condemned him to hell?"

Luc didn't reply. He couldn't. He wondered

the same things, hoping that she had saved him, praying that he could find his way past the vision-induced insanity.

"Oh, Daniel . . ."

The stream bubbled quietly, the night creatures singing their songs. He held her until her tears subsided, until she returned her trust.

Until both of their hearts found some small measure of peace; the wife and the father, united in their love for Daniel.

Twenty-three

The unexpected spring storm had raged fiercely for two days, leaving behind a crystal-clear blue sky and a foot or more of powdery snow. The warmth of the sun promised that this final display of winter's power would disappear as quickly as it had come.

Elizabeth watched the children run toward the sleigh, their hastily donned coats flapping wildly around their legs. Knowing that they had been confined because of the storm, Kal had arrived only moments earlier with the offer of one last sleigh ride. John picked up Elaine and Jenny Sue, settling them into the vehicle before he climbed in. The others all crowded together, Wilson sitting up on the seat beside Kal.

"Are you sure you won't at least ride over to the house?" Kal asked.

"No, I've things to do. Y'all have fun. And stay warm!"

"Don't worry if they're not back by dark."

"I never worry about them when they're with

you." From the doorway, Elizabeth waved until they were out of sight. Their happy laughter floated back to her on the crisp air.

She wondered what she would have done without Kal in the long months since Daniel had left. He was constantly showing up at the door, usually with a surprise activity planned for the children. But sometimes he came after dark when he knew they had settled down for the night. Then he'd sit on the porch and talk to Elizabeth or listen to her plans and far too often, her fears.

Because she knew the children would be back, she cherished the solitude of their absence. The cabin was wonderfully empty with them gone. For two days they'd been confined within its sheltering walls, their natural boisterousness making the roomy structure seem small.

For those same two days she had fought a melancholy sadness at the memories that the same kind of storm had brought Daniel to her last spring.

There had been so many changes in their lives since that night more than a year ago. The children had become a family, secure in their surroundings, blossoming with the love that was given freely by so many people.

Of all the children, John had changed the most. His maturity amazed her. He had become the big brother to all the other children, watching out for them. To her delight, he had become a loving, trusting child. Sometimes he tended to worry too much about things he couldn't change as he had during the storm when he had recognized her sorrow and had done everything he could to lighten her mood.

Adding a couple of logs to the fire, Elizabeth watched them catch hold. "Where are you, Daniel?" she whispered. "Are you safe and warm . . . and as lonely as me? Do you wake in the middle of the night and miss me?" Her voice caught and she briefly closed her eyes. "Hurry home to me, I need you so much."

There had been no word of him or from him, but she knew he was alive, every fiber of her being was aware of him.

At times she felt so close to him, she wondered if he was hidden just beyond her view. At others, she knew he was far, far away. She had felt his pain, his joy, his sorrow. An invisible cord seemed to bind them even through miles of separation.

Forcibly shaking off the lingering sadness and aware of the nervous energy bottled up inside her, Elizabeth spent the afternoon cooking and cleaning. Anxious to begin planting her garden she was disappointed that the ground was too wet to work. It had been plowed before the storm but it would be another day or two before she could get to work in it. But there was always plenty to do in a family with so many children.

By early evening the cabin was spotless, the accumulated mending had been done and two pies, made from apples she'd dried in the autumn, sat cooling on the table.

Before dark, Mark arrived asking her permission for the children to stay the night at the house. Luc and Kal had taken the boys hunting while Linsey entertained the girls and no one was ready to come home.

Elizabeth readily agreed, declining an invitation to join the festivities but sending along one of the pies. As Ethel Mae had predicted, her cooking had vastly improved with experience. She still occasionally burned things and sometimes her cakes where lopsided, but most of her meals were not only edible but delicious.

The temperatures cooled again by dark, but with the fire burning brightly and another lit in the bedroom, Elizabeth was toasty warm. Sitting in the rocking chair that had been her Christmas gift from Luc, she watched as the logs were consumed one by one by the hungry flames.

Her eyes drooped wearily and she knew that she should get up and go to bed. She had long ago become accustomed to sleeping alone in the huge bed that had so briefly offered refuge to lovers desperate to fulfill their final moments together. Now she found comfort in sleeping in the bed that had harbored Daniel's body.

Thoughts of Daniel were always at the surface of her mind, but today they had plagued her continuously. She had felt his anticipation, an eagerness, that was new. He was near, perhaps closer than at any time in all the months that he'd been gone and Elizabeth longed to see him, to touch him, to hear his voice. If a moment was all that he'd allow, she'd fill it with enough memories to help her get through until the next time.

Her eyes drifted closed, Daniel's loving smile in her thoughts as sleep took control.

He entered the cabin quietly, surprised that the night bar hadn't been dropped into place. Subconsciously he was aware that several pieces of furniture had been added and that the room felt like home. But his entire being was centered on the woman sleeping in the rocking chair in front of the fireplace.

Daniel quietly leaned his rifle against the wall, set down his bag and removed his heavy coat. His steps were silent as he approached her. Her blond hair flowed softly around her shoulders, glistened in the fire light. He longed to bury his hands in it, to feel its remembered softness. So many nights he had dreamed of having it swirl around him, creating a cocoon about them as his body united with hers.

When madness had threatened to grasp him in its pitiless claw, images of Elizabeth had brought him back from the edge. The sound of her voice, the feel of her touch, had been his constant companions for months.

Now as he stood gazing down at her, Daniel wondered if she still loved him or if he had driven her away with his obsession. The need to know vied with the desire to remain in ignorance. It wasn't too late, he could leave before she woke and she'd never know that he'd been there.

Even as he knelt in front of her, he wondered if it was better to leave his memories intact or to face the truth. He knew he wasn't strong enough to survive the look of hate in eyes where once there had been only love.

"Ellie." Daniel wrapped strands of her hair around his hand, wondering how it could possibly be softer than he'd remembered. "Wake up for me, sweetheart."

In a dream, she heard his voice and her brow wrinkled as she fought to remain asleep. She didn't want to wake up as she had so many times before only to find that she was alone.

"Elizabeth Jane, open your eyes." Daniel couldn't resist tracing the slope of her cheek. It might be the only touch she'd allow.

"Daniel?" Her voice was filled with longing as a lone tear stole its way from beneath her lid.

His breath caught in his throat as her eyes fluttered. Now that the time was at hand, Daniel wanted to run rather than face the condemnation that he feared would come.

"Daniel . . ." Elizabeth opened her eyes then blinked several times. Surely he was a dream, this man who looked so much like Daniel. Suddenly afraid he would vanish, she held her eyes wide.

"I'm real, Ellie." He smiled at her little-girl expression. "You can blink. I won't disappear."

"Oh God, Daniel."

His strong arms enfolded her, holding her

painfully tight. Elizabeth didn't protest. The beat of his heart was beneath her ear, the warmth of his breath against her cheek.

Then his mouth was on hers. It was a kiss filled with all the lonely months of separation, an urgency of need. Touch met touch, exploration answered unasked questions.

Taking her head between his hands, Daniel studied her beloved face. "I love you, Elizabeth Jane. I need you in my life to make me whole."

"Oh, Daniel." Elizabeth lightly kissed his palm. "You are my life. There's nothing but loneliness without you. I can't face a lifetime of that."

He picked her up, sat down on the rocking chair and settled her into his lap. A contentment he hadn't known in months settled comfortably around him. He rested his chin on her head, rubbing gently back and forth.

"You were right," he said quietly. "The dreams can be controlled."

"Tell me." She raised her head, kissing him repeatedly, burying her hand in his shirt as if to hold him should he decide to leave again.

"I had to stay away long enough to find out if I could have any kind of life or if insanity was still only a step away. I couldn't take the chance of it happening again and this time maybe hurting you or someone else. After I left here, I wandered for months, going wherever I was led.

"At first, I dreaded following the visions." His eyes closed at some memories he'd rather forget.

Forcing himself back to the present, he looked at the flickering fire and continued in a quiet voice. "As soon as I began to have a dream I'd go and I discovered that the pain never grew beyond a mild headache. It seemed almost like once I quit fighting them the visions allowed me to have some measure of peace.

"The visions are as vivid as they've always been, but if I leave soon enough then there is time to prevent some disaster from coming true."

"Thank God," she whispered fervently.

"I haven't stopped everything from happening, perhaps some things are just meant to be, maybe there will always be things I can't stop. But I've been there to save lives and to help rebuild. I've had mothers smother me in tears of gratitude and I've held their children, children that again have a chance to grow up because I was there.

"I can be whole, Ellie." His voice, so filled with relief, lowered with a trace of dread. "With you, I can be whole. But I'll always be forced to leave, to go to some unknown place."

The moment had come and he felt sweat trickle down the center of his back. The decision had to be hers, without influence from him. "Can you live with a man who might get up in the middle of the night or during a blizzard and announce that he has to leave?"

He covered her mouth with his when she opened it to speak, the urgency of his kiss contrasting with the calmness of his voice. "Not so quickly, Ellie. Think before you answer. I may not be here when you need me the most. You'll never know exactly where I am or when I'll come back."

Her warm gray eyes studied him. She saw the dread in his eyes and felt the fear that held him in its grasp.

"You'll always come home? Promise me that nothing will keep you away for longer than necessary."

"You are home, Elizabeth." Pulling her against him, Daniel buried his face in her hair. "I'm only half alive when I'm away from you."

"I love you, Daniel." She touched his face, his neck, the love she felt for him overflowing her heart.

"I've never known lonely until I was forced to live without you. You were always in my thoughts. I'd go to sleep with the image of your face in my mind and I'd wake up with it still there. I've heard your laugh and seen your smile. I've missed you with every breath I took."

Later, she would tell him about the security she had felt because she'd always known he was safe. She didn't know if she could explain it so that he'd understand that even separated she still felt a connection to him.

"I want to love you, Elizabeth, now and for the rest of my life."

Her lips met his in a kiss of promise. He reached for the ribbons at the bodice of her dress but a mewling sound interrupted before he could pull it free.

His gaze turned toward the bedroom and he tensed when the sound came again.

"Ellie?"

Smiling, Elizabeth climbed from his lap and held out her hand. "Come and meet the newest member of our family."

Taking her hand, Daniel stood. "You found a baby?"

Shaking his head with wonder, he knew that he'd have to wait a few minutes to hear the entire story. Elizabeth and her endless supply of love had found another homeless child. He wondered how many rooms he'd have to add to the cabin in the future. At the rate she was going he'd soon need a castle to house the children she'd add to their family.

Hell, he decided, he didn't care if he built fifty rooms. As long as she was in his life he'd do everything in his power to make her happy.

By the time they reached the bedroom the whimpering had become a full-fledged cry of anger. Daniel recognized the cradle beside the bed. Made by Kaleb so many years ago, it had sheltered Daniel and all of his brothers and his sister Dara in their infancy.

"My goodness, are you starving to death?" Elizabeth asked the fretful baby as she knelt to pick it up. "Come meet your daddy, then we'll see about getting you fed."

She wrapped it carefully in a blanket, then turned, her eyes twinkling as she watched Daniel. He looked down at the child, noticing the wrinkled face, red from crying. The tiny hands waved in the air and feet kicked beneath the blanket. It looked like every other baby he'd ever seen, except . . .

"My God! It's mine!" His gaze rested on the bright red hair on the small head. "You've had a baby!"

Elizabeth placed the squirming bundle in his arms. "I tried to wait for you to come home, but you're a couple of weeks too late."

"You had a baby . . ." Daniel looked at the baby who stared intently at him, dark blue eyes trying to focus. Suddenly, he was overwhelmed with love for the infant.

"My son . . ." Daniel raised his face, tears rimming his eyes. "Thank you, Elizabeth . . ."

She reached up to caress his cheek. "Bring the baby into the other room where it's warmer so that I can change the wet cloths. This fascination with you has curbed the tears but it's a situation that won't last long."

Daniel followed her from the room, as fascinated with the baby as the baby was with him.

"Do you know how to change a baby?" Elizabeth laid a small blanket on the table where she had placed everything necessary for the procedure.

"No . . . what's his name?"

"Time you learned . . . I have a couple of ideas but I wanted to wait until you got home. A name is a decision both parents should make."

Carefully lowering the baby to the table, Daniel followed her instructions and began unwrapping the squirming child. Sure enough, just as she'd predicted, the baby began to whimper.

"Just a few more minutes, sweet love, then you can eat."

"My son . . ." Daniel's voice was still filled with awe as he undressed the child. "My son . . . my God! He's a girl!" He looked at her, his eyes incredulous. "Ellie, he's a girl!"

"Yes, Daniel, I know." Elizabeth chuckled. "She's always been a girl. You're the one who decided she was a boy. You never even bothered to ask, so I just decided to let you find out for yourself."

"A girl . . . we have a daughter, Ellie." He was so filled with wonder and touched the baby with such reverence that she felt tears threaten.

When the baby was dry, Elizabeth picked her up and walked toward the rocking chair. Daniel followed her, but before she could sit down, he picked her up. Cradling her in his arms, he sat in the chair, holding Elizabeth and his new daughter.

Elizabeth untied the ribbon on her bodice and exposed her breast. Mewling pitifully, the tiny mouth clamped onto her nipple, while a small fist kneaded the distended skin.

Daniel watched the enchantment of Elizabeth nursing the infant. At some point in time, mysterious to him, she changed the baby to her other breast.

Soon, far too soon for him, the baby closed her eyes and it was obvious even to him that she was asleep. Her little mouth tugged occasionally, until she relaxed completely and Elizabeth's nipple slipped free.

"Thank you for sharing this with me." His voice was humbled by the experience.

Elizabeth rested her head against his wide chest, content at last. He was home.

"I promise you, Ellie, I will never miss the birth of another of our children." He gently stroked the downy fuzz covering the baby's head. "I will always regret that I missed the first weeks of her life."

"No regrets, Daniel. No matter what happens in our future there must be no regrets. If you aren't here it'll be because you're needed somewhere else. Things, good and bad, will probably happen while you're gone, but there'll be no regrets because you missed them."

"I love you, Ellie. What I'm asking of you seems awfully unfair."

"I'll miss you when you aren't here, Daniel, but as long as I know you're coming home I can handle it. And you can do what you have to do knowing that we're safe and well cared for. Your family just about drove me crazy while we waited for the baby to be born."

She raised laughing eyes up to him. "Poor Kaleb! He barely survived Ethel Mae's confinement when he had to go through mine!"

"Ethel Mae?"

"She presented Kaleb with a daughter late in the fall. They named her Mary Belle."

He'd missed so much, he realized with remorse. Never again would he be away so long.

"The last few weeks before your daughter was born I was never alone. Your father or one of your brothers or Kaleb was always within sight of the cabin. They drove me frantic! Your mother offered sympathy but told me that she'd discovered that it was useless to try to fight it."

"I'll have to remember to thank them for watching out for you while I was gone."

Slowly, he lowered his head to hers, kissing her with controlled passion. Until she healed from the birth, he'd have to be satisfied with just holding her and stealing kisses. Lord, it wasn't going to be easy! But they'd have the rest of their lives together. Leaving would never be easy but with her to come home to he could survive their separations.

"I'd like to name her Danielle," Elizabeth said, interrupting his thoughts. "While I was carrying her I thought she'd be a boy and I started calling her Danny. She kept me company on those long, lonely nights without you. I was a little surprised to have a daughter instead of a son, but I'd still like to name her after her father."

He looked down at his daughter who slept peacefully against her mother's breasts. The shape of her nose and chin, especially her mouth, were just like Elizabeth's. His only contribution to her creation seemed to be her hair.

"I think Elizabeth would be a much better choice. She looks just like you."

"Ah, but she has your temper, your hair and I think her eyes will be from the LeClerc side of the family."

"Elizabeth Danielle?"

"Danielle Linsey."

How could he argue with her choice of names. He knew that his mother would be deeply honored.

"Hello, Dani Lin," he whispered to the baby.

"Dani Lin? I think not."

"It'll stick, you know. As soon as I start calling her that so will everyone else."

He was right. It was useless to fight. If she wanted to name the baby Danielle she might as well accept the fact that she'd be called Dani.

And she desperately wanted to give Daniel's first child his name.

Daniel leaned his head back against the chair and closed his eyes. He was home. There was so much to catch up on. He hadn't even asked Elizabeth if the children were all right, or even where they were. It was obvious that they weren't in the cabin. The noise of his arrival would have woke them.

But he was home.

There was time, all the time in the world. There was a future to look forward to. He had no doubt that Dani Lin would be just the first of several children. With Elizabeth at his side, he could accomplish anything.

He looked at the tiny baby, her rosebud mouth pouting. He gently wiped at a drop of milk dribbling from the side of her mouth. Elizabeth relaxed completely against him and he realized that she'd fallen asleep in his arms.

It felt so good—so wonderfully good—to have these two precious bundles in his arms. He knew he should get up and carry them to bed, he'd be stiff and sore in the morning if they slept in the chair.

With a sigh, Daniel closed his eyes. Sometimes a few priceless hours of total contentment were worth a few aches and pains.

Mama?

He smiled as the young voice whispered through his sleepy mind. Without effort or pain, the dream was there, the vision of the future. The rain beat a furious tattoo on the parched ground while in the distance, storm clouds gathered in billowy warning. Suddenly the rain ceased and from the clouds a long, vicious funnel, black as a demon from hell, dropped to the ground. It twirled and swirled in a dance of madness, destroying everything in its path. The small, one room cabin stood no chance against the mightiest weapon of nature. The little girl even less.

Mama. I'm scared.

"You'll be all right, baby," Daniel said quietly to the voice only he could hear. "It's just a big, bad wind and I'll be there to keep you and your mama safe long before it comes. I need just a few days to get to know my daughter and to see my family and then I'll be on my way. I promise."

Mama?

About the Author

A former bookstore owner, Pamela K. Forrest calls herself "an unrepentant daydreamer" and often finds herself spinning plots while tending to necessary household chores—all the while itching to get her ideas down on paper. According to Pam, "Heaven is a place with two bathrooms, maid service, and a cook!" Reared on the beaches of Florida, she now lives in the mountains of North Carolina with Bill, her husband of twenty-four years, and their two teenaged children, Tom and Katie. She is the author of AUTUMN ECSTACY, SWEET SILVER PASSION, and WILD SAVAGE HEART.

FEEL THE FIRE IN CAROL FINCH'S ROMANCES!

BELOVED BETRAYAL (2346, $3.95)

Sabrina Spencer donned a gray wig and veiled hat before blackmailing rugged Ridge Tanner into guiding her to Fort Canby. But the costume soon became her prison—the beauty had fallen head over heels in love!

LOVE'S HIDDEN TREASURE (2980, $4.50)

Shandra d'Evereux felt her heart throb beneath the stolen map she'd hidden in her bodice when Nolan Elliot swept her out onto the veranda. It was hard to concentrate on her mission with that wily rogue around!

MONTANA MOONFIRE (3263, $4.95)

Just as debutante Victoria Flemming-Cassidy was about to marry an oh-so-suitable mate, the towering preacher, Dru Sullivan flung her over his shoulder and headed West! Suddenly, Tori realized she had been given the best present for a bride: a night of passion with a real man!

THUNDER'S TENDER TOUCH (2809, $4.50)

Refined Piper Malone needed bounty-hunter, Vince Logan to recover her swindled inheritance. She thought she could coolly dismiss him after he did the job, but she never counted on the hot flood of desire she felt whenever he was near!

Available wherever paperbacks are sold, or order direct from the Publisher. Send cover price plus 50¢ per copy for mailing and handling to Zebra Books, Dept. 4447 , 475 Park Avenue South, New York, N.Y. 10016. Residents of New York and Tennessee must include sales tax. DO NOT SEND CASH. For a free Zebra/Pinnacle catalog please write to the above address.

DISCOVER DEANA JAMES!